To Mum. Who loved
listening to this in hospital –
and was nothing like Sybil Morris.

SHOOT THE MOON

BELLA CASSIDY

HAPPYSHED
PRESS

ISBN 978-1-7399372-2-5

British Library Cataloguing in Publication Data. A catalogue record for this book is available from the British Library.

With the cutting of the umbilical cord, physical attachment to our mothers ends and emotional and psychological attachment begins. While the first attachment provides everything we need to thrive inside the womb, many psychologists believe the second attachment provides the psychological foundation and maybe even the social and physical buffer we need to thrive in the world.

— *BETH AZAR, 2009*

One's first love is a thread woven into the soul, forever.

— *HOLBY CITY, 2016*

1

—————

ondon, May 2014

L Below the surface, everything slowed. Oblivious to all but the occasional leaf under her fingers, Tassie Morris reached through the water – loving the immersion where nothing else mattered. After the shock of diving in, finishing the first length was always glorious: the cut of cold like silk. Which is why, twice a week, she'd haul herself out of bed and cycle to the lido; the roads still quiet, the century-old pool even more so.

This morning she was one of just seven swimmers. *Thirty-eight, turn... thirty-nine, turn... forty... Or was it still thirty-nine?* Estimating she'd done her time, she pulled herself up the steps, shivering in the pastel light as she wrapped her towel around her torso. Then, squeezing out her silky plait, she watched it drip dark spots on the concrete.

The lido café opened at seven, and the man behind the counter tendered a brittle smile as he handed her a cappuccino. She smiled back. His irascible nature was legendary but they got along just fine; perhaps because her needs were minor in comparison to the burger-loving hordes who would descend on him later.

Outside she chose a table brightened by a triangle of sun and, taking out her phone, scrolled through her contacts to hit 'D&M'.

It rang a few times before her mother answered. 'Hello, Sybil Morris.'

Tassie wrapped her fingers around her cup. 'Hi Mum, it's me.'

'Victoria. How nice to hear from you. Are you calling for your father? I'm afraid he's taking the cows back.'

Tassie looked at her watch. She'd hoped that today – his seventieth birthday – he'd have found someone else to do the milking. 'Oh. OK.' There was a brief silence. 'How is he? Did he get my parcel?'

'Well, something came, which we guessed must be from you. He'll open it later.'

A smile flickered at the corners of Tassie's mouth. She was confident he'd love the Aran jumper she'd sent, and hopefully wouldn't wear it for milking like he had the last one. 'How is he?'

'He's fine, thank you. His hip's been quite bad recently, but summer should help. Always better when the weather's warmer.'

'Yes, of course.' Tassie took a cautious sip of coffee. 'And you? How are you?'

'I can't complain,' her mother said briskly. 'Keeping busy.'

This time the pause was longer, and Tassie twisted in her seat, fiddling with a menu. 'Sorry I've not been home for ages. I've been so busy at work.'

'I'm sure. This must be your peak period. How are the weddings?'

'Yeah, good. Busy. I've got lots on. How's Honey?' She

could hear the clattering and clinking of her mother unloading the dishwasher.

'She's fine. All the puppies found homes. She's a good dog – talking of which—'

'Sorry, yes, I guess she needs walking, or feeding. Bad time to call.'

'Actually, I was going to tell you about a new breeder we're thinking of getting. I've been doing some research into crosses. They're becoming increasingly popular and I've been wondering whether to diversify.'

'And get what?'

'I don't know. I'm still in the early stages of research. But I've been looking at some of the pedigree poodles.'

Tassie snorted. A poodle was the last kind of dog she would have imagined her mother working with.

'You don't approve?' Her mother's voice became self-conscious. 'I thought you liked them?'

'Me, like poodles? Why d'you say that?'

'Because you gave me a scarf once. With poodles on it.'

'Did I? I don't remember.'

'Well, it was a while ago... Anyway, shall I get your father to ring you when he comes in for lunch?'

'I'll be in a meeting. Tonight?' The menu fell through the table's wooden slats and Tassie bent to pick it up, the phone squashed against her ear.

'No, we'll be at the Harrisons. They've invited us for dinner with Sophie and Tom. Tomorrow?'

'OK, I'll try.' Tassie grimaced as she stretched her hand out for the menu, avoiding the dog end of a cigarette. Of *course* her perfect brother and his perfect wife would have been invited to the celebration. Sitting up, she stuck the menu back in its slot. 'Have a good day, Mum.'

'You too, Victoria. Nice of you to call. I'll tell your father.'

The line went dead with the phone still to Tassie's ear.

Someone had turned on the fountain – fashioned like a tiered cake – and water began to trickle down the sides, gathering force as it went. She could picture how the night would unfold. Her mother would tell her father to moderate his drinking, even though it was his birthday; and her brother would say, more than once, 'Dad's fine'.

Thank God she wouldn't be there.

Beaded threads of water sparkled in the sunshine, but the effect was spoiled by the algae that slimed on the fountain. Then she remembered. She *had* been invited – months ago – and had said she'd be too busy. Blowing on her coffee she forced herself to drink it; suddenly keen to get on with her day.

She was just pulling her bag off the floor when something caught her attention outside the pool perimeter – past the fence where she'd secured her bike. She stopped, then straightened. Silvered by sunlight fracturing through a chestnut tree was a little girl, about three or four, dark-blonde hair almost to her waist; standing motionless as a fawn before flight. Tassie blinked, wondering if the light was playing tricks, before glancing at her watch. It was only just gone seven. Hesitantly, she raised her hand and waved. The child's face was transformed by a swift pixie grin as she waved back; although it wasn't quite a wave, more a chubby hand twist.

Delighted with the exchange – yet increasingly worried when no adult appeared – Tassie walked towards the child, scanning for others she was sure must be near. Changing course, she headed towards the pool's exit, her pace quickening as she looked back to check on the little girl, almost running when a building obstructed her view. Rounding the corner she slowed when she saw the child was now sitting on the grass, which was longer than usual for the time of year. Tassie relaxed her pace as she neared. Then, when the child looked at her, their eyes locked, and – deep within – recognition rippled.

She was still a few metres away when she stepped on something narrow and pole-like, which twisted under her foot. Stumbling, she tried to right herself, but as it moved another part flipped up and she fell, wrenching her ankle before she hit the ground. For a moment she was side-tracked by shock, darts of pain shooting up her leg, and when she looked up the child was gone. Wincing, she stood, scared to put her full weight on her foot as she scoured the area: most of it open and affording few places for the child to hide. She went to walk forwards, then glanced down at what had caused her to trip.

It was when she saw the bolt-cutters she knew; although, really, she'd known from the moment she saw the child. She bent to pick them up, feeling their weight in her hand: solid, real. Shaking her head, she limped over to her bike and saw that the chain was almost severed.

Grasping the cutters she gazed into the lido: now just three swimmers, rubber caps bobbing. Looking up, the light was soft as sea-blown glass as she closed her eyes.

She wasn't afraid; far from it. She was enchanted. For this wasn't the first time she'd seen her. Twice before they'd met.

On the first occasion she'd been about four or five...? She searched back through time. She'd been in her bedroom, eyes puffy from crying – a row with her mother over... she couldn't remember, probably something as simple as not wanting to go to bed. That's when she'd seen her, rocking on the swing in the garden, summer rays reaching low. They'd waved at each other and she'd giggled when the little girl had poked out her tongue and she'd done the same. Eventually she'd got bored, waved her good-byes and got into bed, calmer than before. She'd not told anyone about her – not even Tom – accepting that the little girl was there, but not.

The second time she'd been older, maybe just turned seven, playing by the river with her brother while their father dozed. They were stretched out over the water, hoping to catch fish in buckets suspended on string when the branch they were leaning on broke, tipping them into the fast-moving stream. Tom was closer to the bank and had scrambled up, but Tassie wasn't so lucky.

Although she was a good swimmer, the current carried her to where the bank was steeper and when she finally managed to grab onto something and stay herself, she couldn't climb out. The children's cries had alerted their father, but as he came to haul her out of the water – his face pinched with worry – she looked across to the other side and saw the little girl, dressed in yellow, sitting cross-legged, hands catching her giggles. Back on the bank, wrapped in her father's embrace she told him about the child. He stared into the river for a long time, then hugged her tightly before gently suggesting that it was a secret best kept between the two of them. 'For fairies prefer it that way.'

Frustrated, Tassie tried to explain that it wasn't a fairy, 'She was a—' But a sound from her father caused her to pause, surprised when she saw his eyes wet with tears.

The water was April-cold and shivers engulfed her as he wound the picnic blanket around her and kissed the top of her head. Then, once they were back with Tom, they'd busied themselves with getting packed to go home – and she'd never mentioned it again.

It was funny, the things from childhood she'd made herself forget; rationalising those strange events. The little girl had looked different then, her hair lighter, shorter.

Staring at the spot where she'd stood, Tassie opened and closed the rust-stiffened cutters, only now wondering where the bike thief was. She hadn't imagined the attempted theft – so surely not the child?

She hoped not, for the possibility of truth was delightful. Almost too fantastic to believe, but far from chilling. In fact it was a truth that made her senses tingle. Yet as the light began to distil with the movement of the leaves in the trees, her euphoria faded and was replaced by loneliness. Would she see her again? She was suddenly desperate to know.

She undid the lock then wrenched the cutters open as far as she could manage, warping them to make them useless. Then, more hobbling than walking, she threaded both them and her chain onto the fence.

Next, she bound her swimming costume tight around her ankle, hoping to isolate the pain for her cycle home. Perhaps it had just been a trick of the sun – compounded by the stress she'd felt after talking to her mother. She sighed out a smile.

If it *was* a truth, it was one she wouldn't be sharing; she'd learnt that early on. For some things were just too strange to talk about.

2

———

'Looks like it'll be a good one. The vicar's the mother and the reception's in some ancient rectory. Get lots of shots of roses, old crockery – stuff like that. It'll contrast well with the couple being into bikes and tatts. Oh, and they're also something medical. Work in dangerous places. So tattooed *and* saintly. Just up our street.'

Tassie looked at her boss, who was dressed in leather trousers, with a richly-embroidered kimono covering her tattooed arms. It was certainly up Catrina Robson's street, but not really her style. After cycling home she'd changed into her default outfit, carefully pulling on faded jeans and leather sandals before picking out a white linen shirt.

Picking up the brief, Tassie flicked through it – as always impressed by the job Syd had done in putting it together. There was a thorough background and numerous photos of the bride and groom – both in their early thirties and highly photogenic. She frowned when she saw the wedding was in Exeter. She'd been working flat out for the last few months and could have done with a job less far away. Although, these days they all seemed increasingly distant.

'Was there anything else?' Catrina was staring at her, eyes outlined with black kohl under a fringe of electric blue. The team often discussed how much she must spend at the hairdresser, for her bob had the richness of hue you'd normally only get with a wig.

'No, this looks great, thanks.'

Tassie stood. Her editor might run one of the world's most popular bridal magazines, but she didn't achieve it through finding the time to give her staff any cuddly support. Even before she'd left the room, Catrina was back on her mobile: 'Christian, darling, love the new lipsticks...'

Still limping from her fall, Tassie approached a desk situated under ceiling-height windows overlooking Wardour Street. It was the one allocated to the editor's assistant, who was also her best friend.

'Thanks for the brief, Syd. Looks very thorough – as usual.' Tassie glanced at a pile of papers stacked among magazines, diaries and photos. 'Wow. These must be keeping you busy.' Picking up a document with a fluorescent pink cover, she started reading through it.

Syd's face appeared from behind her screen. 'Cat will love that one. It's got some dodgy ex-celebrity, punk hair and piglets.'

Tassie scanned the introductory letter, written in purple capitals. 'As a former, *very* popular runner-up on *Big Brother*, I think me and my fiancé would be the perfect couple to feature in 'Bride Spied'. We absolutely—' She started laughing.

'We *absolutely love* Tassie Morris's photos,' Syd continued. 'What was it? They're so stylish and she makes everything so magical – spelt with a j.'

'Yes, and a y on my name. Bin her.'

'Let's not be spelling snobs.'

'But we know why she's being nice,' Tassie said.

Syd shook her head. 'Even without the magazine, everyone loves your photos, pet. Look how many private jobs you're being asked to do. You're famous.' She took a bite out of a luminous green apple.

Tassie's smile crinkled the corners of her eyes. Sydonie Harper was as cute as she was kind, freckles peppering her cheeks and red curls trailing down the back of her polka dot dress.

They'd originally worked together at the *Independent* before reuniting at the alternative wedding magazine, *Kiss the Bride*. One of the first things they'd devised was a competition whereby each month they'd select a potentially eye-catching ceremony to photograph for free; and now, three years later, 'Bride Spied' was the magazine's most popular feature, attracting thousands of applicants. Tassie glanced through the rest of the file then slung it back on the pile, laughing when Syd immediately straightened it, her fingers topped with silver nails and—

Gasping, Tassie grabbed Syd's hand. 'I can't believe it. I've been here, what, half an hour and you haven't mentioned it?' She twisted Syd's fingers, catching the engagement ring's tiny diamond in the light. 'It's beautiful. Stan's done well. Finally.'

Syd was due to get married in November and her fiancé had been procrastinating for months over getting a ring to replace the beer can pull he'd proposed with. He worked as a cycle courier – which was just about enough to split the rent – while most of his time and passion went on his inventions. Syd had recently been complaining that his current obsession was the ergonomics of spoons.

'What makes you think he chose it?' Syd shrugged. 'I finally took over and he just had to dole the cash. Rather a lot for him; told me he could have bought a new bike for the money. Romantic sod.' She stroked the stone. 'It is lovely isn't it? Although... married? Me and Stan?' She held her hand out. 'I still can't quite believe it.'

'You'll have to come over to celebrate,' said Tassie. 'I owe you an engagement celebration. I'll get Oliver to come too. I've not seen him for ages.' She bent over the desk, giving her friend a loud kiss on the top of her head. 'So happy for you guys.'

Syd leant back on her chair, biting into the apple. 'Thanks, we'd love to. That would be great. Oh, but... Oliver? Not that I don't want to see him. You know he's got a new man—'

'And from the texts he's been sending me, is clearly smitten. Is it Dilak?'

'No, Tilak... hang on.' Syd looked at her pad. 'I wrote it down so we'll get it right when we meet him, Tilakaratne Rajapakse.' She enunciated the syllables. 'Actually, Stan's already met him. Says he's great for Oliver – although *he* called him sound. He's a doctor, a paediatrician? That's someone who works with kids isn't it?'

'Yep. And what I got from Oliver is that they're going to get a dog, and have kids, and a wedding with peonies and white suits – and he's so excited that he can finally plan his own thing. Although perhaps he's getting a bit ahead of himself as they've only been seeing each other for, what, a month?'

'Three months, Tass, keep up. And let's allow him a bit of wedding planner's excitement – hoping that Tilak's as perfect as he says he is. He sounds just what Oliver needs. But anyways,' – Syd polished a mark off her apple – 'can we return to you please? Does this mean that *Josh* is no more?' She fixed her eyes on Tassie.

''Fraid so.' Tassie felt herself redden as she looked out of the window before turning back to her friend. 'Sloping shoulders.' She wrinkled her nose as Syd let out a surprisingly loud guffaw.

'Tassie Morris. Even I, queen of shallow, know you can't not like someone because of their shoulders.' A wistfulness entered Syd's voice. 'He seemed a canny lad, though? I thought, you know, this time it might work?' She continued to stare at her friend. 'Tass, it's got to be a bit about compromise.'

'I know that, really I do. Remember Simon the Fireman?'

This time it was Syd who did the nose-wrinkling. 'With the hazard chest hair? Or Alastair... what was his name? Dagg?' She grimaced. 'Aye, I understood why you would 'na wanna marry him.' Then her face turned serious. 'But Josh was OK, wasn't he? You seemed happy. Even Stan liked him – and he doesn't like anyone, except us and the pug. Oh, and you, of course. And Oliver. And now Tilak. And his mum and... OK, he likes quite a lot of people. But not your men, generally. No offence. Come on. Tell me the real reason.'

Tassie's shoulders fell. 'It just wasn't... he wasn't...' She straightened. 'He just wasn't right. Sorry.' She touched Syd's hand. 'Don't go on about it. I'm fine. Honestly. Right, I've got to go. I've got another meeting.' As she was talking she started backing away, her voice getting louder as she went. 'Don't forget about supper at mine. Lots of the veg are about to sprout. Love to Stan. Oh, and I've never been to Exeter. Looking forward to it.'

'I'm sorry about the B&B.' Syd winced. 'There's not much of a budget.'

'No worries, I'm sure it'll be fine.'

In the doorway Tassie blew Syd a final kiss, aware that her friend was still frowning. As she turned, a sharp pain in her ankle reminded her of earlier, although she hadn't actually stopped thinking about the little girl all morning.

Or him.

For the sense of loss she'd felt had brought *him* sharply into focus. The person she was always thinking about – the one who never left her mind.

She pressed the button for the lift.

Perhaps she was too picky? What if she never found another connection as deep as they'd known?

Syd was getting married, and it now sounded like Tassie might be losing her "partner in cruise" as well – not that she'd ever warmed to Oliver's expression.

She watched the floor numbers decreasing. That wasn't something she'd expected: Oliver getting hitched. She'd thought she'd always have him at least. Her perfect plus one. Better than any not-quite-right long-term relationship. Although... three months?

They really needed to catch up.

Now she thought about it, she'd been so busy working she hadn't really spoken to anyone.

Except, that wasn't exactly true.

There was one person she'd been talking to constantly. And that's probably why she'd been avoiding her friends, Syd having the nose of a bear when it came to uncovering her secrets. Apart from this one.

The lift pinged and the doors slid open.

Compromise.

Wasn't that exactly what she was doing? Still, after all this time.

3

E *xeter, June 2014*
Standing on a narrow street just outside the centre of Exeter, watching her taxi pull away, Tassie's first thought was one of relief that mid-morning sun was finally beginning to filter through the rain. Her second was that she had a hangover.

She stared over the box hedge at a beautiful eighteenth-century building which, despite its city location, was the perfect English vicarage – a Japanese quince winding its way around irregular glass windows and an open front door.

The only thing not in keeping was a lime-green monster of a motorbike parked on the drive. Kneeling beside it, a man with glossy black curls was polishing the bike's already gleaming chrome.

Kawasaki Ninja, together with groom. Tassie remembered her brief.

A window on the second floor opened and a woman stuck her head out, equally black hair pinned in big curls and a glass of champagne waving in her hand. 'Carlos Potel, step away from the bike. There's an issue with the cake. Not straight or something. Honestly, your wheels are fine – and, *mi amor*, it is *I* you are marrying.'

The woman blew a kiss to the man, who stood looking up at her, a hand smearing grease down the edge of his jeans while he rubbed his arm across his forehead.

'Make sure you don't do that when you've got your suit on— Oh, hello.' She noticed Tassie standing in the street. 'You must be Tassie. Are you? Yes, you must be, all those bags. Awesome. I'm Clarissa. The bride, obviously. Hang on, I'll come down.'

Tassie pushed open the gate as Carlos came towards her, his smile embedding dimples in tanned cheeks. 'Hi, I'm Carlos, the groom, obviously.'

He was exquisite. Even better than in the photos.

He held out his hand, then dropped it. 'Actually, you'd better not or you'll get grease on yours.' He examined his fingers. 'Anyway, as you saw I've been summoned, so I'll see you later.' He started to turn, then paused. 'It's great you're here. I know Rissa's delighted.' And with that he walked around the edge of the house to where, Tassie presumed, all the marquee-action was taking place.

Clarissa appeared in the doorway, an emerald satin robe loosely wrapped around her long limbs. 'Has he gone? Good. Sometimes I swear he loves that bike more than me.' Barefooted, she walked onto the drive, her arms out wide. 'Wow, Tassie Morris! I'm so very pleased to meet you. Your photos are stunning. Especially the ones from your newspaper days. I've followed your work for years – loved the piece you did on alligator wrestlers. I sometimes thought we might meet – although abroad, not here at home like this.' She grinned. 'Life can be so unexpected.'

Tassie instantly liked the woman who leant forward to give her a hug, and was pleased that Clarissa knew her early work; something that rarely happened these days. In her previous life she'd worked as a photojournalist. Five years spent travelling the world, shooting stories ranging from blind football championships in Brazil to mud festivals in South Korea.

Eventually, after a second round of newspaper budget cuts, her regular work had dried up. Fortuitously Syd had already crossed over to magazines – *Kiss the Bride* having always been her dream destination – and when a job for an in-house photographer had come up, Tassie suspected her friend might have invented it. It was great to be working together again, and good to have the money. But there was still much she missed about her previous career.

'Here, let me help with your stuff.' Clarissa thrust out her hands. 'We're so lucky to have you. How was your journey? Did you find us OK? You must be needing something to drink. Champagne?' She brandished her glass, now almost empty.

'I think tea might be better.' Tassie laughed. 'I presume you want your photos in focus?'

'Yes, probably for the best. Come.' Clarissa turned and led the way into the house. 'Or even if I don't, your shit-scary editor will.' She glanced back with an amused smile. 'God, Skyping with her was the worst. If it wasn't for the publicity we'll get for MSF – or, Doctors Without Borders as I keep hearing it being called over here. Honestly, you'd think we Brits could manage three words of another language. Anyway, without the publicity I'm not sure we'd be doing this – the magazine stuff. And just how does she get her hair that amazing colour? I have enough problems with the ends of mine.' She saw Tassie's expression. 'They're blue.'

She pointed to the inside of a curl, then motioned for Tassie to set her bags down. 'Let's go into the kitchen. I think Mum's in there. I've no idea where Dad is. Probably hiding.'

In the hallway, faded kilim rugs covered uneven flagstones and contemporary paintings decorated every inch of the dove-grey walls. Music and chatter emanated from a sunny room overlooking the garden and as they entered, a woman was taking a kettle off the Aga. Somewhere in her sixties, she was as tall as Clarissa, wearing a faded T-shirt with *Rev It* across the front.

When she looked over her expression was warm. 'Ah, hello, Tassie is it? I've heard so much about you. Do come and sit down. How about a tea? We're just having breakfast if you'd like some?'

She directed Tassie to an armchair at the end of a table surrounded by women of varying ages, and within minutes Tassie was ensconced in the festive atmosphere; Clarissa holding court as she recounted the hair-raising circumstances in which she and Carlos had first met.

Soon afterwards the conversation turned to weddings: Clarissa's elderly grandmother recalling how the only guest at her wartime ceremony had been the fox she'd worn around her neck. Her eyes misting, she turned to Tassie. 'So dear, are you married?' She looked down the length of Tassie's loosely plaited hair. 'Honey-head. That's what we used to call hair like yours. Beautiful. I'd imagine someone's snapped you up?'

Tassie focused on the slab of homemade bread she'd been buttering, feeling herself blush when she looked up again and found everyone's eyes fixed on her.

'Granny! She *is* beautiful,' Clarissa smiled at Tassie. 'You are beautiful. But really – it's none of our business.'

Tassie grimaced. 'No it's fine, I get asked it all the time. Must be something to do with being over thirty.' She looked at the old lady. 'No. I'm not. Definitely not. Actually, it seems I'm a bit allergic.'

'Oh, I'm sorry. It's a medical issue is it?' The old woman's face creased with concern.

Clarissa snorted. 'I think she means allergic to marriage, Granny.' She looked at Tassie. 'Really? Strange, considering what you do. Have you seen enough to put you off? Or is it just not for you?'

Tassie tensed. Just as she always did when the subjects of her and relationships collided.

'Sorry. Sorry.' Clarissa's cheeks pinked. 'That was even nosier. Just ignore us.'

'No, it's fine.' Tassie forced a smile. 'It might be that marriage just isn't for me. Or maybe I've never met the right person. I don't really know.'

'Well, you're still young, my dear. I can't believe you're, what, much over twenty-five?' Granny Munro peered at her.

'Thirty-two, actually.'

There was a general murmur that she certainly didn't look it, and Tassie felt her face turning red. Normally she was the one doing the scrutinising.

'Come on you lot, stop picking on her or she might leave.' This time it was the reverend intervening.

'Well I hope you do, dear. Meet the one. Me and my Arnold. For fifty-three years we loved each other so very much.' Granny Munro stroked a fragile gold wedding band, which surfed on paper-thin skin. 'I still miss him, even after all this time. Shame we didn't marry until I was older – even older than you. We met on a boat in Norfolk—' The reverend put a gentle hand on her shoulder. 'After that, each year a glory.'

A lady wearing a bright blue pashmina gave a deep sigh. 'Are you sure you're remembering *every* year correctly, Beryl? I doubt it. Twenty-eight years was far too long for me. Miserable bugger. Never thought he'd go. You do right to stay single, miss. You'll be much happier that way. Since Fred left – *thank God* – I've been doing bingo, line-dancing, spinning, everything. *He* never wanted to go out.'

As Tassie joined in the laughter, her eyes moved from Clarissa to her grandmother and her aunts, then over to the reverend, still busy by the stove. She loved watching family dynamics, particularly the kind of affection around this table. So many generations. So much interconnection.

Swallowing her last bit of sausage, she began collecting her crockery together.

'Don't worry about that.' The reverend hurried forward. 'Do you want to go and sort yourself out? We've allocated you the dining room, if that's OK?'

'Yes, that's perfect, thank you. But first—' Tassie walked towards the hallway. 'Let me take some photos of you all. The light's really nice and it's such a lovely scene.'

FOR THE REST of the morning Tassie worked at her usual efficient pace, capturing hundreds of images as she unobtrusively moved around. She always enjoyed this part of the day: the thrill of the preparations, excitement laced with nerves.

When the sound of laughter drew her to the second floor, she found Clarissa getting ready in her old bedroom, faded posters of pop stars curling on the walls. The reverend was with her, along with a very pregnant hairdresser, and Tassie got some great shots of the bride standing in front of a large antique mirror, purple underwear and high boots showing beneath her open robe as she swigged yet more champagne.

Next, she went up to the attic to photograph Carlos, who was attempting to tie his cravat in the cracked surface of an old mirror, while his best man lay sleeping on a single bed.

As she walked around, photographing the obvious as well as the unexpected, Tassie reflected on the conversation at breakfast. Commentary on her single status was something that happened increasingly often these days. And although she found it mildly irritating, the irony wasn't lost on her that in the last three years she'd attended scores of weddings and not one had fuelled any desire for marriage.

In the back garden, a large marquee fitted easily onto the lawn, surrounded by bursts of roses, clematis and daisies. Sitting on a chair near the opening of the tent she scrolled through her photos, trying to picture herself as the one getting ready to stand next to Carlos. She half-smiled, shaking her head. Stunning as he was, that wasn't it. If she felt any affinity with him, it was for him *and* Clarissa. Several times that morning she'd thought how much she'd like to be their friend; there was something about them that had struck a real nerve, making her unusually emotional. Although, she blanched, it could just be a reaction to the seediness of the previous night. She'd not behaved like that for a while.

But *that* wasn't something she wanted to think about.

She wiped her camera lens and snapped the cap back on. Then – standing with more speed than was wise, given the fragile state of her head – she walked in the direction of the church, inhaling deeply.

The cool of the stone building was a welcome change to the increasing heat of the day as she quietly moved around, taking photos of flowers raised high on metal poles at the ends of the pews, then the silver candlesticks on the altar. Walking past the vestry she saw that the reverend had also come over; now looking contemplative as she pulled on her robes.

Tassie watched her, first from the doorway, then moving down into the tiny room. Raising her camera, she tilted her head to request permission and the rev nodded. As she framed the woman's face, bathed in light from a small window, she couldn't help comparing her to her own mother. Different in so many ways.

She gave an involuntary snort, capturing the reverend's quizzical look in her shot. Embarrassed, she lowered her camera and started fiddling with it. 'Sorry, I'm not laughing. Well, not at you.' She looked up, feeling her cheeks beginning to redden. 'I was just thinking. You're so different to my mum. I could never imagine us sharing a day like this. Well, obviously not here, in a vestry...' She looked around, more blood rushing to her cheeks. *For God's sake, shut up.*

The reverend's face was neutral. 'Well, it would be unusual if your mother was also a vicar.' There was a slight pause, then her eyes warmed as their corners creased.

'Yes. No, of course it would. And she's not. Nothing like that. She's a dog breeder actually. No, I mean it's just been so lovely, watching you and Clarissa. Your whole family.'

Oh really, stop now. Tassie examined her camera, then looked away before turning back. 'Anyway, I'll leave you in peace. Good luck for the ceremony.'

Turning, she stepped out through an open side door onto a gravel track, then sped around the side of the church and across the road.

IT WAS ten past three in the afternoon when the organ began blasting its triumphant riff, sound filling every pocket of the vaulted roof. The effect was so arresting, it took a while for the guests to register the cascade of notes as a Guns N' Roses classic.

Slowly the church doors opened, revealing two dark figures outlined against a cerulean sky. With cautious steps they entered the building, their progress sedate as they made their way down the aisle.

Topping a dress of black silk, Clarissa's hair was piled in coils, the cobalt-tipped ends spread in a fan on top. A tattoo of scarlet poppies and vivid green grasses offset the porcelain skin on her chest, contrasting with the cardinal red of her lips. As she moved forward, Tassie saw that the words *faith & hope* were etched in tiny letters onto the base of her neck, and on her back the delicate branches of a bare winter tree meandered above her silver-laced bodice.

Still, the bride looked traditionally radiant as she proceeded – her head flitting from left to right as she picked out friends and family, who shared smiles and whispered compliments as she walked towards the altar.

In contrast with Clarissa's increasing exuberance, her father remained restrained. Dressed in a morning tailcoat and pinstripe trousers, Cedric Rawlings's only flashes of colour were his purple tie and starched silk handkerchief. With his fingers pressing firmly on his daughter's hand, his eyes remained fixed on the reverend until – when they reached the bottom of the steps – he gave the bride a quick kiss, just as Axl Rose would have been banging out the words 'Sweet child o' mine'. Triumphant in their timing, father and daughter smiled.

After the drama of the entrance, silence hung in the air as the reverend stepped forward, the threads of her white and gold robe glittering in a shaft of sunlight that swept the altar. She had stood perfectly still, watching proceedings with little emotion bar a slight lifting of the corners of her mouth.

Now, as she looked down at the couple, her face broke into a slow wide smile. Then she glanced around the congregation, smoothed down invisible creases and began to speak, her voice ringing out. 'The grace of our Lord Jesus Christ, the love of God, and the fellowship of the Holy Spirit, be with you.'

A purple sea of Orders of Service bobbed among the guests, who answered with cheerful vigour, 'And also with you'.

The reverend paused for a few seconds then, as the organ started up again and the congregation stood to sing, she bent forward and touched the couple's conjoined hands, whispering something as she did.

Click.

As she framed the shot, Tassie knew it would be beautiful. It was important that she understood the workings of each family she photographed, for it made such a difference to the results. All morning she'd watched the physical affection between Clarissa and her mother, so she'd been prepared for it happening in the service as well. And, glancing at the back of her camera, she was confident the shot would capture the essence of the day.

She swallowed a sudden rise of emotion as she studied the trio. Normally she photographed ceremonies with detached professionalism, while working hard to capture the uniqueness of each event. Over the years there'd been dogs acting as ring bearers; an entire event delivered in song; and, on one particularly impressive occasion, a celebrant dressed as Henry VIII in a ceremony performed during a storm on a cliff. That had been a cold job. But, striking as they all were, few matched the emotional intimacy she was witnessing now.

If you don't want to be alone, compromise.

Syd's words. Their recall prompted no doubt by the spectacular compromise she'd made last night. Although that certainly wasn't the kind Syd had been suggesting.

Tassie tried to banish the thoughts and concentrate on the job. But it was too late. The night slipped into her mind, like oil on a bedroom carpet.

~

EVEN AS SHE'D rung the bell of *Rose Cottage B&B,* she'd known it wasn't going to be good. Her concerns had begun with the dead roses drooping over the door, deepening when the landlady eventually opened it – a cigarette hanging from the side of her mouth.

Following the woman's wide bottom up narrow stairs, Tassie was shown into a bedroom with satin bedcovers, frilly curtains and an avocado bathroom that looked like it had scurvy.

Only stopping to hang up her wedding workwear – navy culottes and a cream silk vest – she escaped back into the cobbled streets of Exeter, wondering what she could do to delay her return. Pizza came first, followed by a lively looking bar. Then Hamish.

She had an inkling from the start that something didn't quite add up. Still, she found him increasingly attractive as the evening progressed, his tales of growing up as an ambassador's son in Botswana keeping everyone amused. And he was keen, purring keen when he offered to accompany her home.

Outside the bar he slipped his arm around her shoulders, their bodies blending as they walked the empty streets. When they reached the B&B she turned to him and he kissed her, his tongue seeking the depths of her mouth, the alcohol that had freed their reserve now fuelling a joint desire. He told her how much he wanted her as he took her hand, both giggling as they crept up the nicotine-scented stairs. Then, pushing the door with his foot, he rushed to remove her clothing, before standing, quite still, breathing heavily as she leant back on the pillows.

'You're like a... mermaid. Stunning.'

For someone older. She could almost hear him think it.

Languorously he undid his shirt, each button revealing inches more rippled brown chest.

The arrogance of youth. She grimaced at the thought.

Staring into his face she pulled him towards her, undoing the buttons of his jeans before hooking her fingers into his waistband and sliding everything down over his hips. Still staring, she took her time, tying her hair in a loose knot before running her hands over his buttocks, glancing down at his nakedness, then slipping onto her knees.

'MARRIAGE IS GIVEN, that a husband and wife may comfort and help each other, living faithfully together in need and in plenty, in sorrow and in joy.'

Tassie started as the reverend's words pulled her back into the present. For a few moments she listened, frowning slightly as she concentrated on them. Then she moved towards the pulpit to get a different angle of the couple. This time, somehow, the words seemed to have so much more meaning, and she was horrified when tears began to well. She dashed them away. Just what was wrong with her? Maybe it was because the couple were about to go back to Afghanistan – where the dangers were incomprehensible. Perhaps that's what was making her so emotional.

More likely it was her shame regarding the previous night. Exacerbated by her taxi ride that morning, when she'd been surprised but not delighted to receive a text from Hamish.

Hey you. Not stopd thinkg about you or*^! Hope we can meet agn soon.

Seeing his name had only added to the discomfort she'd felt when he'd left a few hours earlier, tripping over himself in his haste to be gone.

Initially she'd put the awkwardness down to a difference in age and experience – his dry-fingered fumblings attesting to that – but seeing the text suddenly made her reconsider.

She typed his name into her search box, and it didn't take much looking before she found him. *Hamish McIntyre, MRes Politics, University of Exeter.* His privacy settings not what they should be, she scrolled through photo after photo. Hamish in bars with friends, Hamish messing about on the moors, Hamish on the beach – in at least half of them with a pretty blonde who, judging by her rapt smiles, must be his girlfriend.

The first wave of nausea had risen as she'd embedded one of the images into her text and typed *I don't think so.* Then, her mouth rigid, she'd blocked his number.

'CARLOS JOSÉ POTEL, will you take Clarissa May Rawlings to be your wedded wife? Will you love her, comfort her, honour her and protect her?' The reverend smiled beatifically as she posed the questions.

Was that what she was missing: comfort and protection? Tassie lifted her camera then lowered it again, a wave of grey washing through her, prompting a weariness that had nothing to do with having drunk too much the night before.

Creeping onto the pulpit steps, she thought about the conversation she'd had with Syd as she took a quick succession of shots. What *had* she said exactly? That she was too old to be behaving like a drunken… teenager. She'd sensed there was a different word her friend had wanted to use.

But. *Fuck it.* Marriage was just a societal convention. Although, Carlos and Clarissa… At that moment their heads were angled towards each other. *Click.* Enough to restore anyone's faith in the existence of true love.

She moved back towards the altar, tightening her focus on Clarissa's eyes, which glistened as she took Carlos's hand.

'To love and to cherish; Till death us do part; According to God's holy law; All this I vow before God.'

As the couple loosed their hands, there was a sharp clatter from the side of the altar and Tassie turned to see the best man scrabbling to retrieve the ring box, his face puce with embarrassment. Despite knowing it would make a great picture she ignored it, for couples could be spooked by things like that.

After the service had finished she was relieved to be back in the fresh air, ready to photograph the bride and groom leaving the church through two boisterous lines of family and friends. Breathing in the sunshine, she trained her camera on the newly-weds as they walked through a blizzard of confetti.

Until, that is, they reached Granny Munro.

At which point, chaos ensued.

For Granny Munro didn't throw her cup of delphinium petals. Instead she threw the cup of water someone had fetched for her, concerned she'd become too dehydrated.

Shot one: the throw.

Shot two: water dripping off Carlos's face.

Shot three: his new wife, doubled up with laughter.

Tassie grinned as she checked her shots, delighted she'd caught it all.

Confident that nothing was going to spook this bride and groom today.

4

London, August 2014

'Yum, smells delicious.' Syd bent to sniff the combination of goat's cheese, griddled courgettes and fresh oregano in the quiche Tassie had placed on the rickety garden table.

'It certainly does,' said Stan, stroking his fiancée's back as the panels of her chiffon top fell forward. 'Is everything from your garden, Tass? Apart from the cheese.'

'Oh my God, I can't believe she's not told you. She's forever banging on about it to me.' Oliver leant forward, his elbows as sharp as his quiff and skinny jeans. 'Not only did she grow the veg but now she's even started making her own *fromage*. I can't believe she hasn't been texting you guys about it. She has me – with photos.'

Tassie bobbed a curtsy as her guests all turned to look at her. 'Dad gave me this book so I thought I'd give it a go. And it seems to have worked. It's actually really easy. D'you want to know how it's done? I can show you the—'

The collective 'no' came from everyone but Tilak, who smiled politely – his smile extraordinarily wide and bright –

then said he'd love to see it before Oliver bumped his shoulder.

Syd laughed. 'Such a country girl, our Tass. I can't think why you're stuck here in London when you'd be so much happier down on the farm.'

'Why does she need that when she has all this?' Stan gestured around them, a muscular bicep covered with a large black cross. 'If we turn the music up, we can't hear the traffic out front or the trains at the back.' And they all laughed when, as if on cue, wheels hissed along the bottom of the garden.

Tassie looked around. They were right: this was the place where she felt happiest. Although it hadn't always seemed like such a good idea. When she'd bought the flat two years previously, she'd willfully ignored all the issues of traffic, trains and the dark, dank interior, focusing instead on the large south-facing kitchen and tangle of vegetation beyond.

Her two front rooms consisted of a just-about-big-enough living room and a frankly-ridiculously small bedroom; although now she loved the fact that her wrought-iron bed and shabby wardrobe virtually filled it.

Both rooms had barricaded windows looking out to a tiny patio – softened by moss and ivy trailing up worn steps to the street above – and Tassie had painted the living room a forest green and her bedroom deep red. Despite the gloom the colours worked, creating a cosy urban cave that was complemented by an eclectic mix of artefacts she'd collected from London markets and her travels abroad.

There were brass lamps; an intricately embroidered Indian bedspread; a cosy leather sofa, its bottom sagging like an old dog's belly; and, Stan's favourite, the vintage gramophone inherited from her Uncle Ali. The kitchen was now equally transformed, with buttercup walls and a battered farmhouse table dominating the centre, and it was only the bathroom that still left much – if not everything – to be desired. Damp and cold, she needed to save enough money to give it a complete refit and, although she was doing pretty well these days, she hadn't quite got there yet.

Finally, there was the garden, which everyone agreed was stunning; not surprising given that Tassie spent every hour she had available working on it. Whatever the weather, she'd once proudly told Syd, she had the wellies to match. Green for rain, yellow for sunshine, and pink Crocs for picking fruit. She'd offered to show them to her, laughing when Syd had firmly declined, stifling a yawn as she'd kicked out tiny feet clad in Chinese slippers.

The sun was now descending behind the roofs, rapidly lengthening the shadows which slanted off the trees screening the railway tracks. Tassie stretched out her tanned legs, sipping her wine which Tilak had just topped up. Surveying the military rows of fruit and veg, she wondered what she would plant next, happily ignoring Oliver, who was telling some scandalous story about a newly married couple. She'd probably already heard it, for she'd been making much more of an effort to speak to him of late.

Unusually big for a town garden, where once there'd been a wasteland of weeds, thorns, old bottles and plastic there was now real beauty, the beds made from old railway sleepers taken from the farm. Her dad had complained bitterly about bringing them to London, but, as she'd pointed out, they'd been cluttering up his yard for years. And she'd loved the weekend they'd spent putting them together – especially as she'd not been back to see her parents in over a year.

Syd gently poked her in the ribs. 'Tass, are you listening?'

Tilak smiled at her as he put his hand on Oliver's shoulder. 'I've already heard this one and I'd recommend it.'

'So,' said Oliver, glaring at Tassie, 'for the sake of Ms Head in the Clouds I shall recap.' He folded then unfolded his arms. 'So, they're starting to walk through the jungle—'

'I think you call it the bush in Africa, Ol,' said Stan.

'Whatever. So they're starting to walk through the bush, and this guide's told them that if they see a lion they mustn't do *anything*. Mustn't shout, move, crouch, jump. Nothing. And whatever they do, they *mustn't* run.'

'I'm not sure I could see a lion and not run,' said Syd. 'Remind me not to choose a safari for our honeymoon, Stan.'

'No chance. We couldn't afford it.'

'Me neither, not run – nor afford it – but... hush you two. Anyway,' – Oliver looked around the table – 'those were the instructions he'd given and they'd been walking for only a few minutes when, would you lark it, a lion appears. So, the guide is standing stock still, doing nothing, like he said. But the couple have turned on their heels and are running back to the truck, fast as their fear will take them.'

'And?' The group was suitably expectant.

'So they reach the truck, the woman first. But the man – her new husband, don't forget – comes running up behind her, yanks her shirt, pushes her aside and scrambles up instead.'

'And?' There was a general intake of breath, then laughter.

'Well, the lion has disappeared – who would blame him – and the guide comes back to say as much. And no doubt shout at them. But the woman, she's busy pulling off her rings, which she throws into the jung— sorry, *bush*, turns to the guide and says, "I want a charter plane out of here.

Now."' He paused, delighted with his story. 'Not a word of a lie. Another planner told me.'

There was more laughter and some amazement as the others absorbed the full juiciness of Oliver's tale.

'That's not actually true is it?' Syd's face was screwed up in disbelief. 'On their *honeymoon*?'

'Not a word of a lie. He had a couple who were on the same safari who told him when they got back.'

'Wow,' said Stan. 'Short marriage. And defo a bit of an overreaction on her part.'

'Really?' Syd glared at him. 'Stanley Matthews, if you ever did that to me I'd not only throw your rings away, I'd chop off your parsnip and throw *that* to the lion. What do you think, Tass, Tilak?'

'I think that would be a fair response on your part,' said Tassie. 'Although I'm not sure it would make much of a meal.'

Tilak laughed along with everyone else – bar Stan – then said, 'I think Syd was asking whether it was an over-reaction?'

Tassie twirled her wine glass, reconsidering the question. 'Well, any relationship is about trust, isn't it? And after that had happened I don't think she could ever trust him again, so it was probably the only answer. However drastic it might seem. After all, when it's gone, it's gone.' She stilled her glass, staring into it, and when she finally smiled, she was aware it was a strangely twisted grin.

With her more considered response, the atmosphere around the table shifted, a stillness descending as everyone sat lost in their own thoughts. Except for Syd, who was staring at Tassie, her eyebrows raised.

Tilak was the first to speak. 'I think Tassie is right. Of course trust is important. But I also think that in times of fear, people behave in ways they'd never want to think they would. We certainly saw that in Sri Lanka during the troubles. Maybe – assuming the couple got together again – it gave them a raw starting point from which to rebuild their relationship.'

He had such a kind, gentle face. Definitely good for Oliver. Tassie looked across at her friend, unusually contemplative as he stared into his plate.

Syd shivered. 'I bet they didn't get back together. And *think* of the consequences. All those wedding presents.'

Everyone laughed, knowing that gifts were currently her big preoccupation. She'd wanted a list at John Lewis; Stan wanted donations for a jukebox. Syd blamed Tassie's gramophone.

'Well, if it had been that wedding in Exeter it wouldn't have been a problem,' said Tassie. 'They just wanted donations.'

She sometimes thought about that weekend, wondering how the couple were doing, back in Afghanistan. She'd been too shy to suggest they kept in touch but wished she had. Especially as the reverend had insisted that she promise to visit if ever she was back in the neighbourhood.

'Actually, I think it's about unconditional love.'

Everyone stared at Oliver, surprised by the weight of his tone.

'I hadn't really thought about it before. To be honest I'd just thought it was a great story. But I think that if you really love someone, love them more than anyone else, then you instinctively put them first. Because you know that life without them wouldn't be worth living. So when something like that happens, it's in that moment you find out the true strength of your feelings.' He coughed. 'And that's why she had to leave. Because in that moment he showed her that he didn't truly love her.'

There was silence for a moment, then he clapped his

hands. 'But what do I know about anything. Come on, let's have seconds. I'm starving.'

Tassie began doling out more slices of quiche, pleased by its popularity as she urged her guests to help themselves to more of her freshly harvested broad beans, potatoes and carrots.

But while most hands were busy with the food, she noticed one of Tilak's moving over to Oliver's. And there it stayed, their fingers entwined – until they each moved to take another sip of wine.

She and Oliver exchanged a quick glance.

'Keeper,' she mouthed.

'TASS, have you got any cheese? No, correction, you always have cheese. What kinds do you have?' Stan looked down at her blearily as he gyrated, barefoot, to Nina Simone's 'My Baby Just Cares for Me'. Tassie and Syd were squashed together on a suede beanbag, while Oliver and Tilak lounged on the sofa.

Syd sniffed. 'There's enough smell going on in here already. Although, Tass, I do need to give you something.' She pushed herself up then held out her hand. Of the group she was the only one still completely sober, having decided at fourteen never to drink again – something to do with a vomit-inducing worm at the bottom of a bottle of Tequila and her foster mother's new white sofa.

Tassie groaned, slipping further into the beanbag as it shifted shape. 'Really? I'm comfortable.'

'Come on.' Syd took her hand and rubbed it. 'It won't take long, then I need to get everyone home.'

In the kitchen she pulled a file out of her oversized tote as Tassie slumped at the table. 'I'm sorry to bring your work home, but I mentioned to Catrina that I was seeing you, and she suggested you might want this. It's instead of the wedding that was cancelled?'

Tassie straightened. Weddings for the magazine were normally scheduled about eight months in advance, but this year they'd had a bit of a crisis for September, with a bride having called off a Mad-Hatter event with just three months to go. She knew Syd had spent a crazy few weeks sorting out a new couple to fill the slot, but she usually only picked up the brief a couple of weeks before each event. She stared at her friend. It was only the beginning of August, meaning the wedding wasn't for another five weeks.

'You might want to open it in the morning?'

'Definitely not now you've said that.' Tassie grabbed the papers. 'Where's...' She looked again, her finger following the text. Maybe she'd drunk more than she thought. 'Sch... ie...hallion?' She read on. 'Two thousand five hundred feet above sea level and only accessible by Land Rover? Sydonie Harper? What the hell is this? Or more like, *where* the hell is it?'

'Er, somewhere spectacular and very romantic?'

'Sydonie. Explain?'

'Scotland.' Syd shrugged. 'Perthshire. About an hour and a half north of Edinburgh. Oh, but Tass, it's beautiful. I can see why Cat wants us to do it.' She took the papers, pulling out a full-page photo of a mountain. '*This* is Schiehallion. The name means Fairy Hill of the Caledonians. Don't you think it's gorgeous? I know it's a long way, and aye, the wedding is actually going to be on the mountain itself... and it might well be raining—' She tried but failed to suppress a grin. 'But I'm so sure it will all be worth it. Don't you think?' She snuggled into Tassie's side. 'Hopefully?'

'Bloody hell, Syd. You and your romantic ideals. It's

going to take me days to get there, days to get back; I'll need a bloody off-roader to get to the ceremony itself and I still won't be paid any more money. And who's going to look after my garden if the weather's still warm? Oh, this is a bit crap.' Tassie put her chin on her hand. 'Really? Has Catrina definitely said it's got to be this one?'

Syd nodded, her grin fading. 'Sorry, pet. If you want the good news, it was either this or one with snake charmers in Swindon.'

'And it's on the first Saturday?'

'Aye.'

'The sixth September?'

'Aye.'

'Shit.'

'Oh no,' Syd was instantly concerned. 'You've not got another booking have you? I checked your work calendar and couldn't see anything.'

'No, I've nothing planned. Not really. But still, shit. There's so much stuff to do in the garden. And I've got all those product shots earlier in the month. Then that private event in Cardiff.'

'Sorry, Tass, I thought you'd relish the adventure. You're always telling me how much you miss your travelling.'

Tassie looked at her friend's face and her voice softened. 'No, it's fine. Really, it's OK. It's just...' She stared out of the kitchen window and after a few moments a smile slid across her face. 'I tell you what, Ms Romance, I've got a brilliant idea. *You* can come and look after my flat while I'm gone. Or – more specifically – the garden. I'll leave you detailed instructions. And all my wellies. You'll enjoy that.' Tassie cocked her head.

Syd pouted, then shrugged. They both knew she'd already agreed the moment she'd pulled the brief out of her bag. 'But I'm only using your yellow ones, with fifty-five pairs of socks. And don't ever expect us to wear those hideous Crocs.'

Tassie laughed as she stood, then put her arms around her friend, nuzzling her chin on the top of Syd's head. 'Deal. Now let's go and find the others. It's all gone very quiet.'

AFTER SHE'D WAVED her friends up the stairs – Tilak and Oliver barely waking to say their goodbyes – Tassie went into the garden and gathered up the last of the dishes from the table. Stan had left his cigarettes. That would upset him. Turning off the lights, she went into her bedroom and retrieved her phone from the floor. Three notifications. When she opened her emails she saw there was one about a shoot scheduled for the following week, one about a wedding she was doing next January. And one that made her heart leap.

Skype me when you get this. Six pm my time would be good.

Tassie looked at her watch. Midnight her time made it eight pm in New York. Way too late to call. He'd be at home with his family by now.

She sat on her bed and typed. Then deleted. Then typed again. Paused. Deleted. Then typed once more. Frowning, she studied what she'd written.

Sorry, saw this too late, try me again? Need to chat through some developments re 6th. We might have to rethink the date. Still, would be great to see you. How long are you over for? Looking forward to it. Definitely. I've missed you. T xx

Pausing, she deleted the last sentence before pressing send, her mind whirling through a maelstrom of recollections.

Many good. Many bad.

Alex Winchester.

Back in her life.

Again.

Going to her wardrobe she grabbed a stool and, reaching up to the top shelf, pulled down a cardboard box. Taking it over to her bed she got a tissue and wiped off the layer of dust that lay like velvet across the top. Inside were stacks of old photos, letters, poems, cards and a little blue and black matchbox. Opening it, she chuckled. Written in tiny spidery letters on a scrap of paper were the words *Je t'aime, Thierry xx*. How she'd fancied the pants off him, aged thirteen and on a French exchange.

As she shifted through the layers, the years of her adolescence, she marvelled at the emotions, smells and sounds that were instantly recreated by everything she touched. Until, finally, she retrieved a thick manila envelope. The ink had faded, but she could still make out the address of her parents' farm on the front, and she pictured the last time she'd looked through its contents: the moment she'd determined to burn everything as she'd sat by the fire, gripping it for what had seemed like hours. But then she'd put the envelope back in the box, of course, just as she always did, chiding herself for her weakness as she'd buried it under everything else.

It had been years since that night, but still her heart skipped a little faster as she pulled out the first thing her fingers touched. It was a small photo, slightly yellowed, a younger version of herself. Eighteen? No, she'd probably just turned seventeen; standing in front of a gigantic

Christmas tree, light cascading out of the surrounding shops – her face glowing with happiness. One window display was all about Cool Britannia, another had lots of Asian clothes. It was the end of the 1990s. A different era.

The era of her and Alex.

5

egent's Park, December 1999

It had been Tassie's idea to take the boat out. Ideas like that usually were. She'd wanted to try it as soon as she'd seen it lying just metres from the lake, bright blue paint crackled over red, its rope coiled loosely in front. Now, as she tugged it towards the water, her breath puffed smoke – illuminated by the low winter sun.

'Come on, it's not tied to anything. It'll be fun.' She stared up at Alex who was watching her from a nearby bench.

He shook his head, his eyebrows raised. 'Really?'

'Come on, or I'll go by myself. You know I will.'

He sighed, dusting the algae from his coat as he looked around the park. In the distance, an old man was shuffling along, head down, a small dog darting this way and that. Eventually Alex shrugged and walked down the bank to join her. Eyeing the boat suspiciously he bent to examine it. 'I bet there's a reason it's not locked.' He dug his thumb into the rim, leaving a small indent. 'See? The wood's gone all soft.'

'Oh, come on, let's just try. What's the worst that can

happen?' With one more pull the bow crunched over stones into the water and Tassie jumped in. 'Look! There's even some oars.' She turned, her enthusiasm rewarded when Alex finally smiled. Bending down she yanked two misshapen pieces of wood from beneath the seats. 'I'm sure these wouldn't be here if it didn't work. And we'll put it back where it was. Come on. It's Christmas.' She cocked her head and blew him a kiss.

A jogger appeared, running in the opposite direction to the old man, his hat clamped by large headphones. But there was no one else visible in the whole of Regent's Park, for winter gloom was just beginning to descend and the weather was cold enough to put most people off a late afternoon stroll.

Gathering up his coat, Alex shook his head as he pulled the boat towards him then clambered in. Still scanning the horizon, he sat, pin-straight, as Tassie thrust the oars into the water and started rowing, straining with each stroke as slowly – but not at all surely – the boat began to move. Soon her face was hot and she had to blow bits of hair out of her mouth as it tumbled down around her, strands of pearl, amber and gold shining in the fading light.

After a few minutes Alex leant forward and, taking her face in his hands, gave her a long kiss. Then, crouching in the middle of the boat, he twisted round and backed up to sit next to her. Nudging her shoulder, he held out a hand. 'Come on. It'll be easier if we both do it.'

It took about eight minutes for them to row into the middle of the lake, a minute to admire the orange sun as it sank behind the silhouetted fingers of the park's trees, and two more minutes to realise the boat was leaking.

Tassie's laughter rang out across the fractured water, soon followed by Alex's expletives. Alerted by the noise, the old man stood and watched, the dog twisting to sniff something between his feet as he strained to make out what they were doing.

They frantically pulled on the oars, racing to reach the shore before it was too late, and as soon as she could Tassie jumped out, soaking her Converse and splashing water over her jeans as she yanked on the bow, flakes of paint coming away in her hand. Alex disembarked more cautiously, trying to avoid his suede shoes getting wet.

Still laughing, she took the lion's share of pulling the boat in, then Alex looked at her, shaking his head.

'Told you.' But his face was amused as he said it and, pulling her close to him, he lifted her chin. 'You're crazy, Tassie Morris – and I still can't believe you came today. But I'm so glad you did. I love you.' He held out his hand, then looked up at the sky. 'Let's get out of here. I think it might actually snow. And I'm freezing.'

WHEN HAD THEY FIRST MET? It had been just an ordinary Thursday – the kind with homework, odd socks and toad in the hole for tea – the day he'd first walked into her life. Or strolled, to be more accurate.

She'd been struggling with algebraic fractions at the kitchen table when her brother had bounced in, followed by a boy she'd never seen before. He'd paused to pat the dog, pushing his dark hair from his face, and while Tom had worked on persuading their mother that there'd be enough toads for everyone, Tassie had done her best not to look up again. She'd not wanted her flushed cheeks to give her away – any more than the faint pink powdering her mother's.

At supper Alex had been charming, explaining how he and Tom had met through the debating society, although he was actually in Tassie's year; asking her father about his

42

cows; commiserating with Tassie about the amount of revision they needed to do – it quickly becoming clear he was doing a lot more than her. Before he'd cycled off at the end of the evening, a trip to the cinema had been arranged with Tom (and Tassie) for the following Saturday; then a week later they'd gone out again, this time just the two of them. And that was it: first love unfolding, with all its exhilarating, palpitating, blood-rushing, head-spinning, heart-crushing emotion.

And there she'd bloody remained.

Tassie carried the envelope through to the sitting room where, sitting cross-legged on the worn brown rug, she tipped out its contents.

Each item carried a memory so strong it almost stung. There were sheets of old paper, postcards, photos, cards, old flyers and – she held them up to the light, amazed they were still intact – two pressed daisies, pristine between squares of faded tissue. Just as she'd done so many times before, she picked up a sheet of paper torn from an exercise book, now yellowed with age, curling letters covering its surface.

My Darling Gorgeous, Hot, Sexy Tassie, I'm sitting in Latin. I'm bored. So bored. So I just thought I'd tell you that I love you. I love you. I love you. I love you… She scanned to the bottom, the same phrase covering the page, then turned it over. *I love you. I love you. I want to make love to you. I love you…* Until the end. *Shit, Smith's prowling the room. Gotta go. See you tonight. Have I told you that I… x*

Sighing, she picked up another photo: Covent Garden's Christmas market, where enormous shiny baubles hung from curved iron beams and scores of goods weighted down tinsel-fringed tables. She and Alex had walked there after Regent's Park, ambling through streets packed with shoppers, quickening their steps when they'd heard music drifting towards them, then gasping with pleasure as they'd stood taking in the scene.

Beneath the church that towered over the piazza sat a jazz band: five old men wearing thick overcoats and Christmas hats. They were belting out a quickstep version of 'Rock Around the Clock', so loud the music bounced off buildings and spun through the air. In front of them people jived their way across the cobblestones, an impromptu dancehall in the open street.

Tassie tugged on Alex's hand. 'Come on!'

For once he didn't need persuading and they slipped into the whirling mass, twisting and twirling until they were out of breath and doubled up with laughter. Still more and more people joined in: children, couples – young and old – even a woman and her dog, up on its hind legs, its tail wagging.

'I've got to take some photos, this is fantastic.' Tassie was breathless as she led Alex out of the crowd and looked for her camera. She quickly adjusted the settings then slipped back into the throng, people smiling at her as she snapped away, the dog briefly back up on its legs, now wearing a Christmas hat. Those she asked happily posed for her, others were so intent on dancing they seemed oblivious to her lens. When an old man grabbed her by the waist Tassie danced with him, her hat sent flying by the surprising vigour with which he spun her round.

Finally she returned to Alex, who'd been leaning against one of the church's pillars watching her.

'That was brilliant,' she said.

'Just like all your other, *brilliant* photos?'

Tassie shrugged as she grinned. He was right, she photographed everything. Flowers in the spring, her dad's cows, the shadows cast by clouds on the fields. Even her mother's dogs – occasionally. Her talent might not be on a par with Alex's academia, but her art teachers loved what she did and were already encouraging her to consider photography at college.

She slipped her hand into his. 'Don McLean. That's me.'

'Huh?'

'I was just remembering something Dad said.' She chuckled. When they'd been discussing her career options a few days earlier, her father had confused Don McLean with Don McCullin.

'What shall we do now?' She stretched up to kiss Alex. 'More dancing? Shopping? Or food?'

'Well, given this was meant to be a present buying trip and we've bought nothing, let's shop.'

'OK.' She reached for her Christmas list. 'I've still no idea what to get Tom.'

'From our conversation last week, I think your brother would like a girlfriend most. Let's see if we can find him a blow-up one.'

~

SIFTING through the scraps of her past, Tassie picked up a photo of her schmoozing a life-sized rag doll. They'd not bought it for her brother, obviously.

Then, she realised – that's when she'd got her mother the poodle scarf. *Before* she'd found out what she had done.

Wincing as she uncrossed her legs to stand, she glanced at a photo of her father on the windowsill. She'd also bought him his tie – blue silk covered in daisies. He'd loved it so much it was the only one he'd worn since, and she'd taken the photo when he'd been made county chair of the NFU. It always made her smile, seeing him leaning over his farm gate, dressed in his smart dark suit.

Next to his photo was one of her and her Uncle Ali: the

bequeather of the gramophone so admired by Stan. She and Alex had arranged to stay with him that weekend in London, and he'd been so lovely when she'd called for directions, telling her gently that her mother had phoned and was furious that Tassie had disappeared, despite being grounded after a dreadful report.

Moving over to the gramophone, she crouched in front of a wooden apple box housing his old record collection, and soon the rich tones of Aretha Franklin were rolling out across the room. She walked back to the windowsill. The photo of her and her uncle had been taken in his flat when she was about ten, the two of them standing in front of walls crammed with books and stuffed animals in dusty boxes. She kissed his image, the glass cold on her lips, then sank back down onto the rug. Picking up a diary, *1999* emblazoned in gold on the front, her lips twitched as she pictured the teenage girl she'd been when writing it. *Couldn't sleep last night. Tried everything: bath, radio, reading, homework. Even tried drawing sheep! Miss Troy forgot to give us homework today. Third time in a row.*

Then. She stopped. *Finally did it!!!!!*

She'd written that after the first time she and Alex had slept together. A new experience for them both, her happiness etched into the messy scrawl. Even now she could remember the excitement: sitting in the alcove of her bedroom window, hugging her knees as she'd watched him walk down the path, feeling happy but nervous, knowing that by the end of the afternoon things would be different; *she* would be different.

But in the event everything had felt so natural, so right. As if being together, as connected as physically possible, was what was meant to be. And if either *had* had any doubts, all post-coital analysis had been lost in a flurry of dressing when they'd heard her mother arriving home unexpectedly early. She pictured Alex hopping around the room, his foot stuck in the pocket of his jeans, his face reddening. How had he managed to regain his composure so quickly? She'd gone downstairs a few minutes later and found him sitting at the kitchen table, innocently drinking a cup of her mother's insipid grey tea, asking about her latest batch of puppies. Bless him.

A small red card fell out of the diary: a bad sketch of a woman next to the words *Hot Honey, Oriental Pleasure, 7 days a week*. Turning it over, she saw where she'd scribbled her uncle's address on the back. And her face hardened.

The card had been one of many splashed across the wall of the phone box, and she'd been giggling when she'd done what her uncle suggested and called home. But that was when the laughter had stopped, soon replaced by fury.

She cringed as she flipped through the diary's pages. *Funniest blow job today. Went right up my nose.* Another entry: *I thought I saw Dad today, in a café in Shrewsbury. Weird. Swear he said he was going to Birmingham. An affair???!!! Wouldn't blame him.* And another: *Ax said he was looking for my E spot. No wonder he couldn't find it!!* Even now, she felt the same sense of outrage she'd felt when her mother had told her that she'd read her diary, just as she could still hear the disdain curdling her mother's voice. And then, her pathetic excuse: that she was worried where her daughter might have gone.

Which did nothing to make her forgive her – then or now. *Condom scare last night, but my God does having an empty house make for good sex.*

How dare she! She flicked through a few more entries. So much about Alex... always Alex.

Collecting a bottle of wine and Stan's cigarettes from the kitchen, she winced when nicotine hit the back of her throat. It was a long time since she'd smoked. Tears pricking her eyes, she picked up a small hinged box and opened it slowly, just as she'd done all those years ago. Inside was a necklace – the silver battered around the edges but the centre still unblemished. Carefully removing it she held it tight, feeling its weight, wanting something more substantial. Needing something more substantial. Still.

∼

AFTER HER CALL HOME, she and Alex had wandered down to the Embankment, her mind still full of what her mother would have read, unable to tell him what had happened; because then it would all become too real.

They sat under Cleopatra's Needle, its tip stretching high into the sky, while across the water the monolithic buildings of the South Bank squatted heavy on the land.

'Tassie?' He cleared his throat, and she saw that he was holding something. 'I got this for you.'

She looked at him, then the package. *Stop thinking about the conversation. It's done. Too late to change it.* The words were loud in her head as she moved to sit on his lap, wrapping her legs around him. 'But it's not Christmas yet?'

'I know, but as we won't be seeing each other, I thought now might be the time to give it to you?' Both his voice and eyes were soft.

'Don't remind me.' She huffed through her nose as her mouth puckered downwards. 'I wish you weren't going away. Another Christmas with my freakin' mother.' She looked at the package and forced a grin. 'But thank you. Can I open it?'

'Er, that's why I'm giving it to you.'

Her heart lightening with expectation, she tore into the pale green tissue then pulled up the lid.

'Oh Alex!' She looked at him. 'It's beautiful. Stunning. What is it?'

'A necklace. You need to take it out to see.'

He reached in and released the tiny object from its base and Tassie breathed in sharply as he held it up under the street light. It was a minuscule camera lens, delicately crafted in silver and black metal. Except, where the lens should have been, was a tiny full moon.

She took it from him, staring in wonder. 'Alex, it's so lovely. How did you find it? When did you buy it? Today?' *She can go to hell. I will never speak to her again – unless I absolutely have to.*

'From that woman with orange hair. When you were buying your parents' things. It's an antique – or second-hand, as Mum would say.'

Tassie circled her arms around him as she kissed him. She always loved kissing Alex. She loved the way she had to reach up on her tiptoes to do so. She loved the taste of him. The way he often smelt of coffee. *Fuck her.* Finally she broke away. 'It's the best present ever. I'll wear it every day. Thank you.' Her eyes were blurry as she stroked his face.

'Glad you like it. Happy Christmas, Tass. Happy New Year and, happy us. I'll miss you.'

'And me you.' She kissed him again. 'Thank you. I love it so much. And...' – she was still embarrassed by the words they'd only just taken to saying – 'I love you.'

Alex hugged her tight, and this time their kiss was long and deep, their tongues entwining as she felt him stiffening beneath her. She moved her hand onto his groin, caressing with firm strokes.

'Tass don't. It's too public.' He shifted, looking around. 'Later, definitely later. If your uncle's a heavy sleeper.' He kissed her again then started to stand, forcing her off his lap.

As he did so, she felt a part of her shrivel. *Maybe he does think I'm too— What a bitch! It* had been a particularly vicious barb from her mother: that she shouldn't get too attached to Alex, as boys like him didn't stick around girls who were easy. *Really. Fuck her.* She stood up, and a cold flake landed on her nose, then another on Alex's cheek.

Snow.

'Told you it would.' Pulling on Tassie's hands, Alex pointed upwards. 'Look!'

Silently they stood, bodies close, arms wrapped around each other as they stared in awe at the millions of snowflakes interweaving like lace. Blinking a flake off her lashes, Tassie looked at him, concentrating on his face, his eyes, his mouth; forcing every other image from her mind. *Don't let her spoil this too.*

She rested her head against his body, breathing in the mustiness of his second-hand coat as they watched the flakes settle briefly on their hats and shoulders before evaporating into dark spots.

While above them, a mass of tiny crystals turned the night sky white: softly dimming the three-quarter moon.

6

Tassie lit another cigarette then held up the necklace. She'd not worn it for, how many years? She counted on her fingers. Six. And he'd given it to her nine years before that.

There was a mirror on the living room wall and peering at her reflection, she compared it with the photo of her at seventeen. Her hair still hung in long heavy waves, although it was a darker blonde now. Her eyes were the same hazel, flecked with green and amber, although, if you looked closely, a little less open, more guarded. She cupped her breasts. Even her figure hadn't changed that much. And her fingers were still adorned with a mix of silver rings, topped by bitten nails.

But all she could really see was misery. Why did it still hurt so much to remember? Like a blunt knife scraping across her heart? Why did she feel like a small child? A rather drunk small child, up late and inexplicably alone. She should go to bed.

She scraped everything together on the rug. So many photos, some bent, most faded. But then, she stopped. The one of the dog. It was still a great shot. Shame to get rid of it.

Or the old couple dancing, their hands waving above their heads. And then – her breathing slowed – there was one of Alex sitting on a bench, looking straight at the camera, a slight smile undermining the intensity of his stare. For a few moments she studied the photo with as much dispassionate professionalism as her swaying would allow. Grey-blue eyes, angular chin, sharp cheekbones... an unexpectedly delicate nose. True, his top lip was a bit thin, rather feminine, but the bottom one was wide and full. Was he as beautiful as she remembered? She sighed. Yes, he was.

She shoved everything into the envelope, then, fetching her phone from the bedroom, searched 'Alex' in her email and scrolled down the thread of messages. When she'd received the first, three months ago, they'd not been in contact for years, and she'd rarely been so surprised, and – let's be honest – thrilled, as when it had appeared in her inbox.

Hi Tass, long time no speak. I hope you're well. I've been thinking about you a lot recently. Must be the time of year – lots of rain... always reminds me of England.

Things are good here. Martha and I now have a little one called Tod, another one on the way. There's the possibility it might be twins. Heaven help me! Work's good. Busy in extremis *but satisfying – well, sort of. Not always easy, working for the family firm. Anyway, I'm in town next month. Got a meeting with some new clients. A premier gin account. It's going to be a biggie.*

So... I'll be in London for four nights and I thought, well, how about meeting up, old friend? You know, clear the air. Lunch is on me – let's call it an apology.

Alex x

She'd resisted answering for a while; but then she'd

broken up with Josh and, yes, she was ashamed to say, during yet another night alone with too much Chardonnay swirling through her bloodstream, she'd sent him a response.

And so they'd met. And nothing had changed. They were as in tune at thirty-two as they'd been at eighteen. And they'd enjoyed a tantalizingly delicious lunch – on his expenses. And talked about lots of stuff, just like old friends. And, halfway down the second bottle of wine, he'd told her that he'd always have feelings for her. 'Very strong feelings...' Then he'd paused and called a waiter over. 'Could this wine possibly go back? It isn't quite chilled.' But, he'd continued after the waiter had gone, he was married now. And had a baby. And another one – possibly two – on the way. And yet he'd still held her hand as they'd walked to the Tube station. Because that was what they always did. And given her a quick peck on the cheek before hailing a taxi. Then a firm hug – held a fraction longer than you might have expected for just good friends. And then he was gone. Again.

Switching off her phone, Tassie grabbed the envelope and went into her bedroom where she pulled on her pyjamas. Lying in bed she closed her eyes, willing sleep to blanket the memories crowding her brain.

Ten minutes later her bedcovers were a swirl of agitation. She got her phone, pulling her knees up to her chest. Was her answer OK? Did she seem too desperate? No, she'd deleted the last sentence. But, oh God, the 'definitely'. Pathetic. She stretched her head back, easing the increasing tightness in her neck, screwing her eyes shut as she twisted her head from side to side. When a tear slid down her cheek she flicked it away.

God knows she'd done all the self-help books. She knew why men preferred bitches, and she had a strong suspicion that Alex just wasn't that into her. But it always led back to one thing: that whether or not he loved her – and she was sure he did, deep down – *she* was still in love with him. She tipped up the envelope and, as she combed through the memories, tears ran down her cheeks. Why was she doing this? She should have burnt the lot, years ago.

Closing her eyes, she counted out her fingers on the envelope. For fifteen bloody years he'd dominated her thoughts, either jumping up and down at the front, or lurking backstage. And they'd only been together for two of them. Which was just pathetic. Of course, during all those years he'd been understudied by others. Many others. Mostly meaningless encounters. Some, nice – a few lovely. Then, an increasing number of not so good. But none had come within even an inch of the long shadow cast by Alex Winchester.

Up on that fucking pedestal.

She wrapped a cardigan around her shoulders – which didn't stop her shivering. Part of the problem was that she still regularly heard about him through the village grapevine – most of it pointedly relayed by her mother. She'd known he'd got into Cambridge, for they'd split up just before he'd gone. She'd desperately tried to persuade him to take a gap year with her but he'd made it clear that he felt such things were a waste of time. Later, she knew he'd got a first – her mother had actually phoned her with that piece of news. Then, after a few years, she heard how he'd moved to New York. Always the same message: how brilliantly he was doing.

She crossed her legs, *making* herself concentrate on the memory she preferred to delete. Because it was ridiculous. She loved remembering everything about that first weekend in London – well, almost everything. So she should make herself think about *that* night too.

Sighing, she searched through the pile until she found a little white notebook with *Covent Garden Hotel* printed across the top. She flicked the empty pages, then stroked the embossed letters. She'd not even got it that night. It was from another time – when she'd suggested another man take her there, hoping to exorcise the memories. Another disaster.

A tear dripped off her chin as she opened up the box again. Taking out the necklace, she wrapped her fingers around it then, shuffling down to lie on her side, she pulled the duvet over herself and curled up her feet.

COVENT GARDEN, *December 2008*

It was possibly the two bottles of wine that had done it. Alex had come over on another business trip and, much as she knew it was wrong, his draw was magnetic. He'd paid the extortionate bill in the austere French restaurant – not that Tassie could have afforded even half of it, particularly after she'd splashed out so much money on her green silk-crêpe dress. At the time she was just starting out as a professional photographer and although the *Guardian* and *Independent* were beginning to take her stuff, it was proving a hard market.

More likely it was the whiskies in the little bar they'd gone to afterwards – her contribution to the evening. For another hour they'd chatted about innocuous things: their jobs, friends, holidays, life for them at twenty-six... Alex was shocked to hear that Tom was already married, and he'd forgotten that her brother was a teacher. After that they'd avoided any of the more personal stuff.

It was late, very late, when Tassie tried to stifle a yawn – anticipation having woken her at five-thirty that morning.

Alex motioned to a smart hotel opposite, his hand faltering only slightly as he did.

'That's me, you know. That's where I'm staying.' He held her gaze for longer than was decent, his eyes igniting a slow burning she knew only too well.

Tassie looked across the road, where the moss green of the hotel's front glittered with tiny lights and trails of ivy, and a Christmas tree twinkled in the cosy reception. Then she thought of her journey back to her flat: in the cold, on the bus. She looked back at him. Different now, with his sharp-cut suit and cashmere coat, but still enough her Alex. And she considered how all this felt so good, so right. Slowly, her breath shallow, she leant over the table as he cupped her face in strong, warm hands.

'It's been a long time, Tass. Too long.'

And in that moment the world stopped moving, along with her heart, and she knew she'd never want anything else.

IN THE LIFT SHE GIGGLED, saying she was feeling a bit *Pretty Woman*.

'Don't worry about that.' His response was casual. 'I said my wife might be joining me when I booked.'

'Alex!' Tassie stared at him, her feelings torn between horror and admiration.

He shrugged. 'Just makes things easier.'

The rest of their ascent was silent, Tassie trying to compute what he'd just said in a brain that was rather too thick with alcohol. Then in the corridor, lifting her face to his, he kissed her – a brief, light embrace – and all was fine again.

Inside the room she took in every detail as Alex headed

straight for the drinks cabinet. Looking up, she gasped. 'I've never been in a room with a mezzanine.'

He chuckled. 'You've clearly led a sheltered existence.'

'No, I mean, not in a hotel room. Not that I've been in many posh ones. It's still mostly backpacker-level for me.'

She ran up the stairs, kicking off her heels before jumping onto the bed and crawling over to the railings, looking down at where Alex was now sprawled on one of the sofas. 'Wow, you do live the life, don't you? Everything you always wanted.'

He looked up at her, smiling faintly before studying the glass in his hand. 'Oh, I don't know, Tass. If you want the honest truth, after a while one hotel room feels pretty much like another, however many mezzanines.'

For a few moments she watched him, then she shrugged off her coat and padded down the stairs. Taking his glass from him, slowly, very slowly she lowered herself onto his lap.

His eyes were sad for an instant, then he kissed her, deep and long, stroking his fingers down her face. Instantly she melted into the kiss, her arms tight around him.

'Come on,' she said, pulling back as she slipped off his tie and began to undo the buttons of his shirt. 'There's *mezze* heaven waiting for us upstairs.'

Alex looked up towards the bed, then back at Tassie, groaning as he bent his head towards her chest. She pushed her fingers through his hair as his hands undid the fastenings of her dress, the silky fabric slipping easily off her shoulders.

'Stand up.' His voice was gruff.

She stood, letting her dress slip down.

'My God, Tassie. You're still utterly fucking gorgeous.' He bent forward and kissed the V of her pants before sliding them down. Then they were on the sofa, working as one, equally urgent, hands, mouths, eyes devouring each other with a voracious need. Soon naked, each explored a body they'd once known so well, that felt instantly familiar. Their breath quickened and deepened, and Tassie felt more alive in that moment than she had for years, her body weightless.

Breaking away, she kneeled before him, unperturbed by her nakedness as she stroked her fingers down his chest, spreading them out through his few soft hairs. Then she took his hand and stood to lead him up the stairs.

By the bed, she turned. 'So, Alex, it's been a long time, how shall we do this?'

He looked at her, then the bed, the railings, then back at her. His eyes danced. 'What was it you used to say? Any instruction to bend over and you'll always aim to please?' As he turned her, gently pushing her forwards, he muzzled his face into the back of her neck. 'I've so missed all this, Tass. I really have.'

Halting his moves, she twisted round, cupping his face with her hands. 'It's been a long time. I've missed it too. I miss you.' Her voice was barely audible. Looking straight at him, she kissed his mouth hard. 'After this long I think I want to be looking at you, all the time.' And she pushed him back onto the bed, sliding on top of him, the soft curves of her frame slipping over the hardness of his, until their bodies were perfectly aligned.

LATER, she woke with a start, taking a moment to wonder where she was. The room was dark and she could hear heavy rain drumming on the street. Then she remembered. She was with Alex. *Her Alex.* Her eyes still closed, she stretched – relaxed and languorous as a cat, her heart swelling at the thought of him next to her. Hearing a movement, she opened her eyes. He was sitting on the edge of the bed.

She stroked his back. 'Can't sleep?'

He didn't turn. 'Tass. I need to tell you something.' His voice was clear, almost sharp, any trace of the warming effects of alcohol now dissipated.

She was instantly alert, the warning bells that rang in her head drowning out any feelings of a hangover. She sat up, pulling her knees to her chest then shrouding herself with the bed covers.

Alex's voice was cracked, dry, like sand on skin. 'Tass, this can't be. Us. We can't...'

She sat, waiting, finding herself unable to speak in the silence that followed.

'I'm getting married.'

'Married?' The word soured her tongue, contaminating her mouth, then a voice sidled into her head. She'd known there was something. Someone. She just hadn't asked.

'Next spring. It's a big thing. I work with her father. He's my boss.'

It was that which finally galvanised her into action. It wasn't the other woman, the damn fiancée. There'd been plenty of other women in the times they'd met. It was his driving, maddening, fucking ambition. Really, that had always been his first love. She jumped off the bed, grabbing her coat and shoes as she tore downstairs.

Alex stood at the railings looking down at her. 'I do love her, Tass. She's not you. But she's right for me.' He carried on staring as she wrenched on her dress. 'I'm sorry.'

And he was still standing there as she slammed the door behind her – the last time she'd seen him naked.

∾

As the cold of the early hours crept through the open window, Tassie stared into the shadows of the garden, her fingers still cradling the necklace. Shuddering, she climbed out of bed and went into the kitchen, turning the kettle on. She'd done it. For the first time in years. Made herself *really* remember that night. Still officially the worst of her life. She snorted. And now here she was again.

She banged the milk carton down, shaking her head. For three months he'd been firmly back in her life with texts and emails. And an invitation to dinner on the sixth. Despite the fact he was now fucking married. And a dad. Alex! A fucking father! She carried her mug into the bedroom, barely caring about the tea slopping over the sides as she yanked open a drawer.

There it was: all her shamelessness. Her *just in case* underwear, sitting pretty in its black and pink box. Not that she'd planned on showing it. She had her standards, her morals. But one felt better if every part of you was best-dressed.

Really?

She picked up her phone, searching for the time in New York. Ten-thirty pm. What would he be doing? She pictured him sitting with his wife and child. No, the child would be in bed. Would it just be the two of them, making polite conversation at a highly polished table? No, they'd have finished dinner and be in the sitting room. Did they even have sitting rooms?

Why had he contacted her again after all these years? Did he still feel the same as her? Had he now realised what they'd had? She searched his work profile, her mouth tightening as she read about his stellar career. Then she searched his wife's name and, there she was: manicured perfection. Blonde hair as straight as dried spaghetti, a direct stare and – in her tailored fuchsia suit and heels – thin as a perfectly sharpened pencil. Clicking along the line of images, there was another of her and Alex at some dinner.

Tassie peered at the screen, studying their body language. The woman had the same stiffness as in the other photo, barely a hint of a smile. Alex's arm was around her waist and his expression was... smug, a tad supercilious. But was she imagining it or were his eyes empty, spent of all that passion? Probably.

Wanker.

She brought up his latest email – *Skype me when you get this* – then checked her phone. He'd not tried to call. Going back into the kitchen she poured a large glass of wine and sat down at the table, her head in her hands. *God!* She laughed out loud. If only Syd knew about this.

Straightforward Sydonie, with her unshakeable belief in the sanctity of happy families; stemming from an impressive ability to recalibrate the sadness of her own past. 'I know I was fostered,' she'd once said when they'd been talking about having children. 'But look at how it turned out. Even after the horror years. Anyone can make a happy family. You, me, anyone.'

Yep, Syd would be furious. But she didn't know about any of this: her guilty secret. No one did – well no one except Tom, and he rarely mentioned Alex. The man was officially taboo. Although try telling her mother that.

Not-a-fucking-gain! She got up and poured the wine into the sink, refilling the glass with water. She just couldn't do this. Shouldn't do this. He was married. And anyway, it was never about her, was it? Someone else would always come first in his life. *Have you no pride, Victoria?*

Going back into the bedroom she picked up her phone and typed fast.

Actually, sorry Alex, but I've been thinking about this a lot and have decided that 'this' is probably not a good idea. It's been nice to be in touch again and good luck with everything. Love always, Tassie x.

Shaking her head, she removed the *love always,* then the *x,* and pressed send, a thrilling sense of control surging through her veins. Moving quickly, she gathered together all the photos, cards and flyers and shoved them back in the envelope. Then she stood poised for... what? It was bin day tomorrow. She could go upstairs, slip everything under the lid and the physical evidence would be gone for ever.

She moved towards the door. Then stopped. Sitting back down on the bed, she held the envelope tight against her chest. She could do that. But she wouldn't. She'd said no to meeting him. That was enough. And she'd give the underwear to Oxfam.

Wearily, she replaced the envelope at the bottom of the box then put it back in the cupboard. Climbing into bed she curled tightly onto her side and began to cry. Slipping into a hole that for so long had trapped her within its walls of loss and ill-conceived hope.

7

---

cotland, September 2014

By the time Tassie reached Aberfeldy it was well after ten, and the end of a long and occasionally painful journey – particularly the two hours spent waiting for a bus in Pitlochry. She'd checked into her hotel room overlooking the town square, and had only just fallen asleep when she was woken by increasingly loud shouts.

The alarm clock read just past midnight as she slipped out of bed and went to the window. Below, a huge, clearly drunk man was fighting to attach another man to a lamp post, while five others stood around, laughing. Even in her sleepy state, Tassie wondered with growing dread whether this might be her first introduction to the groom. If it was, he was furious; loud expletives volleying the air in an accent that was distinctly Australian. She heard the words 'married' and 'fuckin' dead'.

Oh hell.

A few minutes later, an old Land Rover pulled up outside the hotel opposite and a man and woman got out. Surveying the scene, the man shook his head, motioning to the woman to go into the hotel as he strode over to the group. After a quick exchange with the Australian – whose hands *were* now handcuffed to the post – he walked up to the drunk guy and demanded the key. There was a scuffle, the drunk man unwilling to relinquish his prize, until two of the others finally saw sense and joined in helping to persuade him. Eventually the oaf reached into the depths of his jeans pocket. But then, just as he was about to hand it over, he projectile-vomited – all over the ground and the newcomer's feet.

Despite her tiredness, Tassie couldn't help laughing as the men leapt back, one of them stumbling then falling. Ignoring the mess on his shoes, the newcomer released the groom then, following brief introductions, the group dispersed, leaving the drunken slob alone, on his knees in a pool of yellow street light and vomit.

Tassie briefly considered getting her camera and taking her first shot of the wedding, but quickly decided against it. And a short time after that she was back in bed and soon fast asleep.

THE NEXT MORNING, emerging out of the hotel Tassie's heart sank when she saw the road was slick with rain that had been falling for the last hour. She glanced around. On every horizon, grey clouds settled on dark hills.

Hardly ideal conditions for photography. She tutted. Just who would decide to have a wedding up a mountain in Scotland in bloody September?

Retreating into the shelter of the doorway she set her bags down then checked her messages from Syd.

Marcus, BM, will pic u up on morng of 6th @ 9am from outside your hotel. Have fun!! Syd xx

Well, it was now five past and there was no sign of him. She yawned, wondering if she might have time to go back into the gloomy tartan-carpeted breakfast room and grab herself another coffee. She'd not slept particularly well; her dreams – as happened far too often – had been full of Alex.

Remembering the previous night, she peered through the rain at the lamp-post where all the drama had taken place, then wished she hadn't when she realised the lumps on the road were bits of undigested food. She pulled the zip higher on her Rab jacket, wondering if she'd be warm enough in her jeans and cashmere jumper. At the end of the square, the town hall clock ticked round to quarter past nine.

There was a book poking out of the top of her bag and taking it out Tassie studied the back cover. *Mindfulness*. That's what she needed to practise, apparently. According to Oliver, everyone was doing it. She chuckled as she recalled him telling her that he and Tilak had started attending classes and at the first session they'd been asked to carefully hold a razor in their mouths. Oliver had looked confused when she'd looked horrified, agreeing that they would indeed have had to be careful. 'Not a razor, you numpty,' he'd hooted with laughter. 'A raisin.'

He was so happy. She watched the rain, bouncing off car bonnets and dripping down the windows of the café opposite. She was glad for him, and she already adored Tilak.

Slipping the book back into her bag, she imagined the two of them attending their cosy evening classes. Maybe she should actually read the thing instead of just carrying it around. Twenty bloody past. *Where the hell was he?*

Her attention was caught by a door opening in the hotel opposite, and the man and woman she'd seen the previous night coming out. They looked across at her, and, surprised, she stared back.

The man said something to his companion: a tall, heavy-set woman with thick auburn hair and a face that looked as much horse as human. She glanced at Tassie, shrugged, then turned and went back into the hotel.

Tassie felt oddly nervous as the man strode across the street – which was surprisingly wide, so she had plenty of time to take him in. He was tall, well over six foot, with thick dark-blond hair and a tan offset by his denim jacket and frayed V-neck jumper. His face was open, relaxed, with a generous mouth that broke into an amused smile as he watched her observing him. When he arrived in front of her, his eyes were warm with sun-caught crinkles around the edges. Eyes that smiled. Ridiculously, she felt herself blushing as she took his hand.

'I'm hoping you're Tassie? Otherwise this day is only going to get worse.' His voice was deep, well-modulated, the words tinged with a slight West Country burr.

'I am. Are you...' Tassie looked down at her phone, 'Marcus?'

'I can happily say I am not.' The man looked over to the lamp post. 'God knows where he is. Probably still swimming in his own bile. As you'll know from last night.' His eyebrows rose and a smile twisted one corner of his mouth.

'Last night? Oh. You saw me?'

'I happened to notice you as I was driving in. Your hair is quite... distinctive.' Now it was his turn to look uncomfortable. 'Sorry, I'm Dan. Dan Jacobs. And it seems that due to unforeseen circumstances – although if you knew even a smidgeon about that arsehole Marcus, right now wouldn't be so unexpected...' He grimaced. 'Anyway, it seems that I am your driver for the morning.'

Tassie looked across to the decrepit four-by-four parked across the street, a suit hanging incongruously in one of its filthy windows.

66

Dan followed her gaze. 'Yep, meet Daisy, my faithful off-roader.'

'So, I get to drive in my favourite vehicle of all time, *and* I'm saved from a journey with probably the world's vilest best man? I think I owe you a favour.' Tassie smiled. 'Shall we?' Bending to pick up her bags, she threaded her fingers through the various handles.

When she looked up, Dan was grinning.

'Here.' He crouched down at her level. 'Let me take some of those.' His breath was warm, tinged with toothpaste as he took a couple of bags from her. Then together they crossed the road, the rain beginning to lessen but still pattering.

ONCE TASSIE'S bags were secured on the back seat, Dan turned the key in the ignition, generating a sound not unlike the cranking up of an old lawnmower.

'She's a 1969 old dame, but still going strong. Although I hope you don't mind a bit of a bumpy ride.'

Tassie stroked the ripped leather seat. 'She's great.'

As they drove through the town, at first they said little – both taking in the sights, happy to sit in companionable silence. The main square was flanked by quaint shops, an ornate green and white drinking fountain in the middle, and at the end of it was a smart white cinema – surprisingly modernist in style. Tassie smiled as she pointed it out. This was what she'd loved as a photojournalist: photographing a world that was so full of the unexpected.

Reaching the edge of Aberfeldy they approached a wide bridge, four obelisks standing sentry on either side.

'Very fancy,' Dan commented as they drove over.

'A bridge built with no expense spared.' Tassie's response was immediate. 'Cost £4,000 in 1733.'

Dan glanced at her, his eyebrows raised.

'I read about it in the hotel this morning. Although that's where my local knowledge stops.'

What she didn't add is that they'd reminded her of Cleopatra's Needle, which was why she'd bothered to read the blurb.

As they drove further into the countryside the rain stopped, replaced by weak sunshine. Shadows danced across the tarmac, cast from poplar trees lining either side of the road, and ahead of them mountains dominated the skyline.

'So,' Tassie looked over at Dan, 'how come you're involved in this wedding? Are you friends with the groom?'

'Ben and Kirstie actually. We were all at uni together, along with the odious Marcus. I've still no idea why Ben asked him to be best man. I can only think it's because they all still live in Edinburgh and he felt obliged. He always was nicer than he was wise.' Dan shook his head.

'And you? Where do you live now?'

'Oh, miles away,' he said cheerfully. 'On a farm in Somerset. Making cider.'

Tassie wasn't surprised, for it was a job that seemed to suit him. In fact, she was rather pleased; she'd had enough of urbanites where men were concerned. 'Hence Daisy.' She patted the green metal dashboard. 'Dad has one of these, I love them. I grew up on a farm as well. Shropshire.'

'Really?' The corners of Dan's mouth flickered. 'I'm used to telling people I'm a cider maker and seeing them instantly lose interest. What kind of farming do you do?'

'Arable mostly, with a few sheep and cattle. Not that I've lived there for years. And you? How big's your business?'

'We've been producing cider since the 1920s so we're pretty well established. Although we still treat it as a craft. We do taster sessions, corporate stuff occasionally, and have a small café, so it keeps me busy. Keeps *us* busy I should say. Charlotte, who you saw this morning, she works with me.'

'Oh, I see.' Tassie felt a stab of disappointment.

'Yes. We're business partners.'

Was it her imagination or was there a slight emphasis on the word business?

'I've known her since we were children and when she decided to move back to Somerset, with her background in marketing it seemed a good idea to offer her a job.'

Remembering the way Horse Woman had stared at her, Tassie wondered whether it was the job prospects or the potential employer that had attracted her back home.

'Do you work well together?'

'Yes, it's been great. It's like working with family I guess. I've known her so long, she's more like a sister than a colleague.'

Tassie nodded politely.

'That's why she's here, at the wedding. We had some business in Leicester so I invited her as my plus one. We were only meant to be going to the reception – but... well, you know the rest.'

'I do indeed.' Tassie's response remained neutral and she decided to change the subject.

HALF AN HOUR later they pulled off the main road and into a car park. Dan reached for a bag on the back seat, from which he pulled a piece of paper.

'And now our day is going to get a lot weirder.' He handed it to Tassie. 'I hope you're a good navigator. These read like the directions to Neverland.'

Tassie looked at them and laughed. '1. Leave the car park and head due north with the top of the mountain up ahead. 2. After a mile there's a pile of rocks with a barrel on top.'

She read on, her eyes scanning. 'Turn due east here then... this, then that, then over the...'

She looked up, grinning. 'I'll do my best.' Her heart suddenly felt light as buttermilk. 'I love an adventure.'

There were a few cars dotted around the car park, along with a group of elderly male walkers posing for a photo. They turned and stared, clearly surprised when, instead of parking, the four-by-four set off across the grass that sloped for a while before rising steeply towards the mountain.

'Apparently Schiehallion has a perfect conical top,' Dan said, looking ahead.

Tassie was impressed. He'd obviously been practising his Scottish pronunciation.

'But you can't see it from this direction. Only from across the loch. Here goes, hold on.' He put Daisy into a lower gear and they began their ascent.

It had been a while since Tassie had driven off-road, and she loved the thrill of bouncing across the rough terrain. Dan was clearly an expert, twisting this way and that to avoid the dips and sharp boulders. Even better, the sun was still shining, although ahead of them, large smudges of grey were beginning to shade the sky's edges.

'It will be a miracle if we manage to make it through the morning without any more rain,' he said. 'Who would think to have a wedding ceremony up a Scottish mountain, in September, for God's sake?'

As they continued to climb, grass was replaced by ferns, purple heather and bracken, making it harder to spot the sharp boulders that littered their path. Suddenly there was a loud clunk and they were thrown against the dashboard. When they righted themselves – each looking sideways to check the other was OK – the Land Rover was tilting at an extreme angle.

Frowning, Dan slid out of the vehicle, while Tassie

remained inside, straining to sit up straight against the angle of the seat. After a few moments his muffled voice came through the floor. 'I don't believe it; I think the axle's actually snapped. Damn.'

Tassie slid across the seats then jumped out and squatted beside him. His face was creased with concern. She bent down to look underneath Daisy, and saw that the chassis was resting on a devilishly sharp rock.

'Ouch.' She took out her phone. Syd's emergency numbers were on an email and she quickly pulled it up. But, unsurprisingly, wherever she walked there was no signal. 'Do you want to see if you've got any?' She waved her phone at Dan.

Reaching over to the glove compartment, he removed his mobile. 'Nope.' He glanced at his watch, then up the mountain. 'We've got an hour and a half to get there. Although I reckon it's at least a two-hour hike. Are you a fast walker?'

'Do we have any choice? There's no point us just standing here.'

His eyes crinkled. 'I'm liking you. Most people would be heading *down* the mountain at this stage.'

'Most people wouldn't be stupid enough to have agreed to go up it in the first place.'

The crinkles deepened. 'Agreed. All right, let's get whatever we need and go. At least the rain's still holding off.'

Opening up the back of the four-by-four, he grabbed his suit. 'What do you reckon? Are they going to mind that their replacement best man is wearing jeans and a very old jumper?'

'Well, given the daftness of the whole plan, I don't think they *can* mind. But as the photographer I should probably advise you to take the suit.'

He shook his head, then delved back into the truck to

remove his shoes from under the front seat. 'This day gets weirder by the minute.'

By the time he re-emerged, Tassie had stepped up onto a small rock, her senses on full alert as she scanned a shape in the distance. 'You know what you were just saying, about the day getting weirder?' She cocked an ear and narrowed her eyes.

'Yep.' Dan followed her gaze.

'Well, I swear I can hear Dolly Parton.'

Standing quite still, they listened to the faint strains of 'Jolene' trickling across the heather, the music getting louder as it turned into 'Islands in the Stream'. Then they looked at each other and burst out laughing.

'Hang on!' Dan jumped onto a bigger rock, waving his arms. 'Let's make sure he sees us.'

As the rider drew nearer they saw that he was probably in his sixties, perhaps even seventies, sitting astride an enormous black horse. His rust-red face was covered with a dense beard and he was wearing a full-length wax coat and cowboy hat.

Tassie quickly removed her camera from her bag and, taking a couple of shots, saw that Dolly was coming from speakers attached to either side of his saddle.

Removing an iPod from a bag slung across his shoulders, the man turned off the music when he reached the side of the truck. 'You clearly want my photo badly, if you're prepared to jump up and down on a rock like a lunatic.'

His voice was gruff but his smile kindly as he stared down at them. Then his gaze switched to the four-by-four. 'Ah, I see you've got yourselves a bit of bother.' Swinging his leg over he slid down from the horse, holding onto the reins as he bent to look. 'Now that's bad.' He stood up. 'Were you were heading for the bothy?'

Tassie and Dan nodded.

The man shook his head. 'Wedding is it?'

Again they nodded.

'Yours?' His eyebrows rose.

'No,' they said in unison.

'But I'm meant to be photographing it.' Tassie smiled her most dazzling smile, not sure what it would achieve but hoping for something.

'This truck yours?'

Now it was Dan's turn to nod.

'Can you ride?' The man was clearly doing some kind of calculation.

'No. I'm afraid not.' Dan was looking at the horse like it was some kind of saddled alien.

'I can,' Tassie said. 'Pony club, trekking in Outer Mongolia.'

The man's eyes were bright. 'Well that's rather a coincidence. A fellow equestrian. So it would seem best that you take Teela here and get to your ceremony; if you don't want a disappointed bride. After all, it's my bothy they'll be getting married in.' He patted the huge horse. 'Be careful how you go though, she's not used to more than me. Do you think you can handle her?'

Tassie nodded – trying to show more confidence than she felt as the beast pawed the ground.

The man reached into a bag and took out a card, which he handed to Dan. 'Here's my number. Just return her to me as soon as you can, and in the meantime I'll ask for a truck to come here shall I?'

'Are you sure?' Dan's voice was full of gratitude as he stepped forward to shake the man's hand. 'Thank you so much.'

'Aye. We look after each other on this mountain. Give me the keys and I'll do what I can.'

Tassie glanced around. 'How are you going to get home? Aren't we miles from anywhere?'

'I walk this mountain most days. I was only on Teela as I wanted to check out some sheep on the far side. It will be no bother to walk home.'

'Teela.' Tassie stroked the horse's mud-spattered coat as it flicked its head round to sniff her. 'Interesting name.'

'Aye.' Again his eyes twinkled. 'It means strong-willed. I probably should be warning you about that.'

CLOUDS WERE SCUDDING as Dan and Tassie watched the old man stride across the moorland; an isosceles triangle in his long stiff coat. When they turned to each other, incredulity was stretched across both their faces.

Dan looked at the card he'd been given. 'John Drummond, Earl of Perth, Tempar Castle.' He looked up. 'Can this day get any stranger?'

'Yep.'

He looked puzzled.

'Judging by the fear you were showing dear Teela here,' – Tassie patted the horse's coat – 'I'm wondering what you're going to be like when you're on her.'

The horse shifted her feet, tail swishing, and Dan took a step back.

'You guessed my secret. Hate the buggers. Well, don't hate them, we've got two on the farm, but let's say they're not my first choice of ride. But, needs must. Shall we?'

As Tassie removed her bags from Daisy, he eyed them sceptically. 'I'm guessing I'll be carrying those, and mine, so... I can't also carry this.' He held up his suit. 'Do I have to?'

She grinned. ''Fraid so.'

He sighed and started unbuttoning his shirt, shaking his head. 'Weirder and weirder.'

Tassie tried not to watch as he removed his clothing, but failed. Dan's chest was flat and wide, ribs outlined under deeply tanned skin; long, muscular thighs. She suspected he knew she was watching, and suspected he wasn't that bothered.

Once dressed in a dark-blue suit and white shirt, her companion looked very different. And totally ridiculous as he clumsily mounted Teela.

By comparison she was in her element as she expertly adjusted the saddle's stirrups then swung up. The horse shuffled – unused to the sensation of two people – then lowered her head back down to the grass.

Tassie twisted round to look at Dan, perched uncomfortably behind her. Laughing, she patted his thigh. 'Just hold on tightly, dear, I'll look after you. And make sure you shout the directions loudly.'

As they set off she felt happier than she'd done for months; first walking then trotting, enjoying the sensation of Dan's hands around her waist, squeezing tighter the faster they went.

It was just over forty minutes before the tiny bothy came into view, the horse covering the terrain much more easily than a Land Rover could. Bedded in at the back of a clearing, its setting was spectacular: a tapestry of greens, purples and oranges lacing across the terrain as it rose to the top of Schiehallion. Built from narrow slats of grey wood, the bothy itself was more functional than beautiful, so Tassie was relieved to see a hint of sun coming through the clouds, creating a lovely soft light.

As they approached, a couple and a small dog emerged – the man and dog running, the woman walking as fast as her full-length dress would allow. Relief vied with shock on the couple's faces, seeing their photographer and replacement best man arriving on a horse.

'What happened?' Ben was the first to speak.

'Don't ask,' Dan replied. 'We're here now.'

Tassie reined Teela in and slid off her back. Then she held her hand up to Dan, who handed her bags down before stiffly climbing down himself.

Kirstie came to take some of the bags. 'I'm *so* sorry about what I'm guessing has been quite a journey. Thank you so much for making it. I know this was the craziest idea.'

She leant in and gave Tassie a hug. Despite the location, she was dressed in a tight white wedding dress with lace capped sleeves and tiny diamanté flowers studding the fabric. She looked freezing but fabulous.

Somewhat at odds with his broad Australian accent, Ben was in the traditional dress of the Scottish Highlands: a green and red kilt, black jacket, tasselled sporran and a starched white shirt. Even the dog was dressed for the occasion with a gingham bow tie askew around her neck. Tassie crouched to pat her. She was lovely; a brown and cream face, luxuriant tail and skinny body atop even more spindly legs.

'Come in and have a coffee. You must be cold.' Kirstie pointed towards the bothy.

'Actually we're fine, shouldn't we just get started?' Well-trained over the years by Oliver, Tassie was aware how much could go wrong if the day fell too much behind schedule, and she wanted to make the most of the light. 'If you give me those bags back, I'll get sorted.'

Kirstie's face showed her relief. 'Are you sure? That would be great. Poppy, come here.' The dog trotted over and Kirstie straightened her bow tie. 'Right,' she smiled up at Tassie. 'I'd better let the others know we're about to start.'

A few moments later Ben and Dan emerged from the

bothy, Dan now looking considerably more at ease than he had upon dismounting. As they walked towards the edge of the clearing there came a blast of nasal twang and a deep bass drone, then a piper appeared, bending his head in the doorway to make way for his bearskin hat.

Tassie was ready by the door, poised to take her shots as he walked forward, followed by Kirstie with Poppy at her side. Next came a slight, older lady in a long woollen dress – the celebrant, Tassie guessed – and finally a woman about Kirstie's age, dressed in a velvet coat and Doc Martens.

The service went smoothly and quickly. Not least because everyone began to freeze as the sun slipped in and out from behind progressively portentous clouds, making Tassie's job increasingly difficult. After the ceremony had finished she did a quick check on her camera and was relatively pleased with the images of the small gathering, the mountain providing a wonderful backdrop.

Syd was right, this was romantic. But bloody cold – and getting darker all the time.

Inside the bothy, she was initially surprised by its luxuriousness. Looking more closely she realised it wasn't, but was pleased that it had a wood burner and rugs, plus canapés and a couple of bottles of champagne chilling in a bucket. Everyone huddled as near to the stove as they could, and when the piper ceremoniously sliced open the champagne with a long dagger she got some great shots of Poppy lapping up the alcohol spilt beneath his feet.

Soon after the canapés had been eaten, and most of the champagne drunk, a red-haired man in a frayed kilt appeared in the doorway. 'Mr and Mrs McIntyre, your carriage is arriving.' As he spoke, the fast chug of a helicopter's rotor could be heard getting closer.

'Is this a wedding or a James Bond?' Dan murmured as they turned towards the doorway.

'Whatever it is, it's fab.' Grinning, Tassie grabbed her cameras then joined the others, everyone bracing themselves against what was now a bone-cracking wind as they huddled outside the hut.

A bright blue helicopter whirred its way down onto the clearing, flattening the grass beneath, and Tassie took some shots then turned to Dan. Touching his arm, she felt suddenly concerned. 'I'm meant to go with them.'

'I know, Ben's already told me.'

'But what are you going to do about getting Teela back? Will you be all right?'

Dan looked over at the horse, whose head was down as she hoovered up the grass. 'Don't worry,' he said, 'I might not love them, but I *can* just about ride one. And anyway, I've got a guide. Look.'

Around the corner of the bothy a mini version of the kilted man had appeared, his equally red hair squashed beneath a beanie. About eight or nine, he was dressed in a royal-blue tracksuit top with *32Red* emblazoned across it.

'That's the son, Sholto. Mad about Rangers, as you can see.'

Dan patted Tassie's hand, which she suddenly realised was still on his arm. Instantly she felt less nervous, but not fully reassured. It was one very small boy and a very big horse.

'I'll be fine.' Dan's voice was warm with amusement. 'And I'll take my day clothes in case we get lost. Come on, you need to get your stuff together and be off.' He tugged her plait and they both laughed, surprised but not embarrassed by the intimacy of the gesture.

When Tassie re-emerged from the bothy, Dan and Sholto were already up on Teela's back, Dan gripping the reins.

'Come on, girl. Gee up. Come on now.' His voice was

78

more hopeful than masterful and he looked down at Tassie. 'They thought it best we leave before the helicopter does. In case it spooks her.'

Tassie laughed as she raised her camera to take a shot of a fine-looking man in a smart suit trying to get an enormous horse to move, a small boy dressed in football gear sitting behind him, his face a picture of mild disdain as he held Dan's bag against his chest.

By now everyone was watching, revelling in Dan's growing discomfort.

'I'm not sure it's the horse that's spooked.' The guide's face was creased with laughter. 'I reckon ye'll be needing to put Sholto up front. Reckon the horse'll move for him.'

The boy needed no encouragement and, nimbly swinging his leg over Teela's back, he slid down the horse's side then climbed up in front of Dan. Once in position he bent down, ruffled Teela's mane, whispered something, and they were off – Teela lurching into a canter, Dan floundering in his attempts to hold on to the boy.

Ben's laugh was the loudest. 'Sweet as. Reckon he'll never forgive me for today. Although no whinger that one. He'll be all right.'

He looked over at the helicopter, its blades beginning to turn.

'Come on then Mrs Mac, Tassie, let's be on our way. We've got a ripper of a feast to attend and it sure is frostie.'

THE VIEW from the helicopter felt like being suspended in heaven – assuming heaven's a noisy place. A cornucopia of grey, silver and white clouds filled the sky, and the rocky terrain below had the same delicate tapestry of colours that Tassie had seen earlier, now with occasional patches of light glimmering wherever the sun broke through. For miles around, the land looked as uninhabited as it would have done in ancient times.

She tried to take a few photos, but the windows were too thick and dirty to get much so she settled back in her seat, revelling in the ride. Thinking back over the morning she smiled, hoping the horse riding was going OK.

Kirstie turned and grinned at her. Pointing, she shouted, 'Dan's down there somewhere. I hope he's all right.'

'So do I.'

'He'll be fine. He's very capable.' Kirstie's eyebrows raised a fraction. 'You two seemed to be getting on well?'

At that moment Ben tugged on her sleeve and they all looked forward to admire the view. The helicopter was now skimming across a loch, clouds reflected in its silver-lacquered surface. Thick forest and the occasional castle flanked the lake's sides and the water stretched for miles, like a glass landing strip.

Kirstie turned again. 'Isn't this stunning? Hope it makes up for the horse.' She laughed, then kissed her husband's cheek.

Watching Ben put his arm around his new wife, stroking her neck as she leant into his side, Tassie wondered about taking a photo of them. It was a great group – apart from Marcus the Arse. Why did some people keep such awful friends? She leant her head against the window, stifling a yawn, thinking of Dan somewhere down below. Her thoughts wandered over the events of the morning, trying not to focus on the image of him changing into his suit. Then she gave up, closed her eyes and let her mind linger. Syd would be pleased.

Smiling, she got out her phone, took a blurry photo of the loch and pressed send. Almost instantly a message came back, plus a photo of a bowl of apples.

Syd: *OMG, that's amazing! How's it all going? Am I 4given? Garden's looking gd. You have sooo many apples. Stan's obsessing about making cider.*

Tassie: *All good here and yes, you're forgiven. Might have something to tell you after this trip.*

Syd: *What? Tell me now. RU behaving?*

Tassie: *Gotta go. About to land. Talk to you tomorrow xxx*

Syd: *and??!! Ooh, UR so annoying. Love you. And BEHAVE!*

8

The helicopter descended like a giant bluebottle between fat rolls of barley stacked in front of the castle. Tassie's first impression was how tall it was: like a Gaelic skyscraper.

Rising out of the landscape, there was beauty in its starkness, the dark stone and narrow windows topped by grey slate turrets, a line of trees climbing steeply behind. The sun was now completely hidden by black clouds, which billowed across a still bright blue sky, making it the perfect opportunity for photos – despite the temperature remaining chilly.

When they finally got inside, it took about an hour for Tassie to warm up, accompanied by a sense of relief that the main part of her day was over and she had more than enough photos for the magazine.

She was grateful for the glass of whisky she was handed at the end of the blessing ceremony, for it helped fight the chill that permeated every corner of the building. Optimistically, she'd brought a lightweight dress to change into – fine wool and sleeveless – not imagining the venue would have no heating.

Rubbing her bare arms, she looked around the hundred or so guests. She'd still take a few more photos, but luckily in the planning stages Kirstie had insisted that asking her to climb a mountain was enough, reassuring her that her brother was a photographer and would be happy to take over.

She searched the room for Dan, who didn't seem to have arrived yet. She could see Horse Woman – what was her name? She couldn't go on calling her that... Charlotte – talking to Marcus. Although not exactly talking, for that would imply a two-way conversation. She watched Marcus lean further into Charlotte's face with every comment he made, his shirt buttons straining as his fat rolled forwards. Matching each move, Charlotte kept retreating, distaste pulling her back.

Tassie felt a pinprick of guilt – not that she had any reason for it. Apparently, after Marcus had been shunted from best-man duties he'd been asked to bring Charlotte to the castle. And, watching him now, he seemed to think that made her his date.

'Hello.'

Her heart skipped as she turned. Dan was standing beside her, his bag still in his hand.

'Oh, thank goodness for that, I've been worrying.' She gave him a quick hug. 'How was it?'

'Fine, although I'm exhausted. I'm not sure what was more tiring: riding, or riding with a small boy who didn't stop talking.'

'And Daisy?'

His face fell. 'Bit of a problem there. The gracious earl managed to get her to a garage but it will be a few days to fix her. No idea what I'm going to do about that.'

'Dan, you're here. Thank God.'

A voice fog-horned its way through the general hubbub,

and they turned to see Charlotte blasting her way through the guests. Tassie stepped back as the woman gave Dan a lingering embrace.

'I've been hearing the strangest tales about you and a horse. What have you been up to?'

'You hear true. Although it wasn't just me. Charlotte, meet Tassie, my co-rider.'

Charlotte's glance in Tassie's direction was cursory to say the least, and Tassie had to admire the skill with which she held out one hand to be shaken while the other smoothly moved Dan away.

'Let's go and find you a whisky, you must be exhausted. Shall I get you some crisps or nuts as well?'

Dan looked back apologetically as Charlotte led him off through the crowd. And that was that. Where seconds earlier they'd both been standing, now it was just her again. Tassie scanned the room – alive with the animated chatter of friends reunited – wondering who to talk to. After the excitement of Dan's arrival, she felt slightly deflated; aware there was no one else she wanted to meet.

Seeing a balding man heading her way, she shrugged apologetically, then turned and pulled her cameras out from under a table. No client had ever complained about there being too many pictures from their special day.

SHE WAS DELIGHTED with the extra shots she got. At least four hundred years old, the castle was a labyrinth of twisting stone corridors lit by candles flickering in iron sconces. On the ground floor was a stone kitchen with a cavernous fireplace, a bread oven on one side and neatly stacked logs on the other. Next to it was a room painted moss green, dressed for the evening's banquet with silver cutlery and crystal glass that shimmered in the candlelight.

Going up some steep stairs Tassie found herself on the top floor, in a wood-panelled attic with views across the valley. Then, coming back down to the middle floor, she discovered the master bedroom; although she knew no one was staying the night. Peeking in, she saw a beautiful green and silver dress hanging in the window, flowers decorating the A-line skirt, a pair of silver heels on the floor beneath. On the bed, a man's suit was also neatly set out.

She walked over and stroked the fabric of the dress. The label was still attached: Erdem. She sighed. Although she wasn't remotely interested in designer clothes, this was a dress worth going away for.

'You'd look great in that. Why don't you try it on?' The words were slurred.

She jumped, then spun around, embarrassment flooding her face before her heart sank. Marcus. And clearly now Marcus the Oaf again as he swayed in the doorway, leering at her as she did a quick reckoning. It wasn't that different to when she'd once been caught in a field with the family bull: if she tried to leave the room she'd be horribly within reach; if she stayed put, God knows how long he would too.

Ten minutes later she'd decided that Marcus's line of attack was paralysis through boredom. Propped up against the door jamb he'd covered many topics, each more pathetic than the last.

They'd begun with how he'd felt about being deposed as best man ('Fuckin' awful'), moving on to how he'd always suspected Ben liked Dan more than him (prompting a long mucus-filled sniff). The next covered what he remembered of their times at university (good and bad). And finally, wasn't she a bit of a looker, and was she sure she didn't want to try that dress on. (He 'wouldn't look'.)

Tassie glanced at her watch; she was going to have to do

something. Shaking her head with a polite 'I don't think so' to his last comment, she resolutely swung her camera to her front and stepped towards the door.

Marcus might have been drunk, but he was on it within a second. With each step she took, the bull inched forward, until finally they met in the middle of the room and there was nothing she could do but try to side step him. Except she couldn't, because before she knew it his hand was gripping her arm. And it hurt.

Fear and distaste scaled her skin. She'd met this type before: too drunk to have any conscience about what they were doing; too stupid to see their advances weren't wanted.

'Can you take your hand off me.'

Her voice was firm but made no difference. His other hand came onto her bare shoulder: sweaty and hot, his jowls thrusting towards her – stubble coating square edges. His breath was rank, his eyes small and mean. *Like a pig, not a bull.* She pulled at her arm, all thoughts of social niceties disappearing, but the grip tightened as the leer widened. With her free hand she slapped his face as hard as she could. Now the eyes flashed and a hand went towards her face, then stopped.

The bull-pig snorted and twisted away.

When she turned, Dan was standing there, Marcus's forearm clenched in his hand, his face flushed and glaring. 'What the fuck are you doing?'

His anger blazed so fiercely that Marcus retreated, a shove helping him on his way.

Stumbling towards the door he turned and looked at Dan. 'It's—'

'Oh just fuck off. It's men like you who...' Dan shook his head. 'And if I hear one more thing or see one more thing from you tonight, God help me I'll throw you in the moat myself.'

After a few seconds Tassie went out into the corridor and watched Marcus's retreating figure – still stumbling as he lurched towards the winding stairs – part of her hoping he'd fall down them. Returning to the bedroom she found Dan sitting on the edge of the bed, his head lowered. She sat down next to him and touched his shoulder. When he looked up his face was grim.

'Sorry, but I've seen the idiot do that too many times.' After a few seconds his breathing slowed and his eyes softened. 'Are you OK? I'm so sorry you had to experience that. Sorry I left you.'

Tassie laughed. 'You were only expected to give me a lift up a mountain. Not be my chaperone. But I'm glad you appeared. I'm not sure how easy he would have been to handle; all, what, twenty stone of him?' For a moment she found herself a little shaky.

After a beat, Dan put his arm around her and Tassie shifted fractionally into his side. 'Thank you.'

For a few moments they sat quietly, lost in their own thoughts as Tassie scanned back over her years of travelling. There had been similar scrapes in different lands; a male sense of entitlement that appeared to be universal. But each one had only made her stronger.

Straightening, she turned to face him. 'Actually, I arranged all that on purpose. I knew you had some making up to do, so thought I'd stage something so you could be my knight in shining armour. Finally.' Briefly she stroked the lapel of his jacket. 'Or my knight in a dark-blue suit.' She chuckled. 'Oh, and by the way, just in case you do try to throw him in a moat later? There isn't one.'

Dan looked at her, then got up and walked over to the window. 'I can't believe it doesn't have a moat. Rubbish castle.'

Joining him to admire the view, Tassie sensed that

standing there constituted one of those moments when the only logical thing to do was kiss, and her heart started beating just that little bit faster, adrenaline kicking in.

But she was at work, and they were in a bedroom. She looked at Dan, who held her gaze. When she spoke her voice was huskier than it should have been. 'Let's go back down and join the party. I think the banquet's about to start.'

'Come on then.' He touched the side of her cheek and electricity sparked all the way to her stomach. 'As long as you promise me the first dance.'

'Absolutely.' She followed him out of the room. 'Although... Dan?'

He looked back.

'Where's Charlotte? And, thinking about it, how come you came and found me?'

He looked embarrassed. 'I noticed you going up the stairs just now and... well, I thought I'd follow you.'

'Any particular reason?'

'No.' He blushed. 'Just a feeling I needed to.'

Tassie felt a swell of happiness. 'Well, I'm glad you did. Come on, we can't miss the food.'

It was only when they were descending the stairs into the main room that she realised he couldn't have seen her. For she had left the ground floor at least half an hour previously.

ALTHOUGH THEY WERE SEATED at different tables, Tassie was conscious of Dan's eyes on her throughout the meal. She tried to appear interested in the conversation being made by the Edinburgh stockbroker she'd been seated next to, but his attempts to hold her attention were becoming increasingly futile. While she was sure his sailing holiday in

Croatia had been wonderful, she just didn't want to hear about it.

The speeches were funny and touching – except Marcus's, which was short, monotone and excruciating. Afterwards the guests were ushered into the main hall, where Ben and Kirstie were formally welcomed by the caller to start the ceilidh. Tassie considered fetching her camera, then spotted Kirstie's brother taking photos. The lens on his was clearly expensive.

Dan came to join her, his eyes following hers. 'I think you're covered.'

'Yes, Kirstie did tell me.'

Guests were beginning to line up alongside the couple, and when Tassie turned to him he was holding out his hand. 'Shall we? You did promise.'

Tassie scanned the room. 'Charlotte?'

'Don't worry. She's fine. Talking to a nice stockbroker. Apparently they've both just holidayed in Croatia.'

By the fourth turn of the eightsome-reel, Tassie and Dan were just about getting to grips with the moves. She loved dancing with him, the intimacy of her hands in his. Each time the formation whisked her towards another guest, she was aware that she couldn't wait to return to him and frequently they convulsed with laughter as they twirled and jumped around – especially when it was Tassie's turn to do her version of a highland jig. Before dinner she'd pulled her hair out of her plait as a half-hearted attempt at keeping her shoulders warm, and now she had to keep pushing it off her face as she whirled.

When the dance finished, Tassie was finally warm for the first time that evening. She pointed to Charlotte, standing alone at the side of the room. 'Go. You brought her as your guest. It's not fair to leave her.'

Dan looked from Charlotte back to her, clearly torn. 'What about you?'

Tassie nudged his shoulder. 'I'm more than used to being at weddings on my own. I'll be fine. You go. Dance with her.'

For a while she watched them working their way across the floor. Dan had surprising grace, considering his hopelessness on a horse, and the two of them had an easy familiarity. But Tassie also saw the way Charlotte's eyes sparkled just that little bit brighter every time they were reunited. A feeling she now knew too.

Yet again she marvelled at Dan's misreading of his business partner's feelings. And wondered how long they'd been fermenting.

'He'd prefer to be dancing with you.'

When Tassie turned, Kirstie was at her side, now in her Erdem dress. She looked like the Princess of Monaco.

'Oh! You look beautiful,' Tassie said. 'I love your dress. I saw it earlier.'

'Thanks.' Kirstie puffed out the skirt and gave a little twirl. 'It was the only thing I begged for. Ben got the helicopter, I got this. Really though,' – she looked over at Dan – 'he's definitely got the hots for you.'

'D'you think? I don't know. They seem very close?' They watched as Dan and Charlotte bumped into each other and laughed.

'As siblings, maybe. Certainly on his side.' Kirstie's face was suddenly serious. 'They did actually grow up together. Dan's parents were killed in a car accident when he was twelve, and he went to live with Charlotte and her parents. Well, that and boarding school. The best solution for a shit situation, he used to say.'

'Oh. That's so awful.'

'Yep. He's not unaffected by it. It's rare to see him looking as relaxed as he did with you today. Trust me. There's definitely something there. Oh,' — Kirstie looked concerned – 'unless you've got someone else? Sorry, I didn't even think – actually that's a lie, I did check for a ring.'

'No, there's no one. And thanks. For the feedback. Poor Dan.'

Kirstie turned and put her arms out. 'So, welcome to the clan, hopefully... maybe? Anyway, I actually came to say goodbye.' She pulled Tassie into a hug. 'Ben and I are going now. Rather bad organisation with our flight times. I just wanted to thank you for everything.'

Tassie hugged her back. 'It's been my pleasure. And thank *you* for the helicopter ride.'

'And the horse?' Kirstie smiled. 'It's been quite a day.'

'It has. Really fun – and beautiful. Shall I take some photos of you leaving?'

'No, you've done more than enough. Max will take some, I'm sure. Right, I'm going to sneak off now, or we'll never get away.'

OUTSIDE THE CASTLE, the newly-weds climbed into a vintage Austin as everyone cheered wildly, fireworks exploding. Watching the flares lighting up the castle's walls, Tassie wished she had her camera. It had been a spectacular wedding.

As the car pulled away there was a sudden volley of shouting from the straw bales on the edge of the field.

'Arggh. Fuck, fuck, you bastard.'

Illuminated by torches lining the drive, Marcus was spinning round, pawing at his backside, red and white striped boxer shorts now exposed where a piece of his trousers hung loose. Tassie had noticed earlier that – roused from his drunken slumbers to wave goodbye to the couple –

he hadn't even managed to stand during the process, just sprawled across one of the bales.

'Something bit me. Fuck it hurts.'

Tassie laughed, along with quite a few of the other guests, as they watched him tearing this way and that, clearly in agony, until eventually a couple of men took him by the arms and guided him inside, his curses growing fainter but increasingly riper as they led him away.

'There's something called karma, you know.' Dan was by her side, looking delighted.

'Come on, don't be mean. Although... you have a point. What do you think bit him?'

'A rat, probably, frightened by the fireworks. I think he might need to have a tetanus.'

'Marcus, or the rat?' She grinned. 'Waiting in A&E for the night. Oh dear...' She nodded slowly. 'As you say, a fitting end to an extraordinary day.'

As the other guests wandered back inside, Charlotte among them, Tassie and Dan remained where they were, staring at the flares outlining the uncut barley in the fields. High above the trees was a full moon, a disc of silver shining among the stars on a backdrop of midnight blue. Streaking across it, the edges of dark clouds were illuminated like the shells of oysters. 'I should get my camera,' she murmured.

Dan felt for her hand. 'Stop now.' He turned to face her. 'It's late. You've done more than enough.'

'Oh, this wouldn't be for them. I've got a bit of a thing about the moon, I...' She closed her mouth. Alex had suddenly reared into view, along with her portfolio of moon photos. It was something she'd been working on for years, collecting images from around the world.

'You?' Dan's face was close to hers, his breath warm in the night air.

She shrugged. 'It doesn't matter. You're right, I've got enough. Shall we go back in?'

'Well, I would suggest we stay outside, it's so beautiful. But sooo cold.'

Tension stretched between them. Her hand was still in his and her head tilted a fraction.

Suddenly the most extraordinary sound splintered through the trees, like the yucking and yawing of giants.

Tassie jumped, spun around, then whispered, 'If I didn't know better, I'd say Marcus had scored.' The sound came again, followed by a large belch. 'What is that?' Her eyes were wide. 'And why am I whispering?'

Dan began laughing, louder and louder, Tassie joining him, until they were both doubled up with mirth. Still the noises came and eventually Dan stopped laughing, wiping the edges of his eyes. 'It's deer – rutting. We have them on Exmoor.'

'Oh.' Tassie felt disappointed. Really, she wouldn't have been surprised if it had been a giant. Another belch cracked out and she laughed, then shivered.

'Come on, let's go in.' Dan put his arm around her shoulders and they turned and walked back towards the castle, still laughing at each explosive new sound.

In the hallway, Dan looked at his watch. 'We're going back to Aberfeldy now. Ben organised a taxi and thought you could come with us?'

'That's great. Thanks. Will Charlotte be all right with that?'

'Of course. Why wouldn't she?'

Tassie said nothing, but braced herself for the three's-a-crowd journey back into town.

. . .

When they arrived to a deserted Aberfeldy, Tassie was the first to get out of the taxi. As she'd guessed, little but the occasional compliment about the wedding had been exchanged between the three of them on the short journey back across the river.

They watched the taxi depart, then Charlotte spoke.

'Well it's nearly two and we're leaving early in the morning. So, nice to have met you, Tassie.' She held out her hand.

Tassie took it, her hold weak. Dan couldn't have told Charlotte they had no transport. Although maybe he'd arranged something and not mentioned it? Fear of misreading the situation engulfed her. If he'd known they were leaving first thing, why hadn't he said?

'Tassie?'

Looking down she saw she was still holding Charlotte's hand. 'Sorry. Long day.' Blushing, she released it and turned to Dan, who was looking amused. Now it was her turn to hold out her hand, unsure what else to do. The chill emanating from Charlotte was freezing her instincts to hug him – then grab him by the hand and run.

Which definitely wasn't going to happen, judging by the way he was now shaking her hand – equally politely.

'Well, bye. It's all been quite an event and... lovely to meet you both,' she said.

'It was lovely meeting you too...' Dan seemed about to say something else then faltered.

Silence blanketed the moment.

'OK, well... bye.' Picking up her bags Tassie hurried across the road, not once looking behind her.

After she'd eventually found the hotel key – at the bottom of the third bag – she turned back, to an empty street.

9

It was a habit set in stone that Tassie always checked her photos at the end of the day, backing them up onto a hard drive. Despite how good lots of them were – considering the dreadful weather – she felt a real sadness as she looked back through the shots, wondering if she'd misread the whole situation. But Kirstie had said something too; it wasn't just her.

It was after three when she finally got into bed, turned out the light and settled under the duvet. She usually knew exactly what a man's intentions towards her were. But today... today had been different. She'd got it wrong. And she'd probably never see him again. She sighed, snuggling further down – at least the bed was comfy.

Tap.

She turned over on the pillow, lifting her head a fraction.

Silence. She closed her eyes again.

Tap... tap... tap.

She sat up. She hadn't imagined it. Something was making a sound. Turning the light on, she looked around. Nothing.

Tap.

It was coming from the window. Bemused, she got out of bed and crossed the room. Looking down into the street she saw Dan standing there, rubbing his arms against the cold of the night. She felt a shiver of excitement as she struggled to pull up the old sash frame. Unable to lift it far, she had to tilt her head to squeeze her shoulders through the gap. 'Hello, Romeo.'

'Hello... Juliet.' He was half whispering, half calling. 'I would say can I come up? But there's no rose trellis, so can you come down?'

'OK. Just give me a second.'

She gave a delighted wriggle as she slipped her arms into the sleeves of her jacket. Which would look extremely fetching with her rose-print pyjamas. Tying her hair in a loose knot, she quietly slipped down the stairs then, equally quietly, opened the front door.

'I'm sorry to have woken you.'

'You didn't. I wasn't asleep. Come...' She motioned to him to follow her up the stairs, past the silent reception.

Back in her room she was acutely aware of the intimacy of the environment. It was the second bedroom they'd been in that day, and again the atmosphere crackled. Dan went and sat on a chair by the window as she walked over to the table.

'Would you like a cup of tea?'

Shaking his head, he reached into his pocket and brought out two miniature bottles. 'These might make a better nightcap?'

'Ah, yes.' Tassie unwrapped two glasses from the sink and handed them to him.

'So,' – Dan poured the whisky – 'I know this is a bit odd, me turning up like this – although given the day we've already had...' He sipped his drink. 'But I didn't have your number.' He took another sip, longer this time. 'I could have got it from the guys but didn't want to ring them. And I didn't want to wait until they came back from honeymoon because...' Finally, he looked at her. 'That would just have been too long.'

'Too long?' Her eyebrows rose, along with the corners of her mouth.

'Yes.' He coloured slightly, then put his drink on a side table.

The relaxing of her shoulders preceded the relaxing of the rest of her body as she perched on the edge of the bed, wrapping a tartan coverlet around her. 'So you fixed Daisy?'

He looked confused, then understanding flickered across his face. 'Oh, no, I haven't. I just hadn't quite had the nerve to tell Charlotte she'll have to get the train. She wasn't going to be best pleased. Correction, she isn't pleased.'

'And what are you going to do?'

'I don't have any choice really. I'll have to stay on until she's fixed. Which is why I wanted to see you before you go.'

'And why would that be?' She was enjoying this now.

Once again Dan coloured as he picked up his whisky. 'Look, I know it's late and you're probably knackered, but—'

A faint tap on the door made them both jump, then stare at each other.

Charlotte?

Tassie went and opened the door a fraction. In the hallway stood the man from reception, his hair pointing in all directions.

'Madam, I'm afraid you are not allowed to have room guests.' His accent was Eastern European, his approach impeccable.

'Gosh. Don't you sleep?' It was all Tassie could think to say, her face instantly flaming.

'I do, madam, but in the reception, so I heard your friend come in.' He looked as embarrassed as she felt.

'It's all right, I was about to go anyway. I only came for a nightcap.' Dan jumped to his feet and came to the doorway.

'Thank you, sir.' The man looked grateful. 'I will let you out when you come back down.' Bowing his head, he backed back down the corridor.

Tassie and Dan looked at each other. 'Another first,' she said.

Dan put his hands on her shoulders. 'And here's another. I don't suppose you'd like to go for a walk? I was actually just about to suggest it. With this full moon, the valley will be beautiful.'

'A man throws stones at my window in the middle of the night then brings whisky to my room. A walk is the last thing I'd think he'd suggest. But yes.' Her smile was light. 'I'd love to. Just wait there and I'll get dressed – quickly, before Mr Receptionist returns.'

DAN WAS RIGHT, the moon lit the cornfields and a river meandering through the valley in a way that was almost spiritual. And nose-numbingly cold.

Despite her down jacket, Tassie was soon shivering, and Dan put his arm around her shoulders. Now they were walking the conversation had loosened, returning to their earlier goodbye in the street.

'I just didn't know what to say when you left. You seemed so keen to go.' He sounded amused.

'And I suddenly thought you weren't interested,' she said. 'Your handshake was very formal.'

He laughed. '*You* were the hand-shaker if you remember.'

'Oh yes. But Charlotte started it.' Tassie turned to him. 'You do know she's in love with you?'

'Charlotte?' He snorted. 'Don't be ridiculous, we've known each other since we were kids. Grew up together actually. Honestly, there's nothing between us. I've had girlfriends, she's had boyfriends. That's how it is. So, *Tassie*?' He whirled around and stared at her. 'Is that short for something? And how long have you been a wedding photographer for? And do you like the job?'

FOR ALMOST THREE hours they walked and talked. She learnt that he enjoyed his work on the farm – inherited early from his parents – but that sometimes he wished he'd done something different, like medicine perhaps. She told him how she loved taking wedding photos but that she'd preferred her previous career. And they laughed – both somewhat wistfully – acknowledging that life didn't always turn out exactly how you wanted.

She told him about her family, about how her brother and his wife had been trying for a baby for ages and nothing was happening. How her mother didn't seem particularly interested – even though she only lived down the road. He told her about the people he worked with: Silly Billy, the farm apprentice, quickly becoming her favourite as he told her stories of how the boy continually got instructions wrong.

They talked about travel – they'd both done lots, although Tassie aced him with the strangeness of the places she'd visited. And as the night moved deeper into the hours of silence they talked about school; about tennis; about university; about friends; about homes; about food (lots about food, including cheese-making); about cider; about worms (terrible in apples); about Shakespears Sister; about Sly and the Family Stone; about *The Banana Splits*; about tofu and polenta; a bit more about Charlotte; about previous boyfriends and girlfriends (he'd had a few, she underplayed her numbers); about London; about pancakes; about riding; about the light as it began to unfold...

Until, finally, they stood on the bridge, having walked a full circle of the valley and Dan looked up at the moon, receding into the first dawn rays.

'It's not so bad is it? All this...' He turned to her. 'And it's looking better all the time.'

And then they *had* to kiss. For it would have been odd not to. And it was gentle, tender, her arms wrapped around his shoulders, his fingers snaking up her neck and tunnelling into her hair. And the sun's rays rose higher and grew stronger with each passing moment as they carried on kissing, until every part of her tingled with happiness and an unfamiliar sense of peace.

Afterwards they stood staring down at the water, both lost in their thoughts. Although, for once, Tassie didn't really have any. *For once* she was entirely in the moment, where all she could think about was how beautiful the water was, how fresh the morning air smelt, and how wonderful it was to have her hand in Dan's. Right there, in that moment.

Oliver would be pleased.

Back in the centre of town they realised it would be another couple of hours before the first cafés opened. Suddenly ravenous, they charmed a hotel kitchen porter into giving them two croissants: freshly baked, the buttery flakes disintegrating on their fingers as they munched them. Kindly, he gave them two teas as well, saying they could return the mugs later.

Sitting in the middle of the square, Tassie grinned up at Dan as he turned to her.

'Tassie, this is crazy, what I'm about to say.'

'But you're going to say it anyway.'

'*Oh yes*. Right, here goes.' He cleared his throat. 'You know I've got to stay until Daisy's fixed.'

'Yes.'

'And you know they said it will take four days.' He gulped his tea. 'Well, I wondered if there was any chance... although I know you're probably too busy. But, well, I just had this crazy thought—'

Tassie held out her phone. 'Already sorted.'

'Huh?'

'I've already sorted it. Look.'

Dan read the text out loud. 'Hey hon. Is there any chance you could hang on in the flat if I stay away until Friday?' When he looked up, his smile was the broadest she'd seen.

Tassie shrugged and bit into her croissant. 'Sometimes a woman just knows.'

'Really, you'll stay on? Tassie, that's brilliant.'

'And spontaneous. I know. Used to be my middle name. Nice to do something like it again. I won't show you Syd's reply, I've never seen so many exclamation marks.' She smiled. 'But let's not stay in Aberfeldy? Well, maybe tonight. But if we're going to be spontaneous, let's do the rest of it in style?'

They looked at each other, both slightly amazed by the audacity of their decision-making. And both, Tassie suspected, ridiculously pleased.

By the end of the afternoon they'd sorted everything. Tassie had spent a few hours going through her photos, sending a batch of edited ones off to Syd before catching up on admin and clearing her diary for the next five days. Luckily, she hadn't got any proper jobs booked until the following week, but she had to do no end of organising around her garden.

After a tsunami of excitement regarding Tassie's plans, Syd had calmed down and become very accommodating – although she'd balked at Tassie's request to do a bit of manure spreading. Meanwhile Dan had seen an extremely grumpy Charlotte off at the train station, having sweet-talked her into taking on some of his usual work. Tassie didn't ask if Charlotte knew she was also staying; she suspected she didn't.

When they went to pick up the car on loan from the garage, 'do it in style' turned out to be a Barbie-pink Nissan Micra, about which the owner was most apologetic. Apparently his normal loan car was out of action and this one belonged to his daughter, who was currently away. Tassie insisted on Dan pretending to drive so she could take a photo through the open window, 'For posterity's sake'.

That evening, over dinner in an Italian restaurant, they discussed their ideas for the rest of the week, Tassie laughing at Dan when 'spontaneity' was replaced with military planning as he pulled out a bunch of maps and brochures. It turned out he'd been chatting to a local shop owner, who'd suggested they might want to stay with her son and partner in their pub on the Isle of Skye.

'I do love spontaneity,' Dan protested, 'but I was also in the cadets. Taught to always plan ahead.'

And although she teased him, Tassie loved the fact that he'd cared enough to do so much organising.

At the end of the night they returned to her hotel, aware of the receptionist settling down for the night in the back office. Standing in the sitting room, the fire now just embers, Tassie flicked her head in his direction. 'Poor man,' she whispered, 'I hope he doesn't have to sleep there every night.'

Dan kissed her cheek. 'I'd better be going. We've got an early start – and some sleep to catch up on from last night. Is six-thirty OK?

'That early?'

He nodded, his eyes creasing. 'All will be revealed. Just make sure you wear warm clothes.'

The touch of his lips on her cheek left its charge, and Tassie put her arms around his neck. 'I feel like a schoolgirl. Or a Victorian lady – minus chaperone. All this is so...' She pulled back and looked at him. 'Actually, it's all so unexpectedly nice.'

'I know what you mean.' He gently kissed her other cheek, and her stomach flipped. 'Some things are definitely worth waiting for.' Cupping her face in his hands, he softly kissed her lips once, then a second time, his breath scented by whisky. Tassie felt her skin tingling, running from her mouth down through her body. This time her sigh was deeper as she kissed him back.

'You'd better go now, or...' She stopped then grinned, shaking her head. 'Go. Now.'

'Going.' As Dan left the reception she heard him calling a loud, 'Goodnight'.

Chuckling softly, Tassie walked up the stairs to her room. Once in bed she wriggled her feet, trying to warm the sheets. Then she plumped up the pillows, tucked her hair behind her shoulders, whispered Dan goodnight and closed her eyes, slipping into a deep and contented sleep.

10

Early the next morning Tassie waited outside her hotel, full of expectation about what might be happening, glad she'd brought another thick jumper and her favourite old jeans. Dan appeared from the opposite doorway, a square basket in one hand, in the other a – she did a double take – fishing rod. He waved it as he crossed the road.

'Good morning,' he said, stroking a tendril of her hair with his thumb. 'You look...' He examined her face. 'Sleepy. How did you?'

'How did I what?'

'Sleep?'

'Good, thank you. Although it seems not for long enough. What *are* we about to do?'

He grinned, waggling the rod. 'What does it look like? We're going fishing. Mary, in the gift shop...' He stopped, looking slightly embarrassed. 'Well, after I'd told her about us, how we met, our plans for the week, she got quite excited about helping me plan the trip—'

'Oh, so it was Mary, not your military training.' Tassie grinned.

'Anyway, one of her suggestions, and believe me there were many, was that before we leave town we could go fishing. She said the river's famous for it. So...' He bent down and opened the basket, its hinges creaking in the quiet street. Inside were four eggs, some tomatoes, sliced bread and lots of utensils. 'She lent me all this. And it seemed a shame to waste the offer.'

'Are you sure she didn't want to join us? She was being extremely nice to you.'

'Don't be daft. She's about seventy. Said I remind her of her son. Although, as she also told me he's a cross dresser, or "likes to dress like a lassie," as she called it, I'm not sure how.' He looked across the square in the direction of the shop. 'We got close, Mary and I – she's a real character. Anyway, we'd better be going. She told me the fish bite best early on.'

SITTING by the fire they'd made, Tassie watched Dan as he stood at the edge of the river, his shoulders drooping as he wafted the rod through the water. He'd been trying to catch something for half an hour and only managed some rather smelly weeds. Earlier, a heron had landed in the river downstream and they'd laughed when within seconds it had caught a fish then flown off.

In the early morning light, strands of his dark-blond hair were highlighted by the sun and his back and shoulders were broad. He turned to her, his expression rueful. 'You must be getting hungry. Sorry.'

She got up and put her arm around his waist, snuggling her head into his side. 'Actually, I'm fine, and it's so beautiful.'

She loved listening to the flow of the water, the surface

sparkling grey, white and green in the strengthening light, and the sounds of birds – she'd no idea what kind – chorusing in the trees. It made her think about that time when she was a child, playing by the river. She'd thought about the little girl a lot, wondering if she had imagined her. Wondering lots of things... 'Dan?'

'Yes.'

'You know yesterday, when you said you saw me going upstairs, at the castle, when you followed me.'

'Thank goodness I did. My knight-in-shining armour moment. I rather like that image.'

'Yes. Thank goodness. But I don't think it was me. I don't think it could have been.'

'Really? I'm pretty sure it was. Not many people have your hair and, OK I didn't see you, but I definitely heard your laugh.'

She stood for a few moments, staring into the water. Should she tell him about the little girl? She huffed softly. Perhaps it was a bit early in the relationship to start talking about ghosts. Whatever *had* happened the previous day, she was simply grateful.

'Look,' Dan whispered as he pointed to a kingfisher, balanced on a slender branch that stretched across the river. Its brilliant feathers catching the light, it was still as an acrobat about to perform the next feat, before it dived into the stream then flew up into another tree. Suddenly the line started jerking.

'Woah, this is it. Breakfast.' Dan yanked back on the rod. 'It's heavy, must be a big one.' He looked at her, his eyes sparkling, then yanked again, flicking the line out of the water.

There was a splash as the river relinquished his catch. It was indeed a big one. A foul-smelling plimsoll, that doused them with water and weeds as it flew onto the bank.

Staring at it – lying limp on the grass, the laces tangled in the line – Dan groaned. 'I think I'll call it quits.' Chucking the rod on the ground, he pulled a frying pan out of the basket. Underneath was a neatly wrapped package which he opened to reveal thick rashers of bacon. 'Mary thought we might have some trouble. So how about bacon and eggs?'

Tassie chuckled as she crouched beside him. 'Delicious. Shall I make the tea?' She reached into the basket for the tea bags and started filling up a pan from a thermos of water. 'I'm starving actually. I was just being nice.'

When they'd finished breakfast, after a quick shower and change at the hotel, Tassie checked out, then found the gift shop where Dan was taking Mary's stuff back. The old lady was tiny and virtually square, her white hair in a neat bun and her bosom encased in a red hand-knitted cardigan.

'I can see why you've fallen,' she said, looking at Dan as she clasped Tassie's hands, her face softening like a wrinkled apple. 'What a bonnie lass.'

She was thrilled to hear they'd enjoyed their breakfast and made them promise to keep in touch.

'I've given ma boy a ring and he says he'll be delighted to have you stay. He's even given you a discount, on account of you being friends of mine. Three nights I told him. That's right, isn't it?' She patted Tassie's arm. 'Well, off you go now, but mind to come back and tell me how it all went.'

After leaving Aberfeldy they meandered through the Highlands, where first the terrain was relatively flat, autumnal browns and gold stretching all around as Dan commented that it reminded him of Dartmoor. After a while the vista broadened, and soon they were surrounded by an expanse of mountains – often sheering up from the side of the road.

As they travelled through forests, along the sides of lochs and past ancient castles, Tassie was incredulous. 'I've been all over the world,' she murmured at one point, 'but I'm not sure that anything I've seen beats this.'

It was after seven by the time they crossed the bridge onto the Isle of Skye, and when they finally pulled up outside the Eilean Inn the sun had long disappeared. The building was a traditional stone one, long and low, painted white with black-framed windows looking out to the sea. Pushing open the heavy door, a blast of heat hit them as they entered reception. A man was sitting on a high stool behind the counter, cosy in a black roll-neck jumper, Michael Palin's *Around the World in Eighty Days* propped open in front of him.

'Did you know that shredded cobra is a delicacy in China? Have you ever eaten anything like that?' He looked up, waiting expectantly for an answer.

Tassie was the first to speak. 'Er, I was once offered wasp crackers in Japan.'

'And were they tasty?'

'Sort of, although if you got the wrong bit of wasp you still got stung.'

'And did you?'

'Yes. Twice.'

'And how was that?'

'Umm, painful.' She looked at Dan.

A voice emerged from a doorway. 'Laurence! Book the poor darlings in. This is a pub, not show and tell.' The accent was east London, the intonation exclamation mark-heavy.

Again, Tassie and Dan looked at each other, then into the back room. But no one appeared.

'OK, deary, button your trews. There's no formalities to be had.' Laurence beamed at his guests. 'I do believe this is the lovely Dan and equally scrumptious Tassie. Am I right?'

'Yes, that's us, although just Tassie and Dan will do.' Dan stepped forward and held out his hand.

'Och, we'll have no formalities like that. If I wasn't so comfortable I'd bend over the bar and give you a kiss. My mother's told me all about you. Newly hatched lovebirds, eh?' Laurence winked at him.

Tassie joined Dan at the counter, hoping to ameliorate his growing embarrassment. 'You're in the most beautiful position,' she said. 'We can't wait to see the rest of the island.'

'Aye, it is stunning. We love it.' Laurence looked behind him, raising his voice. 'Beats Soho on a Saturday night, doesn't it, Martin?'

'For the whisky and the whelks, definitely.' Martin appeared in the doorway. He was thin and wispy-haired, clasping a red setter puppy that was sniffling his neck.

'Oh, he's beautiful.' Tassie reached over to ruffle the dog's ear.

'She, dear. Jemima, she's called. Rules the house, you'll find. Or eats it, more like. Anyway, as Laurence says, we've been expecting you. Let's get the formals done then we'll show you up to your room. We've given you the Marie Antoinette suite, for the price of a normal double. When Ma Mary requests, we jump, don't we?' He leant sideways and nudged Laurence, who nodded.

THE HONEYMOON SUITE was everything the name might suggest. Done in a style of which Ms Antoinette herself would have approved, it had a four-poster bed swathed in red velvet, antique prints on the walls and a gold and blue bathroom.

'Enjoy,' said Laurence, sweeping the room with his hand. 'If it's windy then close the curtains, it makes a difference.

The fire is real so do feel free to light it. Oh, and we've left you a wee bottle of something.' He pointed to a table as he walked over to the doorway. 'Give us a bell if you need anything. Last orders for dinner are at nine-thirty. If you can make it for then.'

As he closed the door his wink verged on vaudeville, and Tassie and Dan looked at each other, trying to smother their laughter. After flicking through the 'Welcome' file, Tassie walked over to examine the prints on the wall, and took a sharp intake of breath. 'Dan, come and look.' She turned around. 'Dan?'

'There's a Jacuzzi in the bath and the window looks straight out to sea – I guess. It's spectacular. *Come on*, Mary!' He appeared in the bathroom doorway.

'Come and look at these,' she said.

He walked over to her and as he hesitantly put his arms around her, Tassie was aware that once again there was an awkwardness between them.

Which meant the pictures helped.

He burst out laughing. 'That's so rude.'

'I know. They're all the same. I think they must be pornography from the nineteenth century or something. I wonder where they found them.'

For a while they examined the prints, exclaiming at the images of women pulling up their wide skirts to reveal a complete lack of underwear, and men with a plethora of huge phalluses, all indulging in every sexual position imaginable.

Dan snorted. 'They were certainly athletic in the 1800s.' He pointed at one particularly daring pose. 'That's hilarious. As is the whole place. Although I must say I was disappointed by Laurence's jeans and jumper. But again, well done Mary, my new best friend.'

'And mine. Shall we have some wine?' Tassie walked

over to the ice bucket sitting on a suede-topped table. 'Yay, Prosecco. I think I actually prefer it to champagne.'

'Good to know. I'll light the fire, shall I?' Dan was already kneeling by the grate.

Tassie looked at her watch. 'We've got two hours before we need to go to dinner. So definitely.'

DAN HAD OPTED to lounge in one of the green velvet chairs, his legs stretched out, while as usual Tassie was sitting on the floor, her back against the other chair. Flames crackled in the fireplace and an aroma of burning pinewood and expectation filled the room. For a while neither of them spoke, Dan alternating between staring into the fire and sipping his wine.

Tassie looked over to the bed, its four posts looming. Or beckoning? Putting her glass down on the floor she shuffled over to kneel before him. Slowly, she slid her hands up the inside of his paint-speckled sweatshirt, feeling the warmth and softness of his skin.

'Dan?' Her voice was low.

'Tassie?' He looked at her, slowly twisting a lock of her hair.

'There's something I think we need to get out of the way.'

'And that would be?'

'Well. I don't know about you, but I'd quite like to be able to concentrate on dinner.'

'So you want to see the menu?'

'Nope.'

'So you want to eat alone.'

She laughed. 'Nope.'

'Then I'm confused.'

Reaching up, she touched her lips to his, kissed him then drew her face away. She motioned with her head down to the rug. 'Shag pile. Had you noticed? And it's been a long time coming.'

'Ah, now I understand. Or not coming, I think you're trying to say.' He traced the length of her neck with his fingers, then slid his hands round to start unbuttoning her cardigan. 'I've always loved a cardigan. Very sexy.'

'And I've always loved a tatty sweatshirt. But maybe it could come off?' Her breath quickening, Tassie gripped its wide base and, catching his T-shirt, rolled them up over his head. Dan eased forward so she could remove them, then leant back, his face relaxed and content. She traced his chest with her fingers, marvelling at the tanned curves and ridges that were revealed. She nibbled his nipples. 'I've been wanting to do this since the mountain.'

'Really? I knew the suit change was working.' He eased her shirt off her shoulders. 'And I've been wanting to do this since I saw you standing in the window.' Bending forward he slid his hands round to the back of her neck, softly gathering her hair in his hands. Tipping her head back, he kissed her, his mouth covering hers as he gently pushed her back. Together they slipped onto the floor and within minutes had removed the rest of their clothing.

Naked, now they slowed, lying sideways on the rug, languidly stroking the length of each other's sides, both lean, sinuous, their curves like stringed instruments.

Dan butterfly-kissed Tassie's shoulder. 'You really are very, *very* lovely.'

'You too. Golden delicious. Although – no – that's green.' Chuckling, she meandered her hand down his chest. 'How come you're still so tanned?' Her hand moved to stroke his legs, then her head went in the same direction, desire pulsing with each shift of her body.

'Farm wor— Ow!'

She'd bitten his thigh.

The mood broken, soon they were hugging and kissing and rolling across the rug, only stopping when they banged into the ice bucket – water and ice beginning to fly before Dan made a spectacular catch to stop it falling over. More kissing, and then a sensation of cold hit Tassie's back where he'd placed a handful of ice. She tried to do the same but failed and they continued, feeling, exploring, laughing and joking so much that it was almost incidental when two bodies became one. And then they stopped laughing, then talking, as playfulness became purpose, until they eventually lost themselves in a warmth that radiated between them, something that became a tingling that became a growing swell, until both of them rode a wave together so strong that for a moment it engulfed them, spinning them over and over.

Afterwards they edged closer to the fire, the flames now diminishing. Tassie curved her body into Dan's, fitting into him like a pine nut in its shell. 'That was... spectacular,' she whispered, stretching round to kiss his chin. 'And now, my fine man, I can concentrate on dinner.'

'Don't tell me, you're hungry.' Dan stroked his hand over her stomach.

'Always. But we've still got some time. Shall we try the Jacuzzi? Shame there's no more wine.'

'Aha, but look what I have.' Dan rolled away from her and, moving over to his bag, crouched to pull something out.

Watching him, Tassie was delighted by everything she saw, including his shapely buttocks which tightened as he turned to show her two whisky miniatures. He was totally at ease in his nakedness. Not surprising, given how good he looked.

'In my hotel they were darn good at replenishing the freebies— God. I hope they were freebies. No, yes, I'm sure they were. I hope they were. Oh well, they've got my card details.'

Grinning, he walked over to the wardrobe where he unhooked two dressing gowns hanging on the door. Kneeling in front of Tassie, he draped one over her. 'Would you like your whisky cracked open here, m'lady, or in the bath?' He gave her a mock bow. 'And perhaps you'd like it with some wasp crackers? There's a dead one on the windowsill I could mash into the hotel's shortbread. Or maybe a spider? I had some fried in Cambodia once.'

11

_____

Dressing for dinner involved a frantic scrabbling for clothes when they realised they only had ten minutes before nine-thirty.

Tassie giggled as they hurried down the stairs. Dan's hair was wet and in a tangle of knots and her dress was twisted. Reaching the ground floor, she slipped her hand into his. 'I think they might be able to guess what we've been doing.'

'Let's just hope they don't comment.'

When they entered the dining room all the other tables were already occupied, a low hum of conversation filling the room.

'I love the wallpaper,' said Tassie as Martin showed them to their table. The background was pale yellow, almost like silk, with delicate birds and jasmine flowers trailing across it.

'It's fabulous isn't it?' Martin's voice dropped to a stage whisper. 'Don't tell anyone, but you can get the most marvellous things in B&Q.'

'Wow,' Tassie said, genuinely impressed. She should check it out. Maybe for her bathroom.

Martin seated them at a table next to the window and went to fetch some water.

'Good evening, I hope the menu takes your fancy.'

Tassie looked up as a thick white card was held out before her. 'Thank you.' She began to look at the menu then did a double take at the waitress. Laurence, was now more... Laura?

She noted Tassie's double take and smiled, giving a slight curtsey. 'I always dress for dinner, dear.' Her hair, previously dark and greying, was now blonde and in a neat chignon and she wore a plum-coloured silk blouse, a pleated black and maroon skirt and flat patent pumps. There was something of the schoolmistress about her. 'I can highly recommend the crab. Caught fresh this morning. And for you...' She looked at Dan and winked. 'You'll probably be needing a good hearty steak by now.'

Despite her prim attire, the wink was just as lascivious as earlier, and they couldn't help laughing as she turned. Other guests acknowledged their amusement, most smiling with them – apart from one couple in the centre of the room who continued eating their mushroom soup, staring into their bowls as disapproval and awkwardness infused their every slurp.

A woman on the next table leant over to Tassie, her accent Midwest American, her outfit cashmere, shoulder to ankle. 'You get used to her. No one gets away without being commented on. Although it strikes me she's more ruthless as Laurence than she is Eileen. Isn't she, Walter, honey?' She turned and looked at her husband, who nodded. 'We just love this place; it's our fifth visit. You's enjoy your meal now. It's all delicious.'

After some deliberation, Tassie chose toasted goat's cheese salad and Scottish salmon and Dan ordered scallops in oatmeal and steak braised in Skye ale. 'I wouldn't want to go against Eileen's orders.'

The food was spectacular: the scallops fresh and succulent, Tassie's cheese oozing over small rounds of toast. She savoured a mouthful, the creaminess of the cheese enhanced by drizzles of honey. 'I love cheese.'

'I'm beginning to appreciate that you love all types of food.'

'I do, but I particularly love cheese. Much to my friends' amusement I recently started making it.'

'Cheese?'

'Yes, I've made halloumi, ricotta, even some Camembert. Worked pretty well. I'm fascinated by the alchemy of how cream becomes something totally different. Actually,' – she looked at him and felt herself colouring – 'I sometimes have this daydream that I might stop being a photographer and become a cheese-maker instead. Where my parents live there's a lady who makes goat's cheese and I used to love going to help her when I was little. I adored her goats. Such characters.'

'Well, why don't you?' Dan smiled encouragingly.

'Oh, you know. For a long time I didn't have a regular income, but now I do, so that's appealing. I love my flat and my friends. And London's OK.' She shrugged. 'Still, it's a thought I nurture, at the back of my mind. What about you? Any unfilled ambitions?'

Dan pierced a scallop, twirling it around on his fork before popping it in his mouth. 'Sorry, I've not offered, do you want to try one?' He picked up another and held it out to her.

'Not all of it. Just give me a taste.' She skewered some cheese onto her fork and they swapped bites. 'Well?'

Dan gave a small sigh and looked at her. 'I did really want to be a doctor at one stage. I was obsessed with watching *M*A*S*H* re-runs, got into *ER* as well. Didn't every young man want to be Dr Ross? But then...' He looked around the room. 'Actually, I don't normally talk about this stuff as it's all a bit depressing.' He cut into his last scallop. 'How about we return to it later.' He dropped his voice to a whisper. 'It's all a bit Western Front in here.'

Guessing what he'd been about to say, Tassie nodded, taking a sip of wine. 'This is delicious, good choice. Do you know lots about wine, being in the drinks trade?'

AFTER DINNER, they walked along the edge of the sea, the moon painting shards of white onto the water.

As they stood looking out, Dan put his arms around her. 'This is beautiful.' He nuzzled into her neck then kissed up the length of it. 'But there's somewhere else I'd much rather be right now.'

Tassie's body responded in kind. She, it, knew exactly what he meant. She kissed him. 'Come on then. I'll race you.'

They ran back down the road to the hotel, Tassie beating Dan by a short distance, although she knew he'd let her and told him off for doing so. They were laughing as they walked through the door.

Eileen was back at her position on the stool, still reading Michael Palin. 'Nice walk?' She raised an eyebrow.

Tassie nodded. 'Yes, lovely, thanks. And it was a brilliant meal, thank you.'

There was a short silence as she and Dan moved towards the staircase.

'See you in the morning,' Dan said.

'Och, you'll be doing that indeed. Enjoy.' The word was stretched as far as it could go, its suggestive upturn following them around the corner as they almost ran up the stairs.

In the room they moved around easily: undressing, cleaning their teeth, pulling back the bedcovers like they'd done it together a hundred times before. Then, remembering their earlier conversation, Tassie suggested they relight the fire before going to bed.

Sitting on the floor, dressed in the hotel dressing gowns, Dan told her about losing his parents just before his thirteenth birthday. Even now, twenty-one years later, his voice caught as he recounted how they'd been on a business trip, driving down a long straight road in the early evening when a car had lost control on the other side (no one had ever found out why) and crashed headlong into them. Everyone was killed – his parents and the other two people. His mum and dad had been great friends with Charlotte's parents and, having no brothers or sisters who were close, had nominated them as guardians.

'Caused a bit of a ruckus at the time, but eventually it was decided to be the best thing,' he said. 'As I was already at boarding school...' He stopped, then swallowed. 'Actually I'd only just started. Anyway, as I was already there a plan was concocted that I'd remain there in term time and live with the Billingtons in the holidays.' He smiled a twisted grin. 'So you see, Charlotte and I *are* practically brother and sister.'

While he talked, Tassie moved to sit behind him, saying nothing, just enveloping him in her arms, hugging him a little bit tighter every time his voice broke. With the fire spitting the occasional spark, he told her how the farm had been kept in trust; luckily his parents had put plans in place in case anything happened. How, after university, when the farm manager had retired, he'd felt duty bound to return home and run things. 'There's barely any market for selling operations like ours these days.' His voice was wistful. 'Especially now, after the floods.'

'I know.' Tassie squeezed his shoulders. 'Dad was desperate for Tom to take over the farm, I think he just always assumed he would. But he stuck firm about wanting to go into teaching. I still don't know what will happen when Dad retires, if he ever does. He's seventy and showing no signs of it yet. Tom and I don't really discuss it, but it's a real worry. Although hardly a big thing in comparison to what you've experienced.'

'One's issues are always big in one's own life, aren't they? Regardless of comparisons with others.' Dan rubbed her calves. 'But I'm glad that by all accounts you don't have anything major going on in yours. And, right now, neither do I.'

They stared into the flames, each wrapped in their own thoughts, although unease prickled Tassie's neck. Perhaps *now* was the time to talk about Alex? For with that revelation would come annihilation, finally.

But somehow, perhaps because she didn't want to spoil the moment, she just couldn't.

Later, much later, they retired to bed, and this time their lovemaking was just that: tender, slow, Tassie understanding his need for her closeness in both body and mind.

And afterwards they both slept deeply – Tassie experiencing another dreamless sleep.

WHEN DAN WOKE the next morning, it was long after Tassie, who'd snuggled into him, watching his chest slowly rise then fall.

Smiling sleepily, he kissed her, then looked at his watch

and started. 'Wow. Nine o'clock. I never usually sleep beyond six. It's a bad habit of mine.'

For the rest of the day they did very little – spending the time walking along the shoreline, eating in a little café for lunch, enjoying another delicious evening meal, talking, talking.

Just enjoying every element of being in the moment.

12

From: *Tassie.Morris@morrisphotography.co.uk @ 9.15am*
   To: *Sydonie.Harper@kissthebride.com*
   Wednesday 10th September 2014
   Re: *Och Aye the Hellooo*

Hi Sweets

Just thought I should check in with you. There's limited phone reception here and I know you'll be going mad not being able to get in touch so I'm borrowing a computer. How are you? How's Stan? How's my garden?

We're staying just off the west coast of Scotland. And having the nicest time – yes, I know you'll be jumping up and down and shouting for more details. Suffice to say it's all just... perfect.

Dan is just as great as I thought on first meeting (did you get the photo?) I can't quite believe how easy I find his company, and I think he feels the same. He's funny, intelligent (very intelligent), kind, interesting. You'll love him. Oh yes, you will get to meet this one.

Anyway, we're here again for tonight then back to Aberfeldy to pick up the vehicle, then I guess we'll drive back down together, or I'll get the train. Don't want to be too presumptuous.

Syd, I think I finally understand what you've been trying to tell me. About how brilliant it is when you find someone who makes you feel... oh, I don't know. Like everything you were always meant to be. But let's not get ahead of ourselves...

Ha! I can see you dancing around my kitchen – except you'll be at work right now. Hope the Cat Dragon's not too fiery.

Ta-ta for now. Love you.

Tass

xxxxx

Ps: I'll check in on my emails again before I leave.

Pps: He makes cider! And we've discussed making cheese...

Ppps: I presume you got the wedding photos. God I hope you got the wedding photos. I think they've come out all right? I was lucky to get some light, eventually. No thanks to the weather. Never again, Sydonie Harper...

Tassie could almost taste her happiness as she sat waiting for her email to log off. If it was chocolate it would be sweet and crumbly. If it was cheese it would be melting. She chuckled.

'You finished, sweetheart?' Martin appeared, quickly followed by Jemima – who bounded in, sniffing around Tassie's feet.

'I'm so sorry about the Wi-Fi – we've been waiting for months to get it fixed. This one here,' – he bent and tweaked the puppy's ear – 'managed to eat some of the cabling. And no one's come to fix it yet. Island living, eh?'

Jemima nibbled the laces on Tassie's Converse.

'Use our computer any time you want. Although lots of guests tell us that not being contactable is one of the joys of staying here.'

'Thank you.' Tassie eased her shoe out of Jemima's

mouth. 'I'll probably check them again tomorrow before we go. But I agree, it's lovely not having constant messages.'

'Any plans for today?' Martin looked out of the window. 'The weather's going to be rainy all morning but better this afternoon. You could walk up to Waternost Farm. They do a grand high tea.'

'That sounds good. How far is it?'

'Barely anything for youngsters like you. A couple of miles? Maybe three?'

'OK, we'll try that. Thank you.'

'If you come back later, I'll draw you a map.'

Tassie picked up the mug of tea she'd filched from the dining room and walked the length of the inn to the little conservatory. Sitting in the window seat she looked out at Loch Bay, where a small white yacht was motoring across the flint-grey water, green hills behind. It was all so peaceful. She kicked off her shoes and sat cross-legged, cradling her fingers around the mug. Things seemed to be moving so slowly this week, or was it fast? Time just seemed to be happening without her really being aware of it.

Like right now. How long was it since Dan had gone up to have a bath? When she'd said she needed to send an email he'd found a book in the lounge and told her he'd happily amuse himself.

She sighed out a smile. Even though it had been, what, just four days, already they'd fallen into an easy pattern of familiarity, where any plan one made seemed to suit the other perfectly.

Following Martin's directions, they left the inn just after two, soon finding themselves in deserted countryside as they walked past hills covered in crags and boulders, straggling trees bent sideways by the wind.

After a particularly strong gust, Dan pointed to a large opening, low in the rock face. 'How about we shelter for a bit? This wind's relentless.'

Tassie needed no persuading and within moments they found themselves in a large half-lit cave, which felt surprisingly warm given the temperature outside.

'Look, we've got company.' She pointed to the skeleton of a sheep.

Dan went over to investigate, then beckoned to her.

'It must have been sheltering with its lamb. I wonder what happened?'

Lying beside the bigger skeleton was a much smaller one, its skull nuzzling against the carcass of its mother.

'That's sweet. Sort of,' Tassie said. Then she shivered.

'Do you want to go?' Dan put his arms around her and squeezed her tight.

She laughed. 'Are you worried that I'm scared by a couple of skeletons?' She turned and poked his stomach. 'D'you not think I saw enough of them on the farm?' She reached up to kiss him. 'Actually, I've got other things on my mind.'

Pulling him with her, she walked to the driest part of the cave, where she slowly began unzipping his jacket.

'Here's something you don't know about me.' The corners of her mouth twitched. 'I've always loved the smell of damp.'

IT TOOK another half an hour of walking to get to Waternost Farm – both of them grinning, holding the other's hand tight.

The farm was positioned at the tip of one of the island's

peninsulas and as they approached the front door they passed a line of wellies lined up against a hand-built wall, an old sheep dog resting beside it, pink tongue lolling.

Martin had phoned ahead so the woman was expecting them. Tall, gaunt, dressed in a long corduroy shirt and jeans, her silver hair was as tangled as a wire scourer.

'Ahh, good, you're here. I was worried you might have got lost.' She held out her hand. 'Welcome. You've done well to miss the rain.' She looked up at the sky. 'Although I think it might still blow a storm out there. I'm Eva.' She took Tassie's hand. 'And I already know you're Tassie and Dan.'

The house was dark but delightfully warm as they walked into a large room with brown leather sofas and a fire roaring in an old grate.

'I know it's not that cold yet, but nothing beats a fire, does it? Do sit down, the both of you. I hear you'll be interested in the corncrakes, so here's some information to be going on with while I fetch the tea.'

Dan looked at Tassie, who shrugged, mouthing, 'I have no idea.'

When Eva returned with some leaflets they obediently looked through them, and after a while Tassie started reading aloud. 'Corncrakes are extremely secretive, spending most of their time hidden in tall vegetation, their presence only betrayed by their rasping call.' She looked up at Dan and they suppressed their laughter. Just in time, as Eva re-appeared in the doorway.

'Aye, I was lucky enough to hear one this morning; it's been a while.' She was carrying a tray full of square-cut sandwiches, scones and delicate pastries topped with wild flowers.

'This looks wonderful,' Tassie said, as Eva placed the tray before them. 'Martin told us not to eat much lunch.'

'Aye, we like a good high tea on the island. What drink

would you like? We've got Assam, Earl Grey, red ginseng, ginger, chamomile or rooibos. Or I could also make you a red berry tisane.'

'I'll have ginger, please,' said Tassie.

'Rooibos for me,' said Dan.

Tassie looked at him as Eva left the room, raising her eyebrows. 'Eurgh, the first strange thing I've heard you say. How can you drink that stuff?'

'It's an acquired taste, I know. I used to have some stomach problems and Charlotte did a bit of research for me.'

'I think I'd prefer the problems.' Tassie wrinkled her nose. Then felt bad. 'Obviously not really. I'm lucky. I've got the constitution of an ox.'

Once again, the food was delicious. The salmon was local, as were the eggs – freshly collected that morning. As they ate, Eva talked to them about corncrakes and they both politely listened, Dan occasionally asking a question – each one eliciting a long and enthusiastic answer. When they'd finished the tea, Eva walked over to an old television in the corner of the room and bent down to turn it on at the wall.

'The video lasts about forty minutes, so you'll still have time to walk back to the inn, if that's what you're planning.'

They nodded, still bewildered, then politely turned to watch.

THE SKIES WERE BEGINNING to darken as they began the walk back up the hill from Eva's place, turning half-way to wave.

'Well, if there was anything missing in my knowledge of corncrakes,' – Dan's voice began to crack – 'I think that's been resolved.'

Laughter bubbled in Tassie's throat. 'Who would have thought that their nests would be saucer-shaped—'

'Built by the male.'

'Built by the male. And that they eat beetles, snails *and* worms.'

'Indeed. And that new mowing methods mean the flightless chicks can avoid being crushed.'

'Yes.' Tassie frowned. 'Although that is a rather horrible thought.'

They looked at each other, grimaced, then burst out laughing.

'That was one of the weirdest things I've ever experienced. I sincerely feel we missed something in the introduction,' said Dan.

'I know. It was like we were meant to be going there specifically for a talk. Maybe we should have read up on it beforehand.'

'Or *maybe* Martin should have told you when he suggested it?'

'Maybe. But the food was fab and, you never know, it could come in use: our new knowledge of a rare bird. And Dan—' Tassie looked over at him, puffing slightly as she walked up the steep hill. 'I loved the fact that you kept asking her questions. She was so pleased to share her knowledge.'

Dan looked back at her, putting his finger to his lips. 'Don't tell anyone, but when I was a boy I used to be a bit of a twitcher. I'd spend hours wandering the fields, looking for new birds. I found it quite comforting.' Sadness momentarily clouded his face. 'But I must admit, it's a long time since I've studied them.'

A few minutes later a drumroll of thunder trundled across the sky and soon big droplets were falling on their heads, until rain fell like a waterfall.

By now they were in the middle of nowhere, so the only option was to run as fast as they could back down to the inn.

Which they did, laughing about the ridiculousness of how wet they'd quickly become.

'YOU'LL BE NEEDING A BATH. You look like a couple of drowned Chihuahuas.' Laurence was back in his favourite position at the front desk, this time with a copy of *Woman and Home*. 'So how was the tea? How are the corncrakes? You've got to love that woman for her passion for the wee birds, she must give that talk at least twice a week.'

Tassie looked at Dan. 'It was great, thanks.'

Back in their room Tassie picked up a leaflet from a pile on the table. 'Ah, it seems you can't have the tea without the talk,' she called out to Dan. 'That explains everything.'

'*Rrrrrr. Rrrrrr. Rrrrrrr.*' A strange rasping noise came from the bathroom – sounding remarkably like a Scottish bird that was becoming increasingly elusive.

AT DINNER EILEEN was dressed in a fetching black and pink flowered dress with low black heels. 'Marks and Spencer, hen,' she said when Tassie complimented her outfit. 'Mail order is a godsend. Although we do love a wee trip to Inverness. I got terribly excited when I heard they were planning to open in Fort William—'

'So you can imagine her disappointment when she discovered it would only be food.' Martin smiled over at them as he passed with a bottle of wine in his hand, Jemima trotting behind.

Tassie loved the way the couple so easily slipped between Laurence's two personas. Earlier that evening, when she'd asked about the coincidence of the inn having the same name, they'd been enthusiastic in telling her the story.

'It was one of the reasons we bought it. Decided it was a sign,' said Martin.

'Eilean means island in Gaelic, and as I'd already been Eileen for years, it seemed quite the thing to do,' Lawrence carried on.

'Not sure the locals knew what was happening when we arrived. But you're fine with us now, aren't you, Donald?' Martin waved to a man sitting at the bar, who looked up, then nodded.

'Aye, that we are.'

THE NEXT MORNING Tassie woke herself with a body-shaking sneeze. 'Oh dear, I think I've got a cold.' Her voice was pleasingly husky and she shifted closer into Dan.

'Not surprising after our soaking yesterday. Shame we can't keep you in bed all day, nursing you with whisky.'

'I think we've had enough.' She moved her head off the pillow, testing how it felt as she remembered the many nightcaps they'd been plied with the night before. When it had emerged that Martin had omitted to tell Tassie that tea came with a talk, Eileen had scolded him roundly, offering them at least half a bottle of free drinks by way of compensation.

Dan coughed. 'You're probably right.' He ran his fingers over her breasts before kissing each of them. 'And, cold or no cold, we need to get on. It's almost eight. God, I can't believe how well I'm sleeping.' He turned his head on the pillow, his nose almost touching hers. 'I don't think I've slept this well for years. Thank you.'

'For what?'

'Being exactly who you are.' He shuffled forward to kiss

her. 'And exactly who you are is something I'm going to make the most of right now...'

THEY WERE JUST CHECKING out when Tassie remembered she'd not looked at her emails.

'You go and do it, I'll get this.' Dan patted her arm.

'No way, you're not paying.' Tassie reached into her bag and whipped out a card.

'It was my invitation.'

'No it wasn't; I presumed even before you asked.'

'I want to pay. Really. Put it away.'

'Ladies? Whose card shall I be taking?' Martin looked first at Tassie then Dan, a mock frown on his face.

'Mine.'

'Both of them.' They spoke in unison, then laughed.

'No, really,' – Dan grabbed Tassie's card and stuffed it in his pocket – 'I'm insisting. You can buy lunch.' He leant over and kissed her cheek.

'Och, the trials and tribs of young love. How exciting it must be.' Martin took Dan's card, grinning as he put it through the machine. 'And you, young lady.' He looked at Tassie who was now trying to hand over a different card. 'Better you check your emails as you said. Reception's shocking round here.'

As Tassie went into the office, she heard Dan thanking Martin for their wonderful stay before he came to the doorway, bags in both hands.

'I'll see you in the car. Take as long as you need.' He blew her a kiss.

The internet was so slow Tassie wondered if it was still on dial-up. Bending down she stroked Jemima, who'd followed her into the office and was now sitting on her feet.

Finally, her emails appeared. There were four from Syd and, Tassie's heart slammed, one from Alex.

She sat on the chair, staring at the screen. Her feelings for him had always been so visceral, so fixed in her psyche she could reel them off: her heart leaping then racing, her mouth going dry, a sudden rush of blood. But... she looked out of the window towards the bright pink car; things were different now. She should just delete it. Not even bother to read it. That's definitely what she should do.

From: illicitfellacit@hotmail.com

@ 11.15pm

To: tassie@morrisphotography.com

Wednesday 10th September 2014

Re:

Tassie

It was a surprise to get your email – and, I must admit, a great disappointment. I'd been looking forward to meeting. But no such luck. Leading to me sitting here, alone, on a perfectly good Wednesday night, a great bottle of wine beside me (not much left) in a swanky hotel. Is it any surprise I would be missing you?

Tried calling you too, but it went to voicemail. Where are you? Anyway, if you change your mind, I'm now here till Thursday week, staying at Blakes in Chelsea. Something's come up at home, Mum's not been particularly flush of late.

How about a meet up, just for old time's, good time's sake? We've certainly had lots of those. Shame not to?

Alex

Ps: if you get this tonight, feel free to come over. I'll leave a message that my sister might be popping in for a nightcap.

She couldn't stop staring at the time he'd sent the email, and the PS.

There was a time when, wherever she'd been, if it had been physically possible she would have gone to him, thinking it thrilling that there was still such frisson between them.

Although, the thought struck her with force, never had he been so open in his advances. It must have been her message. She'd always known he couldn't handle rejection; she'd just never had the nerve to put it into practice.

Outside, in the carpark Dan was talking to a couple from the hotel. She watched the three of them smiling and laughing. Then, clamping her lips, she pressed delete, then went into her deleted messages and pressed it again.

Things were going to be different now. No longer was Alex Winchester going to rule her life.

She was about to close her emails when she remembered Syd's messages. She opened the last one, then, her heart thumping, opened the rest. The first was an immediate response to hers, telling her how pleased she and Stan were about her news, how they couldn't wait to meet Dan, that he sounded fantastic. The other three were very different. Over and over she kept reading snippets:

Tassie, you've obviously not logged on. Your dad's not as serious as they first thought but is asking for you. Please call home.

Tassie, I'm so sorry, but Tom's just phoned the office. Apparently he's been trying to get hold of you for a while. Your dad's had an accident on the farm and is in hospital. Please call home as soon as you see this.

Sweetheart, your dad has got a bit worse again. I've tried virtually every hotel and inn I can find in the West of Scotland but no luck. I so hope you see this.

'Martin?' Alerted by the tremor in her voice, he instantly came through from reception. 'Please can I borrow your phone?'

'Of course.'

Her hand shaking, she dialled Tom's number. It rang and rang, and as it did Tassie thought back over Syd's emails. The first had arrived at lunchtime the previous day; but clearly the accident had happened some time before that. How could she not have had the sense that something might be wrong? It was her Dad! Shouldn't she have felt something?

Getting no response, she cut the call and phoned her parents' home. This time it went straight to answerphone. 'Hi, Mum, it's Tassie. I've just found out... about Dad. I don't know how I'll get to you, but I'm on my way. I guess I'll stay with Tom.' Tears were already welling as she replaced the receiver.

Martin was still standing in the doorway. 'Bad news?'

'Yes. Very. My dad's had some kind of accident.'

'I'm so sorry to hear that, sweetheart, how terrible. Have you got far to go?'

She felt him squeeze her shoulder as she logged off. 'Shrewsbury.' Her voice cracked as she answered.

'You'd better hurry on your way then.' He gave her a brief hug. 'I'm so sorry your stay is ending this way. Very sad. What hearts you are.'

Tassie bent down, patted Jemima's head then started towards the door. Looking back, she smiled faintly. 'Say goodbye to Laurence from me, and to Eileen. It's been so great, getting to know you all.'

. . .

As soon as Tassie told Dan what had happened he showed no hesitation in suggesting the quickest way to get her home would be for them to drive, first back to Aberfeldy, then on to Shropshire. He brushed aside her protests with a wave of his hand, a hug and a kiss.

Just after they reached the mainland Tom phoned and gave Tassie an update. The pivot belt on their father's rotary mower had sheared off and the blade had hit him in the forearm, cutting through to the bone. They'd thought everything was on the mend, but then an infection had set in and it was touch and go whether he might lose the arm. Still now, no-one could be sure of the outcome.

Gulping down her tears, Tassie relayed what had happened. 'It's the first proper accident he's had in forty years...' She fought hard to contain her emotion. 'He was always so careful.'

As they drove on in silence, Tassie thought about the time her dad had sat at their kitchen table, talking quietly but firmly to her and Tom about the importance of safety after Tom had 'borrowed' the tractor. Trying to impress a girlfriend, no doubt. Lost in her memories, it took a while for her to realise Dan was saying something.

'Sorry? What did you say?'

'No worries – you've got lots on your mind. I was just asking if you wouldn't prefer to stay with your mum tonight?'

'What?' Tassie's surprise at the question made her voice sharp.

Dan glanced at her. 'You've just arranged to stay at Tom's. Wouldn't your mum prefer you to be at home?'

Tassie didn't answer. Now was not the time to explain

that she rarely saw her family, nor that she and her mother barely talked.

'I'm not sure what time we'll get home and I don't want to disturb her if it's late. I'll see her tomorrow.'

After that they lapsed back into silence, Tassie falling deep into her thoughts, aware of a growing tightness in her chest and throat. Something that wasn't just the result of her coughing and sneezing – although she was certainly doing plenty of that.

It was something that happened every time she went home, and one of the reasons she'd stopped going.

In Aberfeldy, Mary met them at the garage with a cardboard box full of home-made food. It was at that point that Tassie cried properly for the first time, touched by the old lady's kindness. Mary hugged her close before turning to Dan.

'Laurence told me it was an absolute delight having the two of you to stay. And asked me to give you this.' She handed him a small package, which Dan then handed to Tassie as they got into the four-by-four.

It was a couple of hours later that she thought to unwrap it. Inside was a tea towel with a drawing of a corncrake surrounded by reeds. As she held it up in Dan's line of vision, tears welled in the corners of Tassie's eyes. 'They were all so lovely.'

He nodded, frowning as an overtaking car skirted too close for comfort on the crowded M74. 'Already seems like another world away'.

⌒

AT JUST AFTER TEN, they finally pulled into Tom's drive on the outskirts of Shrewsbury. It had been an exhausting day: all the roads busy, plus a two-hour spate of heavy rain.

The house was neat and square, surrounded by gardens full of swings and trampolines. Yawning, Dan tipped his head back, stretching his neck from side to side. In the silence, Tassie thought she actually heard it crack. Putting a hand on his leg she leant over and kissed him, rubbing the back of his head as she did.

'Thank you. You've been fantastic. Especially in all that rain.'

As they started to climb down from the Land Rover, Tom came out of the house, Sophie close behind him. Tassie felt her usual pride and affection upon seeing the two of them.

Tom was tall, with blond hair flopping over his eyes, dressed in a brown jumper and faded corduroys. Sophie's spiral-curled hair was piled above a red bandana, a stylish match for her baggy dungarees and stripy T-shirt. She ran past Tom and hugged Tassie, her face creased with concern.

'I'm so sorry you had to hear like you did; you must have been frantic with worry all day.' She pulled back and examined Tassie's face before giving her a kiss. 'We saw him this evening and he seemed a bit better. They think they're getting on top of the infection. So, you can stop worrying so much.' Putting her arm around Tassie's waist she turned to Dan and held out her hand. 'Hi, I'm Sophie.' Then she laughed, a rich, sonorous sound. 'I'm sorry, but we don't actually know your name.'

He smiled as he took her hand. 'Dan. Dan Jacobs. Thank you so much for having us to stay.'

Tom stepped forward to help him with the bags. 'We're delighted. Tassie's not been home for ages, so we're not sure what she's like these days. Maybe a bit too London for our tastes. You, on the other hand, look very nice. Just our type.'

Tassie whacked his shoulder. 'Good to see you too, little bro.'

HALF AN HOUR LATER, the four of them were sitting around the kitchen table.

Tassie picked up one of the books piled up at the end of it. 'How's the studying going, Soph?' She turned to Dan. 'My clever sister-in-law not only teaches but is doing a PhD.'

As if reminded, Sophie tried to stifle a yawn. 'Sorry. Long day. It's fine, thanks. Although a bit intense.'

'What's your subject?' Dan looked at her with interest.

'Well, English is my thing, and my title is...' She took a breath, 'Adaptation as a narrative tool: reflections on the nature of adaptation and a comparison of narrative techniques in the novel and the screenplay.'

Tassie loved Sophie's slow burnishing of each word. Laughing, she rubbed her sister-in-law's hand, then turned to Dan. 'There you go.'

'Interesting.' His response was somewhat awkward. 'I'm not sure what else to say.'

'I wouldn't worry,' said Tom. 'I've got no idea what she's writing about and I live with her. This PhD business is definitely not for me. Tell them about that ridiculous title you saw the other day, Soph.'

She looked at him fondly. 'Yes, that was the best one ever. Something like, some aspects of the vaginal area of a flea.'

Everyone laughed.

'Some?' Dan said.

'Yep. Some.'

'Now that's one I might well read.' He raised his eyebrows. 'But probably not.'

'How are you coping with all this and teaching?' Tassie

looked at the books, then back at Sophie.

'It's OK. Oh... maybe you don't know?' Sophie's smile faltered. 'I went part-time at the beginning of the year. We thought it might, help... you know.'

Tassie put her hand on Sophie's. 'I'm so sorry. Still nothing? Are you any closer to knowing why?'

'Not really. We've both done copious tests. We're getting good at aiming into small pots, aren't we, Tom?'

'Too much information, Soph.' He frowned at her.

'But we'll just keep trying. We have to. They're now talking about IVF, so we've been exploring the options.'

Tassie squeezed her hand. 'You'll get there. The universe *has* to make it happen. You'll be such brilliant parents.'

Sophie smiled at her, putting her hand on top of Tassie's. 'Let's hope.'

Talk returned to Tassie's father and Tom went through the implications of his absence from the farm. Having discovered Dan was a farmer he naturally addressed his comments to both of them, appreciating they all spoke the same language. Apparently it had been an extremely tough few days for everyone.

'We can stay until Sunday I think, can't we Tass?' Dan looked over at her.

Instinct told her that was a bad idea; historically, instinct always told her to leave as soon as she'd arrived. But wanting to help took precedence, so she smiled at him. 'Yes, of course we can. If you're sure that's all right?'

'Really? That's fantastic.' Tom couldn't have looked more pleased – or relieved.

Tassie sneezed loudly then blew into a piece of kitchen roll, having to make the effort to straighten her shoulders afterwards.

It must just be her cold – and the situation with her dad, of course – that was making her feel so morose.

13

---

hropshire, September 2014

The next morning Tassie found Dan's side of the bed empty. Feeling even rougher than she had the day before, she searched for a dressing gown and some thick socks then wandered downstairs.

Sophie was doing the washing up. 'Hi sweetie. We didn't want to wake you as you didn't seem that good last night. The boys have gone off to the farm. Tom wants to be able to tell your dad everything's in order.'

Tassie sat down at the table, hoping Sophie hadn't seen her frown. She was here, and yet it was still Tom doing all the planning? Although, she could have set an alarm on her phone. 'What time is visiting?'

'Not until two, so we've got the morning.'

'Do you think I'll be able to go?' Tassie's voice faltered and she blew her nose.

Sophie turned and stared at her. 'What do you mean?'

'With this stupid cold? What if I give it to him?' When tears welled in her eyes, Sophie came and put an arm around her shoulders.

'Oh honey, you'll be fine, he'll be fine. If you're really

worried we can get you one of those face masks. I know how much he wants to see you.'

Tears now dripped down Tassie's cheeks. 'I should have sensed something, Soph. Surely I should? I, we, were having such a lovely time, and all the time Dad was going through,' – she gestured with her hands – 'this.'

Sophie squeezed her shoulders. 'Don't be daft, you couldn't have known. Then when you did... Well, your dad knows you came as soon as you could. And that's all that matters.'

Tassie looked at her, smiling wanly. 'It's been over a year.'

'I know. And we miss you.' Sophie stroked Tassie's cheek. 'But it's good to have you here now. OK.' She rubbed her hands on a tea towel. 'What do you want for breakfast? I've got some croissants, toast or porridge? Then why don't we go and see your mum. She rang first thing to check you'd arrived.'

Tassie swallowed then blew her nose. 'I guess we should.' She smiled faintly. 'I'll make some toast if I may? Have you got any Marmite?'

'Vile stuff, but probably. Although, first things first.' Sophie sat down, her face brightening. 'Tell me about the gorgeous, and I mean gorgeous, Dan?'

AFTER BREAKFAST TASSIE showered then went back down to the kitchen. She was feeling more together now, her sense of discombobulation finally dissipating.

Sophie was reading one of her books and taking notes.

'Soph?' Tassie sat down at the table as Sophie looked up and smiled. 'What we talked about last night. About you still not getting pregnant. I'm so sorry.'

'Don't worry, hon. I do rather think, like you, that it will happen one way or another. Sybil – sorry, your mum – thinks so too.' She paused, a smirk lifting the corner of her mouth. 'In fact, she's most enthusiastic about the concept of us... inter-breeding.' She entwined her fingers.

Tassie gasped. 'Oh God, Soph, really? She said that? I'm so sorry.'

Sophie laughed. 'There's no need. She's actually been really supportive. We had a long discussion the other day. I'm not sure if you know this, but she also had some problems?'

Tassie shook her head.

'That's all she said. But what she did then do, most enthusiastically, was compare Tom and me having a mixed-race baby to cross-breeding in dogs. Told me how it creates much better results.' Chuckling, she got up and walked over to a shelf overflowing with books, pulling one out. 'She even bought me a book about it.'

Tassie took it from her and read the title aloud. '*Breeding Between the Lines.*' She handed it back to Sophie, shaking her head. 'Really, Soph, I don't know how you do it. You have conversations with my mother I could never have.'

'It's actually a brilliant book, very funny. Although I must admit it made me want a baby even more.' Sophie looked at the cover, then put her hand on Tassie's. 'I know things can be tricky between the two of you. But she's really not that bad. Admittedly she can be a bit blunt sometimes, but underneath, she's very kind. Or she is to me.'

Tassie shrugged. 'I'll take your word for it. At least she's got one daughter she loves.' She stood up then sat down again. 'And I am so pleased she's being supportive of you.' She kissed Sophie's cheek. 'I'm so glad you married Tom, really I am. 'Specially as you're a much better person than me.' She looked at her watch. 'Shall we go?'

· · ·

142

DRIVING to the farm in Sophie's little Fiat 500, Tassie decided that, after a day in Daisy, even a bit of suspension made a welcome change. When they entered the yard the boys were nowhere to be seen, but Sybil instantly appeared in the doorway of the farmhouse. She was dressed in a waxed olive body-warmer, faded jeans and Hunter boots. Her face was lined with fatigue and Tassie was struck by how much older she looked.

'Victoria. Thank you for coming.' Her mother's lips were dry when they touched her cheek, her touch lacking energy.

Tassie thought back to her conversation with Sophie and hugged her; but within seconds her mother was drawing back.

'The boys are up in the top field. A fence has come down so they're fixing it. Really,' – Sybil's shoulders contracted – 'I'm not sure how we're going to cope with your father being laid up. He's barely been off the farm in forty years.'

'Well, we'll do what we can this weekend.' Tassie wanted to put her arm around her mother again, but didn't feel she could. 'And if I can clear my diary a bit, I'll come back whenever I can.'

'Thank you.' Her mother's voice was stiff. 'I'm sure that will be some help. But I know how busy you always are.'

'And Tom and I will do what we can too.' Sophie's voice was gentle. 'I can probably give you more time than him at the moment. Studies can wait.'

Tassie's mum turned and smiled at her. 'Thank you, dear. That will be very helpful. I'd appreciate that.'

As the three of them walked towards the farmhouse, the words *keep calm* played on a loop in Tassie's head. This wasn't about her. It was about her dad. Who needed her.

At the doorway she turned and looked around the yard. Nothing had changed in more than a year since she'd last visited.

Not least the growing tension she felt with every minute of being there.

~

IT WAS JUST Tassie and Tom who went to visit their dad later that afternoon – after much discussion with their mother.

Sybil was convinced Tassie shouldn't go, that her cold would only put Alfred in more danger. Tom said there was no way Tassie could stay at home. Tassie was too furious to say anything.

Tom turned to her as they drove out of the farmyard. 'It's only because she's so worried about him. She knows how much he loves you.'

She didn't respond.

When they arrived at the hospital, having consulted the ward sister, Tassie was allowed to go in, briefly, after she'd washed her hands and taken some miracle medicine that temporarily stopped her sneezing. Acutely aware of the dangers of infection, she determined to keep her distance from her dad, even though she was desperate for physical closeness.

She was shocked when she first saw him, used as she was to him always being so robust and hearty – not this pale, limp figure, dressed in green and white striped pyjamas as he lay propped up by the elevated bed. His bandaged arm was in a sling and as they walked towards him his pain was obvious, although so was his pleasure at seeing them. He winced as he shifted position, then his face adjusted to a strained smile.

Tassie stood behind the rail at the end of the bed, waving awkwardly. 'Hi, Dad.' She sniffed, tears and mucus threatening to block her throat.

'Tassie. Thanks for coming. It's wonderful to see you.'

His smile faltered as he resisted his natural inclination to put his arms out.

She worked hard to keep her voice level. 'I can't hug you, Dad. I'm full of cold and I don't want you to catch anything.'

'But I can.' Tom walked up to Alfred, bent down and gave him a gentle hug, then kissed the top of his head.

Alfred patted his hand. 'Hello, son. How's the farm?'

'All good.' Tom pulled up a chair and sat next to their father, his hand on his arm. 'You won't believe it, but Tassie happened to bring a farmer with her for the weekend, who's a great help.' He looked over at Tassie and nodded. 'I definitely approve.'

Alfred raised his eyebrows. 'Am I going to get to meet him?'

'Maybe,' said Tassie, feeling her cheeks redden. 'Let's see how you're feeling tomorrow. If you're up to it, I'll bring him along.'

'That'll be a first.' Tom laughed, then immediately looked apologetic.

As with most hospital visits, the conversation wasn't exactly scintillating, and the constant beeping from the machine next to her dad didn't help. Tassie told them a bit about the week she'd just had, then talked about how her work was going; Tom filled their father in on what he'd been doing on the farm.

'Oh, and Dad, I made some cheese,' said Tassie. 'From that book you gave me. And it worked.'

'You'll have to bring me some next time you visit.' Alfred smiled at her. Their eyes were normally the same colour, but now his seemed to have dimmed in his pale face. 'It's been too long, Tassie, we've missed you.'

Tassie shuffled her feet. 'I know. Sorry. I'll make sure I

come more regularly.' She felt emotion bubbling in her chest and looked at Tom. 'Shall we go? Dad's tired and I think he's had enough.'

Tom looked surprised but stood up. 'OK, we'll see you tomorrow, Dad. I think Tassie's worried about giving you her cold.'

'I am. But I do wish I could hug you.' Tassie's voice faltered and she looked away, then back at Alfred. 'I love you. Get better soon.'

'And I love you.'

When Tassie turned, her eyes were wet and she was breathing heavily. Thirty-two years, and that was only the second time her father had ever told her that he loved her.

Her mother never had.

Tom caught up with her in the corridor and rubbed her shoulder. 'He'll be all right, you soppy thing. He's a tough old boot. Right, can you drop me back at the farm, then drive the car back home?'

That night the four of them ate an Indian takeaway almost silently. When Tom and Dan hadn't appeared until after dark, exhausted from having spent nearly all day in the fields, Tassie had offered to go and get one.

After they finished, Dan was ushered upstairs to have a bath and Tassie went to make tea for everyone.

She was waiting for the kettle to boil when Tom came and stood by her.

'He was actually far more help than me today.' He put his arm around her shoulders, avoiding her sneeze. 'I think you should keep this one.'

Tassie poured water over the tea bags. 'It's early days yet, Tom. But I agree... he's great.'

It was only afterwards, cleaning her teeth in the tiny bathroom, that she was struck by the weakness of her response.

Dan was great. Pretty perfect in every way. So why wasn't she feeling more delighted?

She thought back over their week away. It had all seemed so wonderful, like something she'd never wanted to end. But now? She shrugged, coughed and blew her nose – for the umpteenth time that day. Her throat was sore and her neck was hurting. She felt rotten.

Slipping into bed she squeezed up close to him, stroking his chest as she kissed his cheek. 'Thank you so much for everything today.' Another sneeze forced her to turn away. 'It's great having you here.'

Dan kissed her shoulder, then grabbed a box of tissues. 'Here. Best you keep these on your side. How are you feeling?'

'Cold-wise or in general?'

'Both.'

'A bit rough. But better than Dad I guess.'

'Hope you feel better in the morning.' He yawned. 'Gotta sleep now.'

He yawned again, and she rubbed his arm as he turned onto his side. Gently, she moulded her body into his and soon his breathing was deep and regular.

For a while she lay there. It was the first night since they'd been together that he'd done that: just turned over, not talked or anything. But – her eyes began to close – it had been a long day.

Finding him too hot to sleep against in the small double bed, she turned, her back against his, one leg falling off the edge of the mattress.

~

Tassie's eyes took a while to focus on Sophie's face, only inches from her own.

'Achhooo.' Her sneeze was loud and violent, waking Dan and causing Sophie to spring back. 'Sorry.' She reached to get a tissue, but Sophie already had one in her hand.

'Here you go.' She paused, waiting as Tassie blew her nose.

As she did, Tassie stared at her sister-in-law. Her hair was wild, which was always to be expected first thing in the morning, but her eyes were... something Tassie couldn't quite work out. Feeling a growing sense of foreboding, she shifted closer to Dan to allow Sophie to sit on the bed. She glanced at her watch. It was only 6.25am.

'Tass. I'm so sorry.'

'What's the matter?' Suddenly, she was fully awake.

'I'm so sorry.'

'What? What is it?'

'It's your dad.'

'Dad? What? Is he worse? Where's Tom?' Dread infused her breathing.

Sophie looked away from the bed, swallowing hard as she hooked a spiral of hair behind her ear. 'Tom's not here. He went to the hospital a couple of hours ago. Your mum texted him.'

Tassie looked at her, then at Dan, who was now sitting up, his breathing stilled in tandem with her own.

'Why did *he* go? Why didn't you wake me? What's happened?' Her voice rose with each new word.

Sophie took a deep breath as she clasped Tassie's hands. 'The hospital phoned to say that something was happening with your dad. I'm really sorry, but I don't know the details. His breathing had changed, they were worried... and... well... I'm so sorry, Tassie, but your mum thought it would be better if you didn't go. On account of your cold. She was still worried about the infection.'

'But I went yesterday. Oh God, you don't think I could have done something?' Tassie's hand flew up to her mouth. 'I don't understand. What's happened?'

'No, honey, I'm sure it was nothing to do with you. I think it was his heart.'

Sophie lifted her hand to stroke the side of Tassie's face, and when Tassie pulled away she placed her hand on her leg instead.

'I'm so sorry, Tass, but Tom just phoned. He tried your phone but couldn't get through. There's no reception up here. I'm so, so sorry... I think your dad had a heart attack.'

'How bad is it?' Tassie pushed the duvet back, frantic to get going.

Sophie put her hand on her arm. 'Tass, he... died. It was very sudden, totally unexpected, that's all I—'

'No!' Tassie bashed her hand away. 'He's dead? He can't be. I saw him yesterday, he was OK. Dead? And I wasn't there. Even though I'm here? What the fuck! Really? No, it can't be true. Show me the texts. No, don't bother. What difference does it make? I can't believe you didn't wake me, Soph. You, of all people. Why?' Tassie felt tears streaming down her face, as they were down Sophie's.

Sophie shook her head and looked at Dan then back at her. 'I don't know why Tom didn't phone earlier. I know there's barely any signal in the hospital. Maybe that's why...' But even as she made the excuse her voice faltered and once again she looked at Dan, as if hoping he might be able to help.

'Don't look at him.' Tassie whipped around, glaring at Dan, then back at Sophie. 'What the fuck can he do? He barely knows us. And certainly can't appreciate the depths of our fucked-up family.' She spat the words out as she stared at them. 'Although he's getting a damned good impression of it now.' Grabbing her jumper from the end of the bed, she ran over to the door and flung it wide, not caring that it crashed against a mirror as it strained on its hinges.

At the top of the stairs she breathed fast and deep, then she turned and walked, more calmly, back into the room.

'Dan. Can I borrow your truck?' She looked at Sophie. 'I presume Tom took your car?'

'Yes.'

'Do you want me to come with you?' He slid out of bed and went to retrieve the keys from his jeans pocket.

'No. Thank you. This is something I need to do alone.'

WHEN TASSIE GOT to the hospital it was still so early she had to wait for ages to be let in through the various doors. Waiting at each one she felt doubly humiliated, knowing that the rest of her family were somewhere beyond, that she'd not been invited.

Her slow progress was probably a good thing, for by the time she'd made her way through to the ward she'd had the chance to calm down and think things through a little more logically. It wouldn't really have been Tom's fault. For decades the two of them and her dad had done almost exactly whatever her mother had commanded. They'd used to joke about it. 'Three Mice and the Ministry,' her dad had called them.

At the thought of her father she was hit by a wave of misery so acute she had to sit on one of the chairs lining the corridor. She bent her head, allowing herself to sob for the first time, until she heard the buzzer of a door opening, at which point she sat up, wiping her nose on her sleeve. It was

Tom. She stood up as he walked towards her, his steps faltering.

'Tass, God, I'm so, so sorry. I've only just managed to get outside and speak to Soph again.'

Even in her anger Tassie still needed him to put his arms around her and she pressed her fists against his chest; a narrow, boyish chest, so unlike the broad security of her father's.

'It was the last thing I would have wanted. The *last* thing. When Mum phoned we had no idea this was going to happen. She just wanted some company. And then...' Still holding each other they awkwardly slumped onto the chairs. 'When it happened, she just went ape shit. Howling, sobbing, screaming. Honestly, it was horrifying. So in a way,' – he took her hands – 'I'm glad you weren't there.'

'Don't say that, Tom. Don't ever say that.' Tassie's voice was tight and as she spoke she stared straight ahead, unable to look at him.

'No, of course, that was the wrong thing to say. Totally stupid. And so wrong for Dad. But you've got to believe me, Tass, it all happened so fast. With Dad. And with Mum it was awful. Eventually the doctor gave her something. I had to give my permission.'

Now it was Tassie's turn to take Tom's hands, her understanding unfolding that there was little her brother could have done. Except, a small sharp voice muttered, to wake her up before he'd originally left the house. So at least she would have been awake. Knowing something was happening. Not that she could have done anything about it. And would that have been worse in a way?

'... and that was the weirdest thing?'

'What?' She refocused on her brother. 'Sorry? What did you say?'

'That they asked if there was anything else. A reason

why Mum might have reacted so strongly. I said I didn't think so. What do you think?'

'I think it's typical of our mother that our father dies and she's the one seeking all the attention.'

Tom withdrew his hand from hers. 'Tass, that's harsh. You didn't see her. It wasn't like that. It was a full-on panic.'

'Whatever. I wasn't there. Remember?'

For a while they sat in silence, watching an old lady shuffle along the corridor, a pot of plastic marigolds in her hand.

'Do you want to see Dad? They've put him in a different room now. Maybe Mum as well – they haven't discharged her yet.'

'I want to see Dad, of course I do. Although there's no saying goodbye now is there. For me.'

'Tassie.' A rare note of irritation flared in Tom's voice. 'The last time he was awake was yesterday, when we both saw him.' His voice broke. 'He didn't wake up at all this morning. So, in fact, his most proper goodbye was to you. When he told you that he loved you. All I got was to keep checking the fences.'

'Oh Tom, I'm sorry.' As the words spilt out of her, so, once again, did the tears, coming in great racking gulps. Tom put his arm around her as images of their father flashed through her mind. Sweet, gentle Dad. Whom she'd never hug again. The pain grew in her chest until it felt like it was constricting her breathing. She'd hardly seen him in the past few years. Suddenly she could barely catch her breath in between her sobs. God, she'd miss him.

After a few minutes, Tom stood up and held out his hand, a frown creasing his brow as he bit the side of his lip.

'Come on, we need to do this. Together.' His voice cracked as he spoke.

Tassie took his hand, wet with his tears, and slowly stood.

They started to walk down the corridor when she stopped and turned to face him.

'Of course I want to do this.' Her voice was flat and cold. 'However hard it is. But, sorry Tom, just Dad. I only want to see him. I have absolutely no desire to see our mother right now. You go, but I'm sorry, I just can't.'

14

Sitting under a solitary oak tree on top of the farm's only hill, Tassie looked out across the valley.

When she and Tom had been children it had been their favourite spot, where they'd soar high on the swing (now long gone), chant gobbledygook while running around the bench, or play I Spy – which Tom always won. As adults they'd often walk up there to share an evening beer. Now, even though it was raining, she was glad to be there, preferring the relative shelter of the tree's canopy to the dreadful tension at her parents' farm. Her *mother's* farm. Who barely seemed to inhabit it now.

Since she'd come out of hospital, Sybil hadn't said a word. Just sat in the kitchen, still in the clothes she'd been wearing, staring into the fire. Tassie hadn't wanted to spend any time with her, but it wasn't an option anyway. Just once, they'd bumped into each other coming through a doorway, and her mother had reached up and touched her cheek – a gesture so unexpected it had made her flinch.

She'd been shocked by how the steel was gone from the grey blue of her mother's eyes, and neither spoke for the few seconds they stood there, before her mother had returned to her seat.

At the bottom of the hill she saw a figure beginning to climb, waving as it approached. By the time her sister-in-law reached her, rain was dripping off the hood of her coat as, panting slightly, she held out a flask.

'Here you go. I thought you'd be freezing so I've brought you some soup.' Sophie sat down beside Tassie, pushing her hood back and looking up as she did. 'It's amazing how much shelter this tree provides. I can see why you and Tom love it.' She looked out across the fields as her breathing slowed. 'He proposed to me, here, on this bench. Did you know?' Her wellies pushed at the grass in front of them. 'Bit clichéd maybe, but still... well, lovely.'

Tassie said nothing, but let her shoulders relax towards Sophie, her head inclining until it was touching Sophie's curls. It had taken remarkably little time to forgive her and Tom. After all, she'd reasoned – OK, Dan had reasoned – now wasn't the time to be falling out.

For a few moments they sat in silence, watching a red tractor plough a flaxen field.

Dan.

Tassie sighed. He'd been brilliant the day her dad had died – and yesterday. But now he'd gone. And she'd been the one to suggest it.

Why? She posed the question yet again. Why had she done that?

She'd said it was because this wasn't his family, his thing to sort out. She'd also been aware of how much it brought up for him about his own parents, and that he needed to get back to his farm.

But it wasn't just that, was it? He'd been hurt. She blanched as she remembered the look in his eyes as he'd stroked her face. But then he'd left, early that morning, and their goodbye had been short, strained. Even as they'd hugged she'd wondered whether she would ever see him again. Yet, rather than feeling intense pain, she'd simply felt numb as she watched him drive away. She just didn't know what was wrong with her.

Sophie touched her hand. 'Have you heard from him?'

'No. He'll still be on the road I guess.'

Sophie twisted around to face her. 'Tass, Tom and I both really liked him. And, despite everything, we could see how well suited you are.'

Tassie found she couldn't speak and when she eventually shrugged her shoulders, Sophie sighed and put an arm around her.

'OK. Now is probably not the time for this. So all I *will* say is, please, think hard before you let this one go. Honestly, we think he's perfect.'

A sudden flash of irritation broke Tassie's silence. 'God, you sound just like Syd. She's always going on about it.'

'Well,' Sophie nudged her. 'Maybe she's also got a point.'

'Yes...' The irritation expanded. 'But I'm the one actually with the person. I'm the one who... I don't know, has to suffer the fact that he doesn't seem to be able to sleep, and he's very quiet sometimes, you know. He often doesn't say a lot, when I need to talk. So he's not perfect. No one is.' She sat up straight. 'Anyway, at the moment *here* is the priority.'

Sophie's face was instantly full of concern. 'But...' She sighed. 'Yes, of course. And there's plenty of time for the two of you and... Well, probably best let it happen in better circumstances.' She cleared her throat. 'Tass, I've got something...'

Tassie watched her push a curl behind her ear, and felt her chest tighten.

'I hope you won't mind how this happened. But–' Sophie

reached into her bag. 'This is for you.' She held out a nondescript white envelope. 'God, Tass, I hope this isn't too weird. It's from your dad. He dictated it to me last week, when we didn't know if we'd be able to get hold of you—' Her voice broke and she pressed her lips together.

Tassie stared at the envelope. It *was* weird: a letter from beyond the grave. Except her dad wasn't in a grave, he was lying in a morgue, his body stone cold.

She took it. 'Wow. Unexpected.' It wasn't very heavy. She stared at it for a few seconds, then looked up. 'I think, if you don't mind, I'll read this when I get home.'

'Of course, you do whatever you want. It's beautif— I think it will definitely help.'

'Thanks. I'm sure. And thanks, for doing it for him. He loved you just as much as Tom and me, you know. And not just for your breeding potential.'

Sophie flinched.

'Sorry. That was a joke. Remember?'

'Yes, I remember. But I also know how hurt you are right now. And I'm sorry if I've had anything to do with it.'

Tassie sighed, resting her head on Sophie's shoulder. 'You haven't, don't worry. The hurt started a long time before you came along. And thank you. When I've got over the strangeness I'll appreciate this.' She held the letter up, then zipped it into her coat pocket. 'Come on. I've still got a few more fences to check. Fancy a walk?'

'Lovely.' Sophie smiled. 'But eat your soup first. Chicken and dumplings. Your favourite. Also known as the only soup I can make.'

Tassie chuckled. 'I'm intrigued as to how you got the dumplings into this flask?' She twisted the top off. 'Ah, you didn't. Chicken and dumplings, without the dumplings? But still good.'

She was pouring some out when her phone pinged. She

pulled it out of her coat, aware that Sophie was watching her as she read the message. 'Dan's back home. I'll just send him a text.'

'To tell him you miss him?' Sophie's voice was hopeful.

'Maybe.' Tassie sipped at her soup, wincing when the hot liquid touched her lips. 'Or maybe, just leave it, Soph.'

～

'TEAS, coffees, mistletoe? Selling it already, you just don't get a kiss.'

Tassie looked up at the train steward hovering with the trolley beside her table, a stellar smile stretching across his face.

'I'll have a tea please. Do you have any Earl Grey?'

He rummaged through a plastic bag hanging in front of him. 'I'm afraid the Queen just had the last one, miss, so it'll be just normal or peppermint.'

She surveyed his goods. 'Actually, I'll have a white wine please, and some cheese and onion crisps.'

She paid for them, then sat staring out the window, trying to avoid looking at her reflection. Although it was better than staring at the woman opposite who kept picking her nose. Which wouldn't be quite so gross if she was less intrigued by what came out of it.

Cracking open the wine, Tassie took a long sip, enjoying the sensation of heat sliding down her throat.

Five minutes later she'd finished the bottle, assuring herself it was only a glass. The man was now pushing the trolley back the other way so she ordered another, hoping it wouldn't prompt any more banter. Luckily it didn't, but she could feel Ms Nose-Picker radiating disapproval.

Her phone pinged, but she went back to gazing out of the window. Probably Syd. Again.

A few minutes later, she opened the second bottle, then idly pressed on the screen. 'Sam Smith'. She stared at the words. *Alex.* Whose name she'd changed after Syd had asked who he was when his name had flashed up once.

Putting her wine on the table, she opened the text.

Tassie, I'm so sorry to hear your news. Mum rang and told me what happened. Your dad was a wonderful man. I'm still in London until tomorrow evening if you want a consolatory drink, or perhaps a hug? It's at times like this when it probably helps to be with people you know. Give me a call when you get this. Ax xx

Her phone rang, making her jump.

This time it was Dan.

She let it ring a few times before she answered.

'Tassie?'

'Hi.'

'Where are you?'

'On the train. I had to come back today. I couldn't cancel one of my jobs.'

'Oh. OK. And how are you?' He sounded as tired as she felt.

'On my second bottle of wine. You know.'

'God, really? You be careful, that's a lot.'

She laughed. 'Miniature bottles.'

'Oh.'

There was a long pause before she spoke. 'How's life in Somerset? The farm? Did everything survive in your absence?'

'Yes, it's all good.' Another pause. 'Charlotte and the boys have done a great job of holding the fort while I've been away. Although I still got the third degree as soon as I got home.'

'Did you tell her about us?'

'Sort of... Or at least she was pretty quick to put two and two together and make ten. Can't say she's best pleased. Although I'd definitely say it was worth it.'

Tassie willed herself to say something. But nothing came out.

'Tass...? Is everything OK? No, stupid question, of course everything's not OK. But, what I mean is, is everything OK, well, with us? It's weird that we've barely spoken. I know I was busy helping your brother, but still, it's silly, I've missed you. If I can do anything? If you want me to come to London – or Shropshire? You know, later on, when you go back? Just let me know.'

His words came out in a rush of emotion, and tears stung Tassie's eyes as she stroked her finger along the edge of the table. She cupped her fingers around her phone as she answered. 'I'm so sorry about how things were when you left. Everything was such a mess. So hard. I don't know, it just seemed easier to cope with things on my own.' She looked out of the window, aware that the woman opposite was listening. 'But... well, everything before Friday. Thank you. It was perfect.'

'It was, wasn't it?' She could hear relief in his voice. 'That's what I've been thinking. Probably one of the best weeks of my life.'

Happy memories flooded Tassie's mind. But, yet again, she couldn't respond.

'OK...' His uncertainty was back. 'I'll let you get back to your drinking. Call me when you get home.'

'I will do, speak later.' Tassie placed her mobile on the table, then picked it up again and brought up Alex's message.

She started to write a reply, then stopped, pressing delete as she glared at the woman opposite.

.   .   .

WHEN TASSIE GOT BACK to her flat, she discovered Syd had left a bottle of wine, an iced bun and some bread and cheese. Stan had left four containers of cider.

Walking around the rooms felt so strange. It was only twelve days since she'd left, but it seemed like so much longer. Not least because she'd left home with two parents, and now she only had one.

Seeing the photo of her dad on the windowsill, a sob caught in her throat.

Going into her bedroom, she changed into her favourite soft harem pants and a hooded sweatshirt, then went out into the garden to examine the proliferation of new buds. Thinking how much deadheading she needed to do – despite Syd's best efforts – she was suddenly hit by the pain of remembering she'd been going to ask her dad how much to cut her apple trees back.

Slumping onto one of the sleepers, her eyes welled as she stroked a deep split in the blackened wood. She would never have guessed, that weekend he'd come down, that it would be the last time she'd see him properly. She felt her chest constrict, quickening her breathing until she was having to inhale deeply to try and slow a growing sense of panic.

After walking around the beds a couple of times, her breaths shuddering in through her nose and out through her mouth, she went back into the kitchen and opened the fridge, glancing at her watch as she did.

Six-fifteen. Surely an acceptable time to open the wine?

Fetching a glass, she carried the bottle into her bedroom then sat down on the bed, scrolling through photos of her dad on her laptop, tracing a finger over his gentle smile.

Most had been taken as he'd worked the land. She'd

always loved one she'd taken years ago: of him feeding hay to a flock of hungry lambs, their coats creamy white, contrasting with their sharp black ears. And the one of him at a local NFU dinner, his suit still a good fit after thirty years, wearing his favourite tie.

'He loves his daisies,' she murmured as she stroked her hand over the photo. In the summer he'd regularly come home with a big bunch of oxeyes and put them in a jar on the table, ignoring her mother's protestations that they gave her hay fever.

Loved.

'How you loved them.' She kissed his image, then, going over to her chest of drawers, lit some incense, took a deep breath, and opened his letter.

Dear Tassie
Hello my lovely.

She stopped. She could hear him saying the words.

I know that folks have been trying to get hold of you, but they don't seem to be able to find you so I just thought I'd take the precaution of writing. You never know what might happen, as they say.

So, this is a pickle isn't it? Here I am in hospital, my arm mashed like a turnip. I knew that I should have got a new part for that machine. I knew something was wrong with it. So, if you learn just one thing from this, Tassie, learn that you always need to take the highest care on the farm – never take chances. Just like I used to tell you and Tom when you were youngsters. Not that you've been on the farm a lot recently. Busy with all your highfalutin London stuff. We've all missed you, you know.

Tassie brushed away her tears, not wanting to risk wetting the paper. Despite her sadness, her mouth twitched, for she could just imagine her dad, lying in hospital, dictating to Sophie as she typed exactly what he said.

And Sophie was right: it did help, for it was almost like he was still alive. Except he wasn't. Her breath caught.

So, what's a man to tell his daughter who he's not seen for a while? Well, first off that I love you. I know I don't often say it, but I always have, Tassie, always will.

Right from the moment you were born – such a very precious moment – it made me feel like I had something to fight for, someone more important than anything or anyone I'd known before. You probably don't know this, but when you were tiny it were just you and me, together for quite a while. What did I know about babies?! But then I figured it weren't that different to calves or lambing, and we managed.

Tassie stopped reading, frowning. She and her dad, together? Where was her mum?

And that's partly why I wanted to write today. I know things haven't always been easy with your mum. And maybe I should have said something earlier, but she were always so certain that I shouldn't. And really it were more her story to tell.

But I've watched how things have gone between the two of you over the years, and now, lying here in this blasted uncomfortable bed, I'm wondering if I did get it right. Really wondering. And thinking maybe not. So, something I need to say to you now, Tassie, is, talk to her. Ask her about what happened before you were born. Tell her I've told you that the time is right, that there's things you need to know.

So, what else can I tell you? How very proud I am of you,

all your talents, your photographs. I've kept every single one of them from your time on the papers, you know. They're all in a file in my desk. The places you've been! Maybe you could take me to some of them one day. Not sure if I'll be able to do a lot of farming now, certainly not unless the arm mends.

Which brings me on to another point – and Tom knows this too. We've been made an offer, a good offer, for some of the farmland. Seems there might be the possibility of planning permission for local housing. Up until now your mother and I have both resisted, but if anything happens then I think you should persuade her to sell. She'll keep the farmhouse but she'll not manage the farm on her own. Truth be known it's been enough of a struggle for me these past few years. Tom has the details, so talk to him about it. After all, it's your inheritance we're talking about.

Well I'm tired now, Tassie girl, and think I probably need to sleep. Don't get a lot of that here, certainly not at night, what with them waking you up all through it. Honestly, I feel more 'observed' than a microscope plate.

Sophie has kindly said she'll print this off for me, so I'll be able to give it to you when next I see you. But, for now, in the words of Don McLean – that famous photographer! – 'And I Love You So'.

Dad x

For a long time Tassie sat holding the letter, reading and rereading it, wishing it was longer. Then she fetched her laptop, searched for Don McLean and found the song her dad had referred to. Watching a smudgy black and white video, she was struck by McLean's constant references to loneliness.

Emotions were something she'd never considered where her dad was concerned; they'd certainly never discussed them. But now she found herself wondering about his happiness, and his relationship with her mum.

There was so much she should have asked him.

It wasn't just in the last year that she'd not really spent any time with him; she'd hardly seen him in the last ten years. Her fault. Her not wanting to go home. And why? Had it really been so awful? Suddenly, she didn't know. And the doubt sharpened her pain.

She scrolled through all her family photos. What did she know about her parents? Not that much, it seemed. And the lyrics from the song, about the lovelessness of life? That cut. Was her dad trying to tell her something else? *No. Don't be dumb.* It was a just a song title he'd mentioned and it was unlikely he'd have known all the words. Although... she pictured her parents' meagre record collection. They did have some of McLean's albums. Was her father's life loveless. Or was hers?

She poured herself a glass of wine, drank it too quickly, then poured another. Standing up, she found herself shaky on her feet, then remembered she'd not eaten anything all day – apart from the cheese and onion crisps; and she wasn't even sure she'd finished those.

She went into the kitchen and found Syd's cheese and bread. Cutting herself big chunks of both she walked back into the sitting room and turned on the TV. Tonight was not a night, she was now realising, to be alone. She should have taken Dan up on his offer. It would have been so lovely to have him here, so much better than... this.

She went over to close her window shutters – just as a pair of feet appeared at the top of her steps.

Her heart leapt.

No, it couldn't be him; they'd only just spoken and he was definitely still in Somerset.

Anyway the shoes were too city: black tasselled brogues.

Then, as they descended, her heart quickened.

The shoes were topped by tailored trousers.

Stunned, she moved backwards into the room, knowing exactly to whom the legs belonged. Although she still jumped when the doorbell rang, then froze until it rang again.

Finally, shaking her head, she stepped forward and opened the door.

'Tassie. Lucky guess you'd be home.' Alex held a single potted orchid in his hand. He looked at it. 'I wasn't sure what was appropriate in these circumstances. So I bought this too.' He held up a bottle of wine.

Tassie nodded at the wine. 'The correct choice. I've already started.' She stared at him. 'What are you doing here, Alex? I didn't call you. And anyway, how do you know where I live?'

'Not hard. It's on your website.'

'Is it? Oh.'

'So...? Are you going to invite me in?'

'Why?'

'Er, because I've just had to get a cab to the back end of nowhere and it would be nice to come in for a chat? Come on, Tass' – he waved the bottle – 'I come in peace, and I know how much you must be hurting.'

Without saying another word, she turned and walked back inside.

'WELL, this is all rather bijou. Very quaint.' Tassie was pouring them a drink as Alex wandered around her living room, picking up various items she'd collected, amusement creasing his face. 'This is?'

'A back scratcher.'

'Made from?'

'Kangaroo.'

'And this?'

'Canned air. From China,' she added reluctantly.

'And this?'

'Snake wine from Vietnam. Alex, stop going through my things and come and sit down.'

Her voice was sharp and Alex obediently sat down on her sofa, avoiding the part that sagged. Stretching out his legs, he extended his arms along the back.

Tassie handed him a glass of wine, then curled into her old chintz chair – another relic from Uncle Ali – watching him sip it before he looked at her with one of his long, intense stares.

'So, do you want to talk about it?'

'Not really.' She drank some wine, picking a thread out of her trouser cuff. 'It was all totally... unexpected. I'd seen him the day before and he seemed fine – well, not fine, but, you know.' She didn't want anyone to know she'd not been there when he died. Her chest tightened and she inhaled.

'Sometimes things happen like that,' said Alex. 'Same with my grandmother – she went very suddenly. Awful. Mum went to see your mother you know? Apparently they play bridge together. Actually, she was worried about her. Seems your mum hardly said a word the whole time she was there.'

Tassie paused before responding, thinking about her dad's letter. Always so vehement in her feelings about her mother, suddenly she felt uncertain. 'I guess she still hasn't recovered from the shock.'

Alex sipped his wine. 'Grief does strike people in different ways. I'm sure she'll be fine. Soon back to her old feisty self.' He grinned – then realised his inappropriateness and adopted a face of concern. 'And you, Tass. How are you? Or how were you before this happened? I was disappointed to get your email. I'd been looking forward to seeing you. I thought we had a good chance of being friends again? You know, make up?'

Tassie stared at him, still not quite believing he was there, in her flat. She glanced over to the box of underwear, still sitting on the side, waiting to go to the charity shop. Blood rose in her cheeks.

'What?'

'Nothing. It's just so weird. You being here. Not really your kind of place.'

'Well, I must say I rather prefer the contemporary look. But this is very *you*, Tass. Very backpacker.'

Tassie felt her blush deepen. 'I like backpacker, thank you. Better than vacuous middle-aged man drinking alone in swanky hotel.'

Alex held her with his slow smile. 'I think you'll find that I'm not middle-aged. And rarely alone.'

She tutted.

'I'm joking, Tass. Joking. I'm a full-on father these days, remember?'

'So how *are* your children?'

Still smiling, Alex pulled out his phone. 'They're great, well as far as we can tell with the unborn ones. Joel's insanely mischievous at the moment, but very cute. Would you like to see a photo?'

'And your wife. How is she?'

Alex glanced at his phone, then put it away again. 'She's good. Keeps busy with all her charity stuff, and the pregnancy, of course. Life in New York can be exhausting. Work is relentless and Americans don't seem to fully understand the concept of time off.' He drained his glass. 'Shall we have another? And maybe we could start thinking about some food? Is there anywhere round here that's vaguely decent?'

'Alex, Dad's just died. I've just got home. And I really don't want to go out for dinner with you.'

'Then we'll order up a takeaway. I know a great Thai in Belgravia that I'm sure will deliver.'

'To Clapham?'

'Come on Tass. Even you must know that anyone will do anything if you pay them enough.'

THE FOOD WAS SURPRISINGLY WELCOME, delivered in an enormous box packed with so much insulation that everything was still piping hot when they removed the beautiful bamboo containers.

Tassie couldn't begin to think how much it must have cost, and didn't want to know. As they ate, seated on the floor picking at the feast between them, Alex began to relax, removing his tie, undoing his shirt, taking off his shoes – with each action becoming more the Alex she could relate to. They talked a lot about her father and she was touched that he remembered a surprising amount about the times they'd spent with him: helping him out on the farm, or sat around the big kitchen table.

'I was very fond of your dad. Always a bit jealous you had him, actually. His quietness, sense of calm. Completely content being a farmer.'

Tassie nodded as tears filled her eyes. 'He was a great dad. D'you know every Christmas he was the one who used to do our stockings?' She laughed, wiping the wet from her cheek. 'Someone who never shopped, unless it was in the farmers co-op. I so loved that about him – and they were great stockings too.'

She paused, wiping more tears as she looked around the room. Many of the books on her shelves had previously been pulled out of a big woollen sock: *Watership Down*, *The Borrowers*, *Animal Farm*, all the Thomas Hardy's.

She thought again about the letter, and blanched. 'I'm glad though, that you think he seemed contented. I'm not so sure, about him and Mum. I actually think there was something quite major going on between them. Something Tom and I never knew about.'

'Really? What makes you say that?'

'Dad wrote me a letter. Just before he died. Said I should ask Mum.'

'Actually, my mother said something strange after she'd seen her. What was it...? She hoped your father's death wouldn't push her into the bad old days? Or I think that's what she said. I didn't query it, but maybe you're right.'

'Well, if I get nowhere with my mum, I could always ask yours. Not that I've seen her for years.' Tassie teased a piece of chicken off a skewer, grimacing as she remembered the awkward times she'd spent with Alex's mother. A woman so cold and haughty she made her own seem like Mrs Darling. Tassie knew she'd been delighted when she and Alex had split up – unlike her own mother, who never seemed to have quite got over his loss.

She looked at him now, leaning back against the couch, a small hole in one of his stripy socks, and the corners of her mouth twitched. 'But I guess I'll try my own first.'

'Probably best.'

And when he looked up at her and grinned, for the first time that night she saw the boy he'd once been.

'So, Tassie Morris.' He scratched the back of his head. 'I know that you're grieving.' He leant over and lightly touched her hand. 'And I'm so sorry for your loss. But I also know the best thing for you right now—' He looked around the room. 'Where's your Scrabble board? You've still got one, haven't you? I bet you do.'

Laughing, Tassie nodded.

'Then come on. Nothing helps mend a broken heart like a game of Scrabble. And I'll even let you beat me.'

It was nearly midnight when Tassie got up to take the glasses into the kitchen, embarrassed to find herself swaying as she did. They'd drunk two bottles of wine and were now well down a third – although Alex had consumed most of it.

She carefully washed the glasses. It was surprisingly nice having him there – playing their usual interminably long game of Scrabble. Cosy, even.

When she walked back into the living room, Alex was standing in front of the fireplace: an open box in his hand and a smug grin on his face. 'This is nice, Tass. Very—'

Walking over, she grabbed the box. He'd pushed back the tissue paper, revealing the black lace and pink satin.

'Our favourite colours. How thoughtful.' His smile had a hint of the superciliousness she hated.

Yanking open a cupboard she threw the box inside, slamming the door. 'I told you to stop going through my stuff.'

'I know you did. Sorry. But the logo was a bit too inviting.'

Still smiling, he moved over to her and put one hand on her shoulder, his other tilting her face towards him. 'Tass. I realise it's not a night for fancy underwear – although God knows I'd like to see you in it. But, well, it's us, you and me. And I know you could do with some comforting.'

'Actually, Alex, what I could do with is you going home and me going to bed. I'm exhausted.'

'But I thought, we could... You might want me to...' His smile was his best slow and sexy one.

'What, Alex?'

'Well, for one thing, it's a long way back to London. At this time of night.'

'For God's sake, you're still in London.'

'Come on, Tass, surely you're not going to chuck me out?'

'Well you'll be sleeping on the sofa. And I'll be locking my door.' She took a step back. 'Because you, me, Alex, are no more. You're married, remember? And I...' She paused. 'Don't want you any more.'

Ten minutes later her duvet was tucked tight around her, her flannel pyjamas coating her limbs like a glove. She couldn't work out how she felt. Irritated, certainly. But also incredulous that Alex was actually in her flat – after all the times she'd dreamt about it. Amazed that he wasn't now in her bed. And strangely elated that for once in her life she'd resisted him.

Liberated even.

He'd been visibly annoyed by the arrangement, snatching the duvet and pillow she'd handed him, then complaining loudly that the sofa was lumpy. She'd wondered about offering him her bed and taking the couch herself, then decided that she'd already offered Alex Winchester far too much.

∾

'TASSIE, TASS, WAKE UP.'

Tassie opened her eyes and sat up, panic hitting her like a mallet. 'Dad. Dad? What's happened?'

'Tassie, you were dreaming. Shouting. I was worried.'

'Alex?' *Alex!* She was confused. What the hell was he doing there? Was he... had they...? It couldn't be... Where was her pyjama top? Panicked she looked around, clutching her duvet to her chest as the realisation dawned.

That she was in her flat. That yes, Alex was there too. Then she remembered that she'd woken up, too hot, and taken her top off.

And that her dad had died.

'Dad.' She looked at Alex, and her breath caught.

'I know, Tass. I'm so sorry.'

And this time she didn't even think to stop him when his arms enfolded her and they lay back down on the bed, Alex pulling the duvet around them.

15

The next morning Tassie woke early, disturbed by the heating knocking as the water started coming through. Another thing to fix.

She turned over – startled when she saw Alex lying next to her, still fast asleep. She softly blew out when she felt her pyjama bottoms against her legs. Although she wasn't wearing the top half.

Shit.

The heating knocked again. Except... it wasn't the heating. She looked at her watch. And it wasn't early, it was half past nine and someone was at the front door. Grabbing her top she slipped it over her head as she went into the living room. Alex's shirt and tie were on the chair, his suit laid out across the beanbag. Unlikely he'd have bought any spare underwear. Although he'd always been a planner where nights of possibility were concerned.

As she pulled open the front door, the light hurt her eyes and she half closed them, then opened them wide.

For there stood Dan.

Dan!

He was wearing his old denim jacket, a bag in his hand.

He looked tired, slightly nervous, but as she stood on the doorstep, recovering from her shock, a big smile spread across his face.

'I was worried about you. Thought I should come.'

He held out his arms and Tassie stepped outside and into them. For a few moments they hugged, then he kissed the top of her head.

'Can I come in? It's bloody freezing and I've been driving for hours.' This time he gently kissed her lips. 'How I've missed you. In fact, I know this might not be the right time, but I've got something I thought I should tell you and... I'm not sure it can wait.' He took her hands. 'Even before you finally invite me inside—'

'Dan. There's something you need to know.'

'I know all I need to.'

'No Dan, you don't.' Tassie almost barked out the words.

He pulled back, his smile faltering. 'What?'

'What's a man got to do for a cup of coffee in the morning.' Alex's voice floated out from the bedroom, infused with sleep.

Dan took a step back, dropping Tassie's hands. His head tilted to the side, his face a sudden frown.

'Shut the bloody door, Tass, it's freezing and I'm practically naked. God your bed's uncomfortable.'

Fuck. Oh fuck.

Tassie turned to see Alex walking across her living room, his hair bed-headed. He was indeed only wearing his boxers, and he draped her dressing gown around his shoulders as he disappeared into the bathroom.

When she turned again Dan was halfway up the stairs, pausing only briefly to glance through the gap in her living room shutters as he went.

'God, no. Dan, you've got the wrong idea.' She was almost shouting. 'Alex is just a friend. From home. He came to see me and stayed, because...' Even as she called out the words, she knew how feeble they sounded.

She ran up the stairs after him, but Dan was already a distance away, striding down the street. Stepping sideways to avoid a broken bottle, she ran again, finally catching up with him.

He looked down at her feet. 'You're not wearing anything. You should be careful.'

She put her hands on his arms. 'Dan, I'm so sorry. You've got to believe me. It's not what it seems.' She could feel his muscles tensing.

'Isn't it, Tassie? Really? So where did he sleep? And actually, who the hell is he?'

'Well, with me. But it didn't start off like that. I promise, nothing happened.'

'And you've known him how long?'

'Well, for ever really. I— We went out together, but when we were very young. And it all ended a long time ago.'

'Did it, Tass? Really? It didn't seem like that to me. And how come I'd never heard about him? You've told me about most of your exes. And I'd certainly remember one you were still seeing. Had known *for ever*.'

For a second she couldn't answer him. She felt she had to tell the truth. And that second was her undoing.

Gently he pulled his arms away. 'Tassie. I'm sorry about your dad, sorry about all this. But it's over between you and me. I see that. Probably should have seen it a few days ago. Idiot that I've been.'

'But Dan, wait. You've driven so far. At least have a cup of coffee before you go. Or I can get dressed and we can go somewhere. Dan. I mean it. I *really* mean it. I... like you.'

Dan's eyes remained soft as his mouth hardened. 'And I'd fallen in love with you.' She saw him bite his lip as he looked away. Then he turned and didn't look back.

She walked back inside the flat to find Alex sitting on the sofa, now wearing her dressing gown and looking at her portfolio.

'I know.' He put his hand up in mock defence, still flicking through the pages. 'I'm going through your stuff again. But these are great, Tass. Really good. Seriously, have you ever thought about getting into advertising? You'd rock.'

She stared at him, surprised he hadn't noticed she'd been gone ten minutes, was without shoes, and that tears were streaming down her face. Eventually he looked up, put the portfolio on the floor and came over to where she was standing, pulling her into a hug.

'Oh baby, I'm sorry. Is it your dad again? It will come in waves you know, that's what happened when Martha's grandfather died. Although he was the holder of a rather large fortune, not enough of which went to her. So that might have had something to do with it.'

Tassie pulled away. 'Yes, it's Dad. Sorry, I just need to do something.' She went into her bedroom, picked up her phone, and started typing.

Dan, I am so, so sorry about what happened. You do have to believe me that nothing was going on. But yes, you are right, it's complicated and I probably should have told you about Alex. Like, he's married with kids and lives in New York. It's just that he's over at the moment and came to see me last night as his mother told him what had happened. He knew Dad. Please can we speak? Maybe when you've had a chance to calm down? God, I hope you're not driving all the way home. Tassie xx

She pressed send, then went over to the window, staring at a blackbird skipping around the garden table. She had really liked him, in a way she'd not felt for years. Not since... well, since Alex. Or so it had seemed at the time. But perhaps it hadn't been real, given how quickly he'd reacted. *Overreacted.* She snorted. The bird looked up, then carried on picking at the table. Wasn't she worth a bit more than that?

'Come on, mopes.' Alex was leaning against the door frame. 'I know exactly what you need right now. Get dressed. I'm taking you out for the day. How about we go to Regent's Park?'

Tears smarting, Tassie looked at him for a few seconds then slowly nodded. 'OK.' She shivered, her feet cold on the bare wooden floor. 'Why don't you go and make us a coffee – there's some real stuff in the cupboard.'

When she turned back to the window the bird had gone, and she stood for a while, waiting to see if it would return. If she did really like Dan, then what the hell was today about? Why was she now spending it with Alex?

'Where's the coffee?' He was shouting from the kitchen.

'In the cupboard next to the—' She shoved her feet into her slippers. 'Hang on, I'll come.' She snorted, her mouth fixed in a line. Because that's what she'd always done.

He'd call and she'd run.

Clouds were beginning to obscure the sunshine as they entered the gates to Regent's Park. They passed a couple leaving, but apart from them and two people on roller skates, the park was empty.

Tassie thought back over the day as they walked towards the lake. It had been surprisingly fine – although she'd heard nothing back from Dan. After getting a Tube into town – clearly the first in a while for Alex – they'd mooched around the National Gallery, then gone to a Greek restaurant in Soho. Afterwards, walking through the streets, they'd laughed as they'd recalled visiting a porn cinema as teenagers, where she'd chosen a film according to the poster displaying the biggest breasts.

'And then,' – Alex nudged her shoulder – 'when we were watching it, you got cramp and started writhing around. The man behind thought it was his double lucky day.' He stopped laughing and looked at her. 'But we didn't stay to the end. Better action in that cheap hotel room.'

And later, when he'd taken her hand as they walked, she hadn't resisted.

'Do you remember?' He was now pointing over to the lake. 'You insisted on stealing some wreck of a boat and made me go out in it. Almost sank. Lucky I wasn't drowned.'

'Don't be so dramatic. And I'm sure it's not that deep.'

Alex turned to her, the ghost of a smile around his eyes but the rest of his expression serious. 'We used to have some fun, Tass, didn't we? Real fun. I'm not sure why I've allowed myself to forget so much of it.'

They walked along in silence, easy in each other's company, although Tassie was acutely aware of Alex's hand, close to hers again. Ahead of them, a group of teenage boys swaggered along the path, pushing each other and laughing loudly. When they came alongside, one of them walked straight up to Alex, dropping a match box as he did.

'Hey mate, you got a light?'

Alex shook his head and tried to walk around him, but the boy quickly shifted to block his way. He was small and wiry, hair shaved on one side, stringy as spaghetti on the other. Letters spelling out *THUG LIFE* were tattooed down his neck.

'Oh come on, Beaks. Leave it out will ya.'

Tassie looked across to his friend: tall and spotty, greasy ginger hair slicked back.

'I'm only asking for a light, ain't I?'

'We don't smoke.' Tassie looked at the boy and smiled, then wished she hadn't when he immediately came to stand in front of her.

'Probably a good thing, girlie. Wouldn't want smoke going in this lovely stuff. Like Goldie-fuckin'-locks you is.'

She flinched as the boy grabbed a lock of her hair and dragged two fingers down the length of it. Jumping back, she looked around. The other boys had spread out in a semicircle, like a well-coordinated pride of lions, obscuring what was happening from the rest of the park.

'Beaks, come on. We'll miss the start of the film.' Again it was the ginger guy. Now the only one left outside the circle.

'Who needs fuckin' zombie tits when you've got this beauty.' Beaks went to put his hand out again, lower this time, but Tassie stepped sideways and moved to walk around him.

'Fuck off, you little tosser.'

As soon as she heard Alex's words, Tassie's heart stopped.

The boy's reaction was instant. From his pocket he pulled a knife, the blade flashing like a snake's tongue, and, grabbing Tassie's arm, he pulled her towards him, yanked a fistful of hair, then sliced a section off the bottom.

Tassie was so shocked she couldn't move.

And neither did Alex.

The boy slouched over to him, slowly cutting the knife back and forth as he waved Tassie's hair in front of Alex's face. 'You see this, mate. *This* is only the fuckin' start. Unless you say sorry, we'll be cutting a lot more shite off your bird.' His face twisted as he spoke. 'Wankers like you in your fancy suits. Think you own it all. Well not 'ere. This park is our patch, mate, and you're going to have to pay to be in it. So, be nice, open your wallet.'

Alex glared at the boy. 'There'll be CCTV, you'll be done for this.'

'Nice try, mate, but we know every camera. *Our park*, see. And nothing will happen. So, are you going to do what I ask or am I going to have to do a bit more persuading. Tezzer, come 'ere.'

Another boy stepped forward, a stupid grin spreading across his face, the crotch of his tracksuit bottoms stretching just above his knees.

'Why don't you just hold onto Goldi' over there, 'til this 'ere wanker decides how he's gonna pay.'

The boy came forward and grabbed Tassie's arm. He was breathing heavily, the air around him rank with alcohol and stale tobacco.

Tassie held her breath as Alex looked at Beaks, then the rest of his mates, some of whom took small steps towards him. Slowly he removed his wallet from his pocket, turning slightly as he did. He pulled out some notes and thrust them at the boy.

'All of them, mate.'

Furious, Alex hesitated again, then pulled out the rest. 'Dollars,' he said flatly. 'I hope you know a good exchange place.'

Beaks laughed, then gestured towards Tassie. 'So *just* what's it worth that we don't *cut* any more off?'

'For fuck's sake. I've given you my money. Now fuck off.'

Beaks pointed his knife under Alex's chin then stroked it down his chest. 'Now let me see. Nice suit, nice shoes. I'll be damned if there ain't a nice fuckin' watch somewhere.'

Alex instinctively put his hand in his pocket. 'I am not giving you my watch. You've got my money.'

'Your Rolla or your girlfriend's hair, mate. Seems a fair swap?' His friends laughed, egging Beaks on. 'Terry, you got your knife there, mate? How's your 'airdressing?'

Tassie's fear was instantly overtaken by anger and she tried to wrench her arm out of Terry's hand, but he was too strong. For a few seconds no one moved. Then, in the distance, they heard the sound of police sirens. Still far away, but definitely heading in their direction. The boys started muttering, some of them backing away.

Tassie tried again to free her arm, but Terry's hand still gripped her.

'Beaks, we gotta fuck it, mate. If I get done again, that's it.' Ginger's voice was shrill and imploring.

Beaks looked at Alex once more, then at Tassie. 'Well, we got the moola I guess. And darlin',' – he spat on the ground – 'find yourself a proper fuckin' geezer, why don't you.' He turned back to Alex and punched him hard in the stomach. 'Not a tosser like this one'. Then he spun around and within moments he and his friends had disappeared into the bushes.

Alex was doubled up in pain when he looked up at Tassie. 'God, I thought they were going to kill us.' His voice was shrill, his eyes narrowed. 'The bastards took so much money. About six hundred bloody quid.'

Tassie stared down at him, her breath shaky. She knew she should hold out her hand, or bend down and comfort him. But somehow, she just couldn't. She was transfixed by Oliver's voice floating through her mind. *If you love someone, you instinctively put them first. Because without them life isn't worth living.*

And she knew, without a shadow of a doubt, that the last person on Alex's mind just then had been her. For God's sake, she wasn't even worth his watch.

She waited until she could feel confident her voice wouldn't shake. 'Alex, I'm going to go. I'm sorry, but I have to.'

'Of course we need to go. Bloody Regent's Park? Worse

than bloody Central.' Alex started pushing himself up then stopped and winced. He held out his hand. 'Come on, help me up. Let's get out of here. Find a bar. I need a large drink.'

'No, Alex, *I* need to go. On my own. Right now. I'm sorry, I know you're hurt, but... I just can't be with you. Not any more. Sorry.'

And she turned and walked away, leaving him squatting on the ground, staring after her in amazement.

As she half-walked, half-ran through the park, tears streamed down her face. She stopped just after the gate and sat down on a bench, suddenly feeling intensely lonely, her stomach knotted and painful, her legs trembling.

She pulled her parka collar up, shrinking back into the comforting softness of its fake fur as the tears continued to flow.

Her dad would have done anything to protect her. Dan would have done anything to protect her. Syd's pug would have done more. Then she thought of the little girl in the park. She would have too. She knew that.

But not Alex. Never Alex.

Finally, she saw that.

16

---

*L*ondon, *November 2014*
        'Have a doughnut.'
        'I don't want a doughnut.'

'No really, have one. You've not eaten all morning and that's your second glass of champagne.'

Tassie glared at Oliver. 'I'm fine.'

He shrugged, but stayed close to her as they watched Syd and Stan circling the room.

It wasn't a surprise that Syd was dressed in a white fifties-style dress, with a bodice made of intricate French lace and her cornflower blue Louboutin matching the flower in her hair. What *was* unexpected was how Stan had been dressed when he'd arrived at the registry office that morning – looking uncharacteristically nervous. He normally wore his locs in a ponytail, but he'd cut them short for the occasion and his smart grey suit was teamed with a stripy city shirt, topped with a pink tie and a large pink and yellow boutonnière.

They looked relaxed and happy as they moved amongst their friends and relatives, receiving and delivering hugs and kisses. Spotting her friends, Syd waved then shimmied through the guests, dragging Stan with her. The four shared a brief hug as Syd motioned to the doughnut, still uneaten in Tassie's hand.

'D'you like them? Bless them, my nan and auntie made them all. Had the most impressive production line going.'

Tassie bit into it and nodded her approval. Actually, it was delicious.

'How are you guys? Have you had a drink?' Syd looked at their hands. 'Silly question. Tass, how does it feel to be a guest for once, instead of taking the photos?' She stroked her hand down Tassie's dress. 'This looks beautiful. Thank you so much for being my bridesmaid.'

'My pleasure. I was honoured you asked.' Tassie kissed Syd's cheek, then turned to Stan. 'And you, Mr Matthews, don't you scrub up well? I like the bob. You both look brilliant.' She took their hands. 'I'm so, so happy for you.'

'What time is Tilak getting here?' Syd looked at Oliver. 'What a bummer he couldn't change his shift.'

Oliver looked down for a second. 'I'm not sure, not too long I hope. He'll hate that he's missing all this.'

Tassie glanced at him.

Syd was also frowning. 'But last time we—'

'Well, I'm sure he'll be here as soon as he can.' Stan leant forward and kissed Tassie. 'Thanks for being here, guys, and Tassie, you do look lovely. Almost as beautiful as my new wife.' He turned back to Syd. 'Come on, missus, I promised my Auntie Irie a family photo.'

'It must be a relief,' Oliver said, adjusting his bow tie as they watched the couple walk away. For their friends' wedding he'd excelled himself with the tightness of his buttoned shirt and trousers.

'What must?'

'Not having to take the photos. I know I'm loving not being the organiser.'

'Oh, I don't know.' Tassie looked down at her dress. 'I think I'm discovering I prefer being on the other side of the camera – in my own clothes.'

'Meow.'

'Oh shush. It's very Syd, but hardly me – is it?'

Oliver looked at her and laughed. The dress was vintage polyester: coral, with a bow on the waistline. Her shoes were also coral, low with a pointed toe.

'Well, I must say it's not your best look, but make sure you smile for the photos. And it's a great do. Hats off to Syd and Stan for having done it on a shoestring.'

'Isn't it. I love the sweets bags, and the champagne's good too.' She reached out to grab another glass from a young waiter walking past.

'Tass. Bloody eat your doughnut. Syd will be extremely unhappy if her one and only bridesmaid gets rip-roaring drunk before they've done the speeches. Particularly as you're giving one of them.'

'Shit. Yes, where is it?' Panicked, Tassie opened her clutch. 'Oh, here.' She blew out a breath, then turned to face her friend. 'So, tell me what's up with you and Tilak. Something's clearly wrong.'

'Why do you say that?'

'Because I'm sure he could have swapped his shift?'

'What do you know of his work commitments?' Oliver snapped out the question.

'Er, nothing. I'm just surprised he couldn't make it.'

'Well, he'll be here later. He knows how important today is.' Oliver's voice was tinged with uncertainty. 'Stop worrying about it. Why don't we talk about *Dan* instead? What's happened there? Syd told me you'd said he was perfect.'

Tassie felt her mouth droop. 'Nothing. Absolutely nothing. That's all over. I thought he was, but turns out he wasn't. Let's drop it.'

'So what happened? Was it your dad?'

'Dad?' The word still caught in her throat. 'What's he got to do with it?'

'Well, I just thought, with it all happening at once, maybe you... I don't know, maybe meeting Dan got mixed in with your dad dying? That's why it didn't work?'

'Excellent analysis of the situation, Oliver. But no. It just didn't. OK? No Freud necessary.'

'But Syd said—'

'Syd's just being Syd. You know how desperate she is to get me married. It was all over before it began.' Tassie looked over to where Syd and Stan were talking to the wedding photographer. 'I've got to go, I think they're about to do group photos.' She kissed Oliver's cheek. 'I'll see you later.'

As always it took ages to get the groups sorted, and for a while Tassie watched the photographer, who began with photos of the couple and Stan's mum and dad. As his mother was wheelchair-bound with late-stage Parkinson's, Stan had worried that she wouldn't be able to make the wedding; so everyone was thrilled that she had.

Tassie winced as she watched the photographer firing off photos, for the woman's illness meant it took her a long time to smile, which the man just didn't seem to notice.

She decided she'd do some of her own of the four of them.

Waiting for her turn to be called, she thought back over the two months since her dad had died. Was Oliver right? Was it the shock of his accident that had meant she'd started doubting her and Dan? Possibly. But then she'd fucked it up anyway.

Bloody Alex. She'd not heard from him since she'd left him in the park. Not that she wanted to. In fact she'd hardly spoken to anyone, throwing herself into work, taking any jobs she could. Looking around, she saw a table with a bottle of wine on it and went over and poured herself another glass.

It was now just Syd and Stan posing, Syd's foot in the air, her bouquet held aloft as her husband leant in to give her a kiss. How lovely she looked; how happy they were.

She'd lied, of course. She was desolate about the fact that she'd not heard from Dan, despite having texted him four more times and phoning him twice. Finally, she'd sent him a postcard, a delicate watercolour of an albatross, with the words *Miss you* on the back. And left it at that.

Her eyes began to water and she gripped the stem of her glass. This was Syd's day.

She watched her friend, now standing between her mum and dad, both so proud of their daughter. That hurt. She'd now never be able to do that with her parents. Not that she'd ever get married. Nor would they have shown the amount of pride that Syd's parents were currently expressing.

Glancing up, she saw Oliver looking at her, frowning and shaking his head. She raised her glass, beamed, then held up the rest of her doughnut and popped it in her mouth.

She chewed, appreciating the sweet dough, thinking about the conversation she'd had with her mother soon after the funeral. It had taken a long time for Sybil to start speaking again, but then it wasn't long before she was back to her usual crisp self.

Tassie licked the sugar off her lips. She hadn't wanted to talk to her. Had only done it to honour her father's wishes. And it hadn't gone well.

~

HER MOTHER HAD BEEN in the laundry room, preparing a den for the puppies Honey was expecting, so it had seemed like a good time to ask.

Initially she seemed pleased when Tassie offered to help, talking about her plans for each puppy, where they were going, stuff about their new owners.

However, as soon as she bought up the subject of her own birth her mother visibly stiffened.

'Tassie, I really see no point in discussing things from the past. Can you pass me those towels.'

Tassie handed the large pile over and then, in the silence that followed, went and knelt down next to her mother, holding out her hand for a towel.

'Thanks, but it's easier if I do it myself.'

Tassie sat back on the floor. 'It was something Dad said, when he wrote to me.'

'He wrote to you? When?' Her mother carried on unfolding.

'In the hospital. He dictated it to Sophie.'

'When no one could find you.'

'Yes, then.'

Her mother spent a long time making sure the towels were tucked into every corner of the den and Tassie could only see the back of her.

'He said that I should talk to you.'

'We do talk.'

'No, about when I was born—'

Sybil stood up, went over to the sink and started washing her hands. Tassie leant forward and replaced a towel that her mother had kicked out of the den when she'd got up.

'Tassie.' Her mother dried her hands with her back still to her. 'I'm sorry, but I have no idea what your father meant. All that was a very long time ago and, really, I have enough to think about right now, given his death. Far *too* much to think about, in fact.'

Honey waddled into the scullery and nuzzled Sybil's legs. Sybil knelt and stroked the dog's swollen belly for a few seconds. 'You're a good dog, aren't you?' Her voice softened as she talked, and when she looked up her face had softened too. 'Do you think you might like to make some lunch? Anything but chicken soup would be good.'

'Of course.' As Tassie moved to leave the room, her mother touched her arm.

'Actually, I'm done here. Let's make it together.'

And they'd made lunch, and eaten it, and barely said another word.

'TASSIE, YOUR TURN.' The voice speared her thoughts and she looked over to where Syd was gesturing to her to put down her glass. She put it back on the table. It was good that it was still full, for she did have a speech to give. But shit that she still didn't have any answers.

'ONE of the good things about Syd's dad being in the alcohol trade is all the free booze.' Oliver swayed gently, holding up a magnum of wine. 'Can you believe the size of this beauty? Come on, let's get pissed.'

'Oliver, I think we already are. I need some more food.' Tassie looked around the room, observing that most of the guests were in various stages of inebriation: activities ranging from wild dad-dancing, to a woman, draped in a feather boa, snogging a man considerably younger than herself. Meanwhile two children were going around the tables, hoovering up any remnants of wine they found. 'These two families certainly know how to party,' she said.

'Don't they just. Oh look. Stan's ma is dancing.'

In the middle of the dance floor, Stan's dad was gently moving his wife's chair back and forth, the white blonde of her hair haloing her fixed smile as they swayed to the beats of Bob Marley. Tassie was struck by how, with his pork-pie hat and neatly styled salt and pepper beard, Stan's dad looked every bit as stylish as his son. She turned to Oliver and bumped his shoulder. 'Don't they look lovely. What? Why are you looking so miserable?'

'I thought I was drunk.'

'You are. But you're a miserable drunk, and I'm not sure I like it. Come on, what's up?'

Oliver sighed. 'Tilak.'

'Ha! I knew there was something wrong.'

'OK clever clogs. But still not talking 'bout it.'

'Come on. This is me.'

'Exactly. Ms Tighter than MI5 when it comes to information. Pot, kettle.'

Tassie sighed. 'Right. I'll tell you my sad story if you tell me yours. On the condition you don't tell Syd. She'll kill me.' She took the magnum from Oliver and filled up their glasses. 'I'm thinking we might need a bit more of this.'

Oliver rubbed his hands down the sides of his face then took several deep breaths. 'Tilak's family don't know about us. Don't know he's gay even, and he won't tell them. And if he doesn't, well, there's no future for us.'

'Oh. Is it a cultural thing?'

'Yes, well, no, lots of people have issues telling their family. But the stupid thing is that, from what he's told me, I'm sure they already know. And it's killing us, causing so many rows, but he's adamant he can't do it.' He looked into his glass, then up at Tassie, his eyes bright. 'So that's it. Not so incredible. Not even that unusual. But pretty bloody shite.'

'Oh, Oliver.' She rubbed his leg. 'You never know, he might change his mind?'

Oliver dabbed the corner of his eye. 'Tass, he's thirty-six. If he's not changed it by now, I don't think he will. And the sad thing is, he really is the one. *Was.* I just don't know what to do.'

Tassie kissed his cheek. He looked so miserable. Much smaller than his usual flamboyant self.

Oliver forced a grin. 'So that's mine, and you can't do anything about it, so hit me with your misery.'

It took Tassie rather longer to tell Oliver about every-thing that had happened, and by the time she'd finished his face was incredulous.

'Oh my God, Tass, and you never said anything. Wow!' He looked her up and down then, picking the bottle up, poured them more wine. 'Well, look at us, both fucking up *the ones.*'

'I'm not saying he was that. There wasn't long enough to tell.'

'You're lying, sister. I can see that.' Oliver took out a tissue and blew his nose. 'Buggering Berties, look at us. What messes we are.' He downed his glass in one. 'More drink?'

More drink led to more drinks, a bit of cheese and biscuits, then some bad slow dancing. By midnight the wedding was beginning to dwindle in noise and vitality, a few guests having fallen asleep around the tables, others having left.

'Tass, you know I love you.' Oliver stopped dancing and stroked her hair back from her face.

Tassie smiled. 'And I you, Oliver, even though you're standing on my toes.'

'Shit. Sorry.' Oliver stepped back – and into someone. 'Oh, shit, sorry I...'

He turned, and as he did Tassie saw Tilak standing behind him, smiling broadly. He stepped forward and gave Tassie a hug then turned to Oliver, kissing him briefly on the lips. Tassie watched the surprise flit across Oliver's face as Tilak pulled away.

'I thought you couldn't get off?' Oliver said.

'I managed to. But then I had to go somewhere before I came here. Dad's going away tomorrow so I needed to go home.'

'And...' Hope lit up Oliver's face and Tassie held her breath, waiting for the answer.

Tilak nodded. 'You were right. I'm sorry. They did already know, were fine about it. Just said they hoped whoever it was made me happy. I'm so sorry for having put you through... everything, for nothing.'

'Well, thank fanny for that.' Oliver sprang forward and, putting his arms around Tilak's neck, kissed him hard.

A man with a Newcastle United tie propped on his barrel stomach spluttered into his beer as he walked past.

'That's great, the absolute best,' Tassie said. But neither Tilak nor Oliver had heard her.

Quietly, she stepped away from the two of them – lost in the wonder of their new beginnings, their arms tight around each other – and went to get another doughnut.

'HEY, that's good news; I didn't think he was coming.' Syd put her arm around Tassie's waist, staring at Oliver and Tilak, who were now slow dancing.

This time Tassie was sure Oliver wouldn't be stepping on Tilak's feet; he looked like he couldn't weigh more than a feather.

'You having a good time?' Syd squeezed her side. 'You seem a bit subdued.'

'Yes, it's been brilliant. And I'm so happy for you.' Tassie nodded vigorously.

'Thanks, it has been great hasn't it? But Tass, I'm worried about you—'

'Syd, this is your wedding day. Of all the days to worry about me, this isn't it.'

'I know, pet, but I'm so happy and just want you to be too. Come on, let's go and take a seat on the couches. I'm knackered and God knows where Stan is.'

Soon they were joined by Oliver and Tilak, the four of them squashing onto the round banquette, all facing inward.

Oliver laughed. 'Feels like we're in some weird rugby scrum.'

'Or a Scottish country dance,' said Tassie.

'Dressed quite unusually for it though.' Syd patted her dress. 'Do you like my theme, Oliver? Doughnut banquettes to match the doughnuts.'

'Yes Mrs Matthews—'

'Mrs Harper-Matthews.'

'Sorry, Mrs H-C,' Oliver bowed his head. 'I must say that I hadn't noticed that finer detail so I stand... sorry, *sit* corrected. But anyway, your powers of observation aren't that good either. You've clearly not done your normal inquisition on Tassie.'

'Oliver! No!'

Tassie started to put her hand over Oliver's mouth but, laughing, he pulled away.

'It seems she hasn't been entirely honest with us about that Dan guy. *Or* someone else. Seems she *is* in love with him, but truly buggered it all up.'

Syd stared at Tassie. 'What? What's this all about? Tass, what have you not been telling me?'

Syd looked at Oliver, then Tilak, who looked amused as he shrugged his shoulders and put his hands up. 'I know nothing I'm afraid. I've just arrived.'

Syd frowned. 'I knew there was something wrong, I *knew* it didn't add up. Tassie, what's happened? Is that why you've been so bloody miserable?'

'What is this, a private party or an epithelial cell?' Stan's face appeared over the top of them, his tie now undone and his rose wilted.

'A what?' Oliver said, while Tilak raised his eyebrows and smiled.

'We're just finding out exactly what's been going on with Tassie, and why she's been such a right wet rag for the past two months. Well...' Syd stopped and put her hand on Tassie's knee, looking both embarrassed and apologetic. 'Apart from missing her dad.'

'All right then, I love a good story, budge up.' The others moved over as Stan jumped over the cushions. 'Especially when it's a Tassie one.'

Delighted to be the centre of attention – delighted full stop – Oliver repeated Tassie's story, making the most of the bit when both Alex and Dan had turned up at the same time – even though Tassie had majorly underplayed the Alex part.

It was strange, hearing her story recounted, and Tassie could see how Dan must have felt. As Oliver continued, the group oohed and aahed in the appropriate places, Syd hugging Tassie tightly when he got to the bit about the park.

'And you've not heard from him since? Dan, I mean, not the other guy.' Syd managed to looked both upset and disapproving.

'No.' Tassie shook her head. 'I've written, texted. I even

sent him a card with an albatross on it.' She felt her cheeks burning as they all looked at her enquiringly.

'Because they're extinct? Deep, Tass.' Oliver looked at her and shook his head.

'No,' she blushed even deeper. 'Because they mate for life. It was... is, was my...' She wanted to say it was her last attempt to show him how much he meant to her; but as they all stared at her, all she could actually do was cry. Although at least this time, as tears trickled down her cheeks, she felt the love and warmth of her friends surrounding her.

'Syd, I'm sorry to intrude.'

Tassie dabbed her eyes then looked up. Standing there was an older woman, her hair in two long plaits, a maroon and orange dress, patterned with strange swirls, wrapped around her portly figure.

'I've got to go now, and just wanted to say goodbye.' The woman smiled apologetically.

Syd touched Tassie's knee. 'Sorry, pet, I'll be back, but I just need to say goodbye to my Auntie Jeannie.'

'That's fine. Really, go and see everyone else. It's your wedding day.' Tassie sniffed. 'And it's about time I danced again, I love a bit of *Grease*. Oliver, Tilak, shall we?'

The following track was 'Dancing Queen' and the three of them were twirling and jumping, their hands waving in the air, when Syd came up to Tassie, her face flushed. Pulling on Tassie's hand she beckoned to Oliver.

'Boys, you come too. I have the *best* plan.'

Stan was standing behind her, shaking his head.

Leaving the dance floor they followed Syd to where her Auntie Jeannie was standing, coat in hand, near the exit.

'Tassie, meet Jeannie; Jeannie, meet Tassie.'

Smiling politely, Tassie held out her hand as Jeannie did the same.

'Now, Tass, my Auntie Jeannie is a bit of a witch.'

Jeannie shook her head and frowned. 'Not a witch, Sydonie, a Wiccan.' She looked at the group. 'I practise witchcraft as a kind of religion. All as a force for good.'

'Anyway, the thing is, Tass, Auntie Jeannie lives in Glastonbury, in *Somerset*,' – Syd gave a dramatic pause – 'where she's driving back to *now*.'

'And?'

'Well, when she mentioned she had to drive all the way back, I remembered that *Dan* lives in Somerset. And, well, then I told her a bit about your dilemma and – being able to tell the future as she can – we decided it would be a good idea for you to go with her. Go and *see* him.'

She beamed at Tassie. Stan was still shaking his head.

Jeannie touched Syd's arm. 'I didn't say I could see the future, dear, I just said that I would be delighted to give your friend a lift.' She turned and smiled at Tassie encouragingly.

'What? Now?' Tassie was bemused as she looked from Jeannie to Syd.

'Aye, now. Isn't that what true love is all about? Spontaneity?' Syd's grin grew ever wider.

'In my bridesmaid's dress?' Tassie looked down at her pointy shoes.

'Oh I'm sure Auntie Jeannie will have something you can borrow. And a coat... suitable for... a farm.' Syd looked briefly at Stan, then back at Tassie. 'You've got your handbag haven't you? A credit card?'

'Yes.'

'Well,' she nodded, mainly to herself. 'That's all you need. Anything else you can buy along the way. Go on. Auntie Jeannie and I both feel this is the correct path for you. You need to go and see him. And all will be good.'

Looking at Syd's fixed grin, slowly a warmth spread through Tassie. She looked at Jeannie. 'Are you OK with giving me a lift?'

Expectation began to tingle.

'I'd be glad of the company. I didn't want to go back tonight, but tomorrow's an important day in our calendar so I had to.'

'Oliver? What do you think? Tilak?' Tassie turned to them.

Tilak shook his head. 'And to think... I could have missed out on all this.'

Oliver shrugged. 'I think you only have one life, dearest, and if this is the path that's been opened up for you, then you'd better damn well take it.' He pulled her into a big hug, whispering, 'Just be sure you're not drugged and put in a big pot when you get there.'

Tassie stood in front of Syd, who clasped her arms then kissed her cheek.

'Honestly, Jeannie's always been my favourite auntie. She might be a witch, but she's also a pharmacist. Works in Boots. You'll love her.'

Tassie laughed, then looked around the group. 'I guess... it looks like I'm going now. To get my man back. On the broomstick of a witch.'

'It's a Honda Civic, dear, and as I said, I'm a Wiccan.'

THE HONDA WAS a smart new red one, with a star-shaped air freshener hanging under the mirror and two pillows and a rug neatly folded on the back seat.

Jeannie saw Tassie glancing around it and chuckled. 'Were you expecting a cauldron?'

Tassie was embarrassed. 'Maybe a black cat at least?'

'I do have one of those actually. Briony. But I don't tend to bring him on long drives. So... Tassie is it?'

'Yes. Short for Victoria, but only my mother calls me that.'

'I was christened Margo but got called Jeannie at school. Not that Jeannie was a witch, she was a genie, obviously. But anyway, the name stuck.'

'So you've been into witchcraft since you were little?'

'Yes, always been fascinated by it.'

'Can you put spells on people?'

'No dear, although some Wiccas do believe in that. I follow the path laid out by our founder – a retired civil servant from Lancashire. There are witches everywhere, you know, you just need to be able to spot them.'

'And you have a ceremony tomorrow?'

'Heralded by the moon. It's one of my favourites of the year.'

Tassie looked up at the sky. There was just a sliver of moon on show, barely visible above the London skyline. 'I love the moon. I've always taken photos of it.'

'Are you a photographer?'

'Yes. And the moon has always been one of the things I've been most drawn to. Which is ironic as it's so hard to capture.'

'And not without its powers, despite the distance. It's a new moon tomorrow. Which means a time for new beginnings, when an energy is harnessed that will help to create new relationships.'

'Well, that's good news for me then.'

Jeannie was silent for a while. 'Yes, but it's also a Snow Moon. Which means it's a time to reassess what it is that truly works in your life, and what doesn't. A time to honestly appraise everything.'

Tassie tried to smother a yawn. Over the past few months she'd been doing rather too much honest appraisal: constantly cursing herself and not being able to find joy in anything. Not her work, nor her friends – whom she'd barely seen as they were all too wrapped up in their own lives – and certainly not her non-existent love life.

What the hell was she doing? Driving down to Somerset on Syd's whim. Dan hadn't spoken to her since the incident at her flat, so why would he now? She shifted around in her seat, the boning in her dress sticking into her sides.

After a few minutes Jeannie glanced at her. 'We've got a long way to go, and you need to be looking your best for the morning. Why don't you grab the pillows and blanket from the back and get some sleep? It's after one.'

'Will you be all right?'

'Yes, of course. I've always been a bit of a night owl.' Jeannie smiled. 'Now *that* is someone I'm looking forward to seeing.'

'Sorry?'

'As well as Briony I have an owl, called Saffron.' She chuckled. 'What did you expect?'

17

G lastonbury, November 2014

'Tassie, wake up, we're here.'

For a few moments Tassie was confused as to where she was. Then she remembered. 'What time is it?'

'Just after five. We made excellent time. Come in and have a cup of tea. Then you can wait until a more decent hour before you set off on your adventure.'

'OK, thank you.' Tassie looked out of the window. From the light of the street lamps she could see they were outside a tiny cottage with a pink front door and irregular leaded windows.

'Home.' Jeannie sighed contentedly. 'Come and meet my family.'

As she pushed open the door, a large black cat was already waiting on the other side. It wound itself around Jeannie's legs and she bent down and stroked it. It had the most startling green eyes.

'Meet Briony.' She grinned at Tassie. 'And now's a good time to meet Saffron too. She'll still be awake.'

She led Tassie through a tiny kitchen, past dark pinewood shelves crammed with copper pots of every size, dried herbs hanging on hooks. Opening a door to the back yard she whistled, a low melodic sound, and suddenly Tassie heard the fluttering of wings as a white owl swooped down from a tall post, landing on Jeannie's outstretched arm. Gently, she stroked its feathers and murmured, 'Saffron, meet Tassie.'

Tassie stared at Jeannie in amazement. 'You mean she's wild, but just stays here and doesn't fly away?'

'Oh, she flies away every night but always comes back early in the morning. I hand-reared her from when she was a baby. Her mother was killed and I got her from the sanctuary.'

The owl sat quite still, her eyes locked forward, claws curled loosely around Jeannie's arm.

Jeannie nodded conversationally at the silent creature. 'Did you get any mice tonight, Saffie? How was your flight?' The owl turned its head towards her and blinked. 'Good? OK, well, I need to give our visitor a drink. So you go back to sleep now, or whatever it was you were doing.'

Jeannie raised her arm and the owl launched itself again, a quick fluttering of wings before she soared silently through the air, back up to her perch.

'I wish I'd brought my camera.' Tassie stared after her. 'That's one of the most beautiful sights I've ever seen.' She started. 'My camera. Shit. I had my camera, where is it?'

Jeannie smiled. 'You gave it to one of your friends to look after. The one with the amazing teeth.'

'Phew. Thank God.' She paused. 'And thank God I gave it to him.'

'Yes, he was the only guest still sober I think, apart from Syd.'

Tassie looked up at the owl. 'But I do wish I could take some photos. She'd be stunning in this light.'

'Best thing that ever happened to me, my Saffie,' said

Jeannie. 'Although Briony has never been keen. Come on, let's get you a cup of tea. And I think I probably need to lend you some clothes. That dress is appalling – I hope you don't mind me saying. Syd did always have the strangest taste.'

TASSIE SIPPED HER CHAMOMILE TEA, staring at the walls of Jeannie's sitting room. They were painted emerald green and crammed with colourful paintings and wall hangings. When her host appeared, carrying a wodge of clothing, Tassie could see that nearly all of it was of the orange, green and maroon tie-dyed variety.

This was going to be interesting.

'Here you go, I think these could all look great on you.'

'Thank you so much.' Tassie started looking through the pile, politely exclaiming how lovely everything was, while getting more and more desperate by the second. She eventually chose a long, tiered denim skirt, an orange stretch T-shirt and a moss green jumper.

Jeannie nodded approvingly. 'Lovely choices. I'm bigger than you, but you're taller, so I'm sure they'll be fine.' She pointed to the ceiling. 'If you go upstairs, my room's the first on the left. It'll be warmer than elsewhere.'

Tassie was surprised when she walked into the bedroom. After the cosy clutter of downstairs she'd expected to find something similar. But it was painted in creams and whites, the bed covered with a rose-chintz duvet and matching cushions on a white rattan chair.

Behind the double bed was a large photo of some kind of ceremony: eight naked women standing in a circle. Tassie bent over the bed to look more closely. The balanced rocks looked like Stonehenge, but the landscape was wrong. Peering more closely she spotted Jeannie in the same pose as all the others: one arm out, her other hand crossed over her breasts, long black hair streaming down around her. It was a beautiful photo, the rising sun streaming through the cracks in the boulders, the undulating land misty behind them.

Tassie removed her dress, relieved to be released from the boning, then pulled on the skirt and jumper. She looked at herself in a narrow mirror hanging on the wall – and laughed. She looked, well, not dreadful, but pretty dreadful, and nothing like herself. Folding the skirt's waistband to try and make it fit better, she did the same to the arms of the jumper so they were no longer hanging in points. At least the colour was nice.

'YOU LOOK LOVELY; I thought that jumper would suit you. Alpaca, knitted by a friend of mine.' Jeannie was sitting with Briony curled on her lap.

'Thank you again.' Tassie forced a delighted smile.

'Right, we need some shoes now, don't we?' Jeannie pushed the cat off her. 'What size are you?'

'Six.'

'Great, I thought you might say that.' She held up a pair of green boots with black cork soles that looked like stunted wellies. 'They're vegan and I love them. Sadly they're a bit too small for me – I knew that when I bought them in a sale. Daft I know. So, here you go.'

Tassie pulled them on. They were far worse than anything else she was wearing.

'Oh yes, that's perfect. You look like a proper Glastonbury girl. Just the part. Now, would you like some breakfast? How about avocado on sourdough? The bread should be fine if it's toasted.'

Tassie could hear the cheerful chatter of the morning DJ as the car-hire man twisted his sign to open. She'd decided that there was no other way she was going to be able to find Dan's farm, for it seemed to be situated in the middle of nowhere. She arranged to bring the car back that evening, leaving the keys in the exhaust if she arrived after closing.

As she drove out of Glastonbury, sun shone on the mist that lay low on the ground. The road was very straight, fertile wetlands on either side. After she'd gone some distance, looking in the car mirror she saw Glastonbury Tor rising above the town and was struck by its beauty. Pulling over, she got out of the car to better appreciate her surroundings. There was a stream running alongside the road and she frowned as she remembered Dan's stories of the devastation the floods had caused.

Dan.

Her mouth went drier than it already felt after the previous night's alcohol, which still soured her stomach. How would it go? Would he even be there? Anticipation fluttered as she looked down at her outfit. Which she'd briefly considered replacing, but had decided she wouldn't bother doing – partly because she didn't want to wait for all the shops to open.

Pulling out her phone, she studied Dan's contact details. When she'd searched for cider farms she'd been amazed at how many had come up: Harry's Cider, Rich's Farmhouse Cider, The Tricky Cider Company, Sheppy's... Clearly the business to be in around here. She checked the directions.

Jacob's Cider was just over half an hour away.

The first thing that struck her was that Dan's operation was much bigger than she'd expected, for there were half a dozen cars parked at the end of the drive. By the entrance was a beautiful vintage Bedford truck: bright green with *Betty* written on the side in black letters.

The operation consisted of three long prefabricated buildings, where she guessed they made the cider, and a quaint timber and brick restaurant – hardly the small café he'd described – plus a cider shop signposted behind. As she eased the car into a space, a red tractor trundled past, stopping just behind her. She looked at the boy driving it – slight, with blond hair and freckles – and had an inkling who he was.

'Billy, why did you bring it back here? Martin said to leave it in the top field.'

Tassie turned her head in the direction of the voice; although she didn't need to look, to know who it was.

Charlotte was standing outside one of the buildings, wearing green wellies and an oversized cream jumper. She was about to go back inside when she saw Tassie. She turned anyway, then slowly turned back. Tassie took a deep breath. It was unlikely she'd recognise her.

Her movements still slow, Charlotte began to walk towards her. 'Do I know you? Is it...?'

'Yes. Tassie. We met, in Scotland.'

Charlotte stopped a few metres away, her posture distinctly uninviting as she put her hands behind her back; a Wonder Woman pose that was somewhat at odds with her jumper and wellies.

Well, maybe not the wellies.

Tassie took a few steps forward. 'I was wondering if—'

'He's not. He's away.'

'Oh.' Both air and hope drained out of her. 'Will he be ba—'

'He's in Ireland.'

'Oh.' *Come on. Say something apart from, oh.* Except, what to say? Or do?

Suddenly Tassie felt intensely foolish, standing there in her weird outfit, on a cider farm, in front of someone who clearly thought she was the devil. As they stared at each other, she was struck by the fact that the woman really did look remarkably like a horse. All that was missing was steam coming out of her nostrils.

'As I said, he's not here so—'

Tassie took a step towards her. 'Can you just say that I came. That I'm sorry. That I need him to forgive me.' *Shut up. She so doesn't care.*

Charlotte stared at her, her face deadpan. Then she straightened and walked closer.

'No, I'm not going to tell him that. I'm not going to tell him anything. I know your type: flightier than a sparrow. Unfortunately, Dan's always been far too attracted to women like you. But things are different now. He was broken when he came back from London. *Broken.* I've never seen him so bad. Didn't talk for days. Don't you think he's already been through enough?' She snorted. 'Oh yes, I know every sordid detail of what happened with you. Because I was here for him, just as I've always been. Just as I always will be. So, no, I won't be telling him anything. And you might as well go.'

When Charlotte put her hand up to smooth her hair it seemed an unnecessary gesture, for it was already pulled into a tight ponytail.

Until Tassie saw it: a small ruby and diamond ring.

'Women like you,' Charlotte continued. 'Always think you can have whoever you want. Do whatever you like. Well, Dan's not the man for you. I can assure you of that.'

Then she turned and walked away, back into the building from where she'd come.

As Tassie walked back to her car she saw Billy staring at her.

'Sorry about the… Could you move your tractor?'

The boy nodded mutely, continuing to stare at her as she reversed out from behind him. And, blinking back the tears, she didn't look at him again.

18

Speeding back along the road, Tassie couldn't believe she'd been so stupid. What had she been thinking, coming down on the spur of the moment? And, yuck, how awful that the only person she'd seen was Charlotte.

But of course it would be so. And... oh God... engaged? *What the fuck?* Well, he couldn't have been so serious after all. *I've fallen in love with you this week – but I'm happy to get engaged to someone else two months after.*

Damn fast work.

Her chest tightened as a slow rage burned. Although... It was her who'd begun the process that had led to this. Broken, Charlotte had said. Dan was broken. And all because of Alex.

She stopped the car, pushing open the door, needing fresh air in her lungs. Stamping up and down at the side of the road she didn't care about the strange looks she was getting from people driving past.

Eventually a woman was kind enough to stop and ask if she was all right, three children jostling to look out of the back window.

'Yes, thank you.' Tassie stopped stamping. 'Well, no... but, really, I'm fine.'

The woman looked suitably confused as she got back into her Volvo.

Watching her pull away, Tassie glanced at her watch. It was still only ten. She stared across the grass to the river, where reeds lined the water's edge. What was she going to do, miles away from anywhere? She didn't even know where the nearest city was. She looked at the map on her phone. Exeter.

Exeter.

She watched the occasional car drive past. The reverend lived in Exeter. The lovely rev, who'd given her an open invitation to visit any time she was down. And it was only an hour away.

Suddenly she couldn't think of anything she'd like to do more than see her again. She didn't have a number, but she had her email. She typed fast then pressed send, hoping the reverend would see it before she got there. In the meantime she'd just start driving.

TASSIE STOOD in front of the vicarage's red front door – the quince now an intricate twist of bare wood – smiling when she saw the outline of Carlos's bike in the courtyard, covered by a thick tarpaulin. What a wonderful day it had been. She pushed on the gate, which squeaked as it opened, then rang the bell.

She'd been standing there for a few minutes, wondering if anyone was in, when the door opened and there was Clarissa's father, looking exactly like he had the previous summer, except now he was in an old grey woollen jumper, faded cords and tartan slippers.

'Yes, can I help you?'

'Hello, Mr...'

'Rawlings?'

'Yes, Mr Rawlings.'

'I'm sorry, do I know you?'

'Yes. Well, no. Not really. I'm Tassie, I took the photos at your daughter's wedding. And well, the rev— Mrs Rawlings suggested I should come and see you if ever I was in Exeter again.'

'Oh.' For a few seconds he stared at her, the colour in his face visibly draining.

'I'm sorry. Is this a bad time? I'll go, shall I?'

Tassie took a step backwards as the man moved towards her, his hand half out.

'No. No, it's all right. Sorry. Come in. Come in.' He motioned to her to come forward. 'I'll just go and get Angela. Have you come from far?'

With each movement he seemed to recover his manners, and finally, as he ushered her into the large kitchen, he smiled.

As instructed, Tassie made herself a mug of tea with the heavy steel kettle, briefly enjoying a sense of familiarity as her parents had the same one. Then she sat down at the table – and had drunk most of her tea by the time the reverend appeared.

When she did, Tassie was shocked by the change in her. The previous summer her hair had been glossy black, just a few strands of white; but now it was almost completely grey. Her eyes were tinged red, and Tassie suspected she'd been crying.

The rev stepped forward and when she enveloped Tassie in a hug, Tassie could feel her body shuddering. She had a horrible feeling she was crying again.

After a moment the reverend pulled back, motioning for

Tassie to sit down. Her face was wet with tears as she pulled a hanky out of her jeans pocket, before sitting down beside her and straightening her shirt.

'I'm so sorry, this must all seem strange to you. It's just, you caught me off guard. Normally I'm— Anyway, I'm so delighted to see you. Delighted. It brings back such wonderful memories of the day.' The rev's eyes went to a large photograph on the kitchen wall. It was the one of Clarissa laughing at Carlos, soon after her granny had covered him in water. 'I love that photo so much. Thank you for capturing the moment.'

Tassie sat silent, unsure of what to say, trying to guess what had changed so much.

The reverend blew her nose then took Tassie's hand. 'It was such a beautiful day.'

She smiled again, and it contained so much sadness that suddenly Tassie knew.

'Clarissa?' Even as she said the name, she couldn't bear for it to be true.

The reverend nodded. 'I'm so sorry. I assumed you'd seen the news?'

Tassie desperately scanned through the last twelve months. She remembered there'd been reports of an MSF hospital having been blown up, several in fact, but none had been in Afghanistan.

Watching her, the reverend shook her head. 'They'd transferred to Sudan.' She sighed. 'To Frandala. Where I knew the hospital had previously been targeted, so I did try and persuade them not to go. But Clarissa just laughed, said it was beautiful, up in the mountains, that it would be like an extended honeymoon.' She frowned, looking up at the photo again. 'Not that they got to see much of the beauty. I think it was pretty dire from the moment they landed.'

A single tear rolled down her cheek and Tassie resisted the temptation to wipe it away.

'We always knew this could be one of the outcomes. That God's plan for them – as Clarissa used to call it – was always a risky one. At least they were taken together, and I believe were saved any pain. Or, that's what I tell myself.'

Tassie could only stare at the reverend, who was still mourning the loss of her beloved daughter and son-in-law, yet could already find a positive. She knew enough about the situation in Sudan to know that Clarissa and Carlos would have died for nothing: deaths that were deemed so inconsequential their photos hadn't even made the national news. She leant forward and hugged the reverend, who, this time, didn't cry. Just hugged her back.

When she eventually pushed Tassie's arms away, her smile held no hint of grief. 'So, Tassie. It's lovely to see you. What brings you to this part of the world? Will you stay for some lunch? Please say you will. Cedric's made boeuf bourguignon.'

'Thank you. That would be lovely.' Tassie looked up at the photo. 'And maybe...' She considered the practicalities. 'You might like to see all of my photos from the wedding – there's loads you never saw. I can log into my account online and show them to you?'

'Oh, what a wonderful idea. Thank you. Really, it's very nice having you here. And so unexpected.'

'I'm sorry, I did email.'

'Oh, don't worry about that. I only check them once a day. I'm doing nothing important this morning, although I do have to go and visit one of my parishioners just before lunch. A real character of ninety-six. Maybe you'd like to come with me?'

. . .

Tassie loved spending the morning at the vicarage. As they looked through her photos she felt pleased she could do something to bring back happier times. The Reverend and Mr Rawlings spent ages looking at each one, discussing family members, remembering who'd said what, done what, worn what on the day.

After they'd chosen a selection – Tassie offering to make up an album – the reverend suggested they walk to see the old lady. 'It's such a beautiful day.'

They ambled along the road, passing another church which was smaller than the rev's. She glanced at it. 'We had a joint funeral for them.' Turning, she smiled. 'It was so beautiful. I think at first Carlos's family weren't sure, him being Catholic, but in the end everyone who came said it was wonderful.'

'Did you—' Tassie blanched, unable to finish.

'Take it? Yes, yes, I did. I had the privilege of bringing my beautiful child into this world, so it was wonderful to have the privilege of helping her through to the next.'

What serenity. Tassie looked back at the church. Perhaps it was her faith that gave her such strength? It seemed quite similar to the sense of peace she'd felt with Jeannie earlier that day. Was religion the way to go – be it Christian or Pagan? She smiled, and the reverend looked at her quizzically. 'I was just thinking, you seem so incredibly... resigned to your loss. If that's not the wrong thing to say.'

'Oh, I've not lost my child – children. They're just working in a different way. In a different place. For me, heaven isn't so very different to the Nuba Mountains. The communications being pretty poor with both.' The reverend put her arm through Tassie's. 'But you're right, my faith does make everything bearable. God's path often takes us in directions that don't immediately seem obvious. But there's always a plan. Always.'

'I don't think there's much of a plan for me.' As soon as she'd said the words Tassie was mortified. 'Sorry. My problems are minuscule. Not that they're really problems anyway.'

'Everyone's problems are relative, Tassie—' The reverend broke off when she saw Tassie's face fall. 'Sorry, did I say something?'

Tassie shrugged. 'No, not at all. It's just somebody else said that to me once. You just reminded me.'

The reverend gently squeezed her arm. 'Well whoever said it was obviously very wise. And there's nothing I like better than talking about other people's issues – whether large or small. So why don't we talk about yours? After we've seen Miss Maisie.' She pointed over a low wall. 'Look, she's waiting for us in the window – I knew she would be.'

In the window of a large white house, a tiny lady was leaning on a stick, her head straining to look up. When she saw them, she turned and shuffled out of view.

'If I know Maisie she'll be on her way to open the front door.' The reverend's voice was thick with affection. 'If you want to see a wonder of the world, this is definitely one of them.'

WHEN THEY RETURNED to the vicarage, lunch was ready in the Aga. It was delicious, the sauce rich with wine and herbs, the meat as tender as marshmallow. The two women did most of the talking, Cedric only responding when asked a direct question, despite his smiles and nods.

The rev winked at Tassie. 'My husband's not known as much of a talker.'

Cedric harrumphed as he pushed a pile of mash onto his fork.

'As you see, Clarissa definitely got her chatty side from me.'

After lunch had been cleared away, the reverend motioned to Tassie to follow her. 'Let's go to my office.'

In the quiet, dark room, two identical chairs were placed on either side of a fake log fire. Both were covered in faded brown linen, with high backs and arms, and Tassie noticed a box of tissues on a little table next to one of them. She laughed. 'It's like being at the therapist.'

'Well, counselling does constitute a large part of my job. And it's probably the thing I enjoy the most.' The reverend smiled at her encouragingly as she crouched down to turn on the fire, then took one of the chairs. Leaning back, she put her elbows on the arms and crossed her hands. 'So, what really brings you here today, Tassie? And, more importantly, how can I help?'

WHETHER IT WAS the feeling that it would be helpful for the reverend to hear about something different, or because the chair was so comfy and the rev so easy to talk to, within half an hour Tassie had told her just about everything she could think of: Dan, her dad dying, Alex – always Alex, how she'd failed to get Dan to listen to her again. She even told her about the other men – not all the other men, obviously. But the fact that she'd never seemed to be able to settle down; to commit. The reverend listened quietly, only interjecting with the occasional question and when Tassie had finished, she sat silently for a while.

'Tell me about your mother.'

Tassie was surprised. Out of everything she'd said, her mother was the last thing she'd expected to talk about. 'My mother?'

'Yes. You've spoken a lot about your father. Tell me more about her.'

Tassie frowned. 'Well, there's not a lot to say. We don't get on. Never have. It's like... like... there's this barrier between us that can't be breached. Not that I particularly want it to be. I'm used to things as they are, I guess. I had Dad, and Tom, and, well, that was always enough.'

'Really, Tassie? Everyone needs their mother.'

'But what if their mother doesn't need them?' Tassie was surprised that tears instantly smarted.

'It's clear that she loves you, from things you've told me.'

Tassie snorted. 'I'm not sure how I've done that...' Again the tears welled, along with the doubt. 'She's never actually... told me... she loves me, you know. Not once.'

'Well, that's a generational thing. Parents haven't always been so openly affectionate with their children. You also need to consider, perhaps, that our generation were children during a war. Meaning that things were very different.'

Reaching across for a tissue, Tassie blew her nose. She knew her grandfather had been posted to Crete just after her mother was born, so she'd not actually met him until she was four. It was a story that was occasionally told at family gatherings, and Uncle Ali had talked about it too: how strange it had been for her mother when her grandfather had finally returned, how much easier it had been for him. For by the time he'd been born their father was home again.

Her beloved Uncle Ali. He'd never told her he loved her either. But *that* she'd always known.

The reverend was watching her intently. 'When did things get bad with your mother? Can you remember?'

'I can't remember a time when they weren't.' Tassie huffed through her nose. 'Although... My father said something strange to me, in a letter he wrote before he died. That there'd been a time when Mum had been away, when I was a baby. That it was just him and me.' She laughed. 'He compared looking after me to lambing.'

The reverend nodded. 'And have you asked your mother about this?'

'She won't talk about it.'

They both sat for a while, then the reverend leant forward and put her hand on Tassie's knee. 'From the little you've told me, it's obvious your mother finds it hard to express her feelings. But I think you should talk to her. Find out about this time. I'm not a therapist, but over the years I've done a lot of reading around the subject. And one of the things psychotherapists believe is that what happens from when you are born to the age of three is crucial. Particularly in the first year and a half.' She shook her head, 'Sadly, just like poor old Eve, women have always carried a heavy burden. For a lot of it seems to fall on the mother. But I do believe the bond in those months is vital. In fact, I think I've got a book here somewhere...'

She scanned her shelves for a few moments then, unable to find what she was looking for, turned back to Tassie. 'It doesn't matter. But I think there might well be something in your past that you need to understand.' She paused, her face reflective. 'There's something called attachment hunger. And it's surprising how often I've seen it affect people.'

'So I'm hungry to be attached to my mother?' Tassie snorted. 'I don't think so.'

'As I said, everyone needs positive attachment. It's a fundamental. And if that isn't allowed to happen, if it *can't* happen, then sometimes people look elsewhere.'

It took barely a minute for Tassie to make the connection. The same eyes. The same ability to make her feel completely worthless. Both as unattainable as the moon.

'Alex.'

The reverend nodded. 'Well, obviously I can't be sure. And, as I said, I'm not a psychotherapist. But from what you've told me, I think that it could be.'

'So... what? You mean, it was never about Alex? It was always about my *mother*?' Tassie's short burst of laughter was harsh.

'Possibly.'

'Well, thanks, Mum.'

'Tassie.' The reverend shook her head. 'I don't think it was her fault.'

'But whatever happened, it's too late now isn't it? I've spent fifteen years mooning over some idiot – who I've finally begun to see is an idiot. I've lost the potential love of my life – who's now engaged to someone else. And all because of my mother!' *Shut up, Tassie, the woman's in mourning.* 'I'm so sorry. It's just...' She slowed her breathing, then put her hands on her knees, smiling weakly. 'It's a lot to take in.'

'I know it is. And I'm not saying I'm right, and I'll say again that I'm not strictly qualified in this. But sometimes, if it feels right in your gut, then it often is.'

Tassie looked at her watch. It was nearly three and she still had to get the car back to Glastonbury and somehow make her way back to London. 'Listen, I should go. You weren't expecting me and I'm sure you've got things to do.' She stood up.

The reverend also stood. 'Nothing that couldn't wait.' She took Tassie's hands in hers. 'Tassie Morris, you are a good person. And I hope you can resolve this.'

Tassie was surprised when the rev stepped forward and kissed her cheek.

'Talk to your mum. Because right now, I can assure you, she needs you. Whatever you might think.'

19

———

When Tassie dropped the car back in Glastonbury, she discovered that the station was miles out of town and she'd have to get a taxi. At the station, the office was shut and the platforms deserted – with no information, that she could find, about trains. For half an hour she'd sat on a bench, wondering what on earth to do, before deciding she'd just have to get on the next train that looked like it was going east.

Then, when a man finally appeared – pulling on a station master's coat as he came out of a tiny cottage – he told her that there were no more fast trains to London. So she'd made the snap decision to head for Shropshire instead.

She yawned. She'd been on various trains for nearly five hours and it was getting very late.

The whole time she'd been mulling over her conversation with the reverend. Had things always been so bad between her and her mother? Should she have cut her some slack? Possibly. But who was the adult?

And what about her years with Alex? The times he'd let her down, humiliated her, treated her like some kind of lackey. Although... She was always so willing to follow on behind, fit in with his plans. So, was it him treating her like that? Or was it her, desperately clinging on, ignoring all the signs.

It was a whole new perspective that made her cringe with embarrassment.

Now she could see things more clearly, she had to admit that it wasn't all his fault. Alex had his own issues, his own insecurities, and she guessed it must be hard not to take advantage of someone you know is willing to do anything, put up with anything, just to have your company.

And then she thought about Dan. And the thought of having lost him was almost too painful to bear, as the full wonder of their week together came flooding back. She missed him. God she was an idiot. And humiliated. And stupid. So friggin' stupid.

She was feeling all those emotions when she stepped down from the train.

'Hello, sis, bit of a surprise visit?' Tom was waiting in the carpark, leaning against his car. Above him, bugs flitted around the station lights.

Tassie hugged him tight, until he pulled back from her, laughing as he looked her up and down. 'And, may I ask, what *are* you wearing? Don't tell me: this is one last goodbye before you set off to join a cult?'

She looked at her sleeves – their points now fully exposed. With everything else that had happened, she'd forgotten she was dressed like a hippie.

'Long story. Really long story. I'll tell you over a mug of hot chocolate. Maybe. Come on, let's go, I'm knackered.'

THE NEXT MORNING Tassie was up early, sitting alone in the kitchen. She'd barely slept, thoughts having continued to whizz around her head. But with the early light, a few more things had begun to slot into place; and for the first time in months, she was beginning to feel like she'd got things a little more in perspective.

'Tassie, what a fantastic surprise.' Sophie appeared in the doorway in a spotty nightie, her screw-curls sticking out all over the place. 'I'm sorry I didn't see you last night, I was so tired I went to bed early. Have you helped yourself to tea? Breakfast? I left the Marmite out for you. Did you find it?'

A few minutes later Tom could be heard running down the stairs before he burst through the door.

'Shit, shit! I forgot that I'm on gate duty this morning. Have you seen my bag, Soph? See you later – hope to see you too, Tass.' He grabbed a banana, spotted his bag in the corner of the room, waved, and was gone.

Tassie and Sophie looked at each other, and laughed.

'Still the same old Tom, then. Dad's death hasn't suddenly made him the super-organised man of the family?'

'Still the same.' Sophie smiled gently; and in the momentary silence, reference to Alfred hung like an old coat.

'So how have you been, Soph? Any news?'

'What, about my PhD? Still plodding away.'

'No about...'

'About school? Still working hard – new GCSEs coming in this year. Nightmare.'

'No—' Tassie was unsure whether to continue.

'You mean about the baby? Oh that.' Sophie beamed. 'Well, I do have a photo you might want to see. Although it's a little out of focus. I had it early, because... you know, all our problems. So it's not quite up to your standard.'

Tassie jumped up. 'You're not...?'

'I am. All that peeing into pots finally paid off. Confirmed two days ago.' Sophie squeezed Tassie's arm. 'So I'm so glad you're here.'

'Oh Sophie. *Sophie*. I'm so thrilled. So very happy— But, hang on—' Tassie frowned. 'Why didn't Tom tell me?'

Sophie took her hands. 'I asked him not to. I know it's selfish, but I so wanted to see your face. After all, it is me who's carrying the munchkin. And me who has to stab herself with a needle every day.'

Tassie's frown became concern. 'Why?'

'To help stop my blood from clotting. It's OK. Once you've done it a few times it becomes remarkably inconsequential. And so worth every needle. I keep suggesting to Tom that he does it to himself with a pin, so we can experience the same. But, strangely, it seems he doesn't want to.' Sophie laughed as she stood. 'I'll show you the scan. Or shall I make some tea?'

'Scan, definitely. And let's not have tea. Let's have champagne. Oh—' Tassie went to stand, then sat down again. 'I'm guessing not a good idea for you.'

'No. And, Tassie.' Sophie's voice was stern. 'Never a good idea for anyone at seven-thirty in the morning.'

'OK, but let me make the tea. You sit down.'

They spent a couple of hours luxuriating in talking about the baby: what it would mean, how Tom was feeling, how Sybil had reacted – with pure delight, apparently. Tassie avoided talking about her news and Sophie was too excited about her own to ask.

After a bath, Tassie borrowed some jeans and a top from Sophie's infinite choices of stripy ones, then went back down to the kitchen.

As usual, her sister-in-law was working at the table, and Tassie put her arms around her shoulders. 'I can't tell you how happy this makes me. You and Tom were born to be parents. You'll be brilliant.'

'As will you, Tass, one day.'

Tassie sat down opposite her. 'Yeah, right. I can't even keep a boyfriend, let alone make a baby.'

Sophie looked at her sharply. 'What about...' She saw Tassie's face. 'I'm sorry, I've been so busy telling you my news we've not talked about your—'

'And nor will we.' Tassie stood again. 'Gotta go, honey, I said I'd see Mum at eleven. Are you sure it's all right for me to borrow the car?'

'Yes of course. But we'll talk about this when you return?'

'And once again you sound just like Syd. Bye, Soph. I'll try not to crash.'

In the farmyard, her father's absence was immediately obvious. Tiles were coming off one of the barn roofs, there was green moss on the edges of the tractor trailer, and bags of feed in the courtyard that probably should have been put away.

Tassie scrutinised everything. She could still picture him coming out of the barn, wiping his hands down his overalls as he always did, his face lighting up upon her arrival. Meaning that she had to take some deep breaths before opening the front door.

Her mother wasn't in the kitchen, and she'd walked through most of the house before she found her in her father's office. Sybil was sitting at his desk, reading through some papers. She looked up, frowning.

'So much paperwork. So many things your father doesn't seem to have records for.'

Tassie gave her a hug then kissed the top of her head.

She could smell Honey's fur. 'What are you doing?' She looked over the papers: deeds from the farm, estate agent's letters, other official-looking documents.

'Well, given that I've decided to sell the land, I'm trying to get everything sorted. Although, I must say, none of it is easy.'

'I could help, maybe? Go through some of the paperwork?'

'No, that's fine. Tom's going to do it on Sunday. He knows the mechanics of the farm better than you.' Her mother gave her a brief smile. 'But thank you for the offer.'

'So, is it good money, what you're getting for the land?'

'It will be enough, I'm sure. But let's not count anything until it's done.' Sybil looked back down at the papers and started piling them together. 'I think I'm done here for the morning.' She looked up. 'So, what's brought you here so suddenly? It's lovely to see you, but a little unexpected?'

'Erm...' Tassie floundered. 'I just thought I'd... Well, you know. See how you are. Shall I go and make some tea?'

Her mother stood, rubbing the back of her neck. 'Sounds like a good idea. It feels like I've been doing this for hours. But I did say, didn't I, that I'll need to be gone by twelve-thirty? I'm taking one of Honey's pups to a lady in Middletree.'

'Yes, that's fine. You did.'

As Tassie followed her mother into the kitchen, she worked out she had an hour-and-a-half time slot. *Think of the reverend. Just think of the reverend. And stay calm.*

Her mother handed her a mug of tea then sat opposite her at the long oak table. 'I was surprised when Tom phoned last night to say you were on your way.' She pushed a plate towards her. 'Biscuit? I made them yesterday, orange and cardamom.' She paused. 'They were your father's favourite.'

'Thank you.' Tassie was surprised to see tears in her mother's eyes and she reached for her hand. Sybil looked down and, after a pause, slowly slid her own across the table.

'Mum...' Tassie took a breath. 'I know that I've brought this up before, and you didn't want to talk about it.' Instantly she felt the hand stiffen. 'But for me, for my sake, do you think we could? You see, whatever it was that happened, I think it affected me, is still affecting me, and I need to know.'

The hand slid out from under hers.

'For goodness' sake.' Her mother's voice was sharp. 'What is it with all this nonsense, obsessing about everything going back to childhood? I do think one needs to take responsibility for one's behaviour as an adult.'

The third-person delivery of the sentence didn't make the pill any sweeter and Tassie breathed deeply. 'I am taking responsibility, Mum. But that's why I'd really like to have this conversation. I was talking to someone yesterday—'

'You talked to someone? About us? About what exactly?'

Tassie flinched. Her mother's greatest horror was having anyone talk about her. The words, 'For God's sake, don't repeat it' had been a mantra of her childhood.

'Well, not about you specifically, but—'

'I should hope not. Really, I've said it before and will say it again. I don't have any desire to bring up the past, none of it, especially now your father's gone. And I would ask that you don't either. Also, please don't go discussing our family business with other people. Who were you talking to?'

'It was a vicar, in Exeter. I photographed her daughter's wedding.' Tassie kept her voice low and steady. 'She said that I might have something called attach—'

'Really, Victoria.' The veins in her mother's face darkened. 'All these ridiculous theories. I can't believe you were discussing our business with someone you barely know. And a vicar? What if she knows our vicar and sees fit to contact him? Really, why would you do such a thing?'

Tassie snorted. 'Mum, I'm sure she won't contact anyone. It was just a chat. That's all.'

'Well, it doesn't sound like that to me.' Sybil got up and walked over to the Aga, its rail lined with clothes that were drying. Including, Tassie noticed, two old shirts of her father's.

Her mother began removing them, folding then placing them in a basket. When she turned, her face was set. 'Was there anything else you needed to discuss? If I'm going to get to Middletree by twelve-thirty I do need to start getting things ready. It's always so hard for Honey when she has to have her pups taken away.'

With the last words her voice broke slightly and she turned back to the Aga. Almost immediately, she turned again.

'It's lovely to see you, but next time you need to give a bit more warning. I'm very busy, far too busy, especially now, running the farm *and* the dogs. It would be lovely to chat more, but I can't.' She briefly stroked one of Alfred's shirts before folding it. 'Now, would you like to help me get the puppy ready? She's an utter delight. I'll be sad to see her go.'

As Tassie drove back to Tom and Sophie's she felt sadness weighting her heart like an eiderdown. It hadn't been awful seeing her mother; at least things hadn't ended in silence or with her storming off. But neither had it got her any closer to knowing what had happened.

To her surprise, Tom was in the kitchen, sitting at the table eating an overstuffed sandwich.

'I've got two free lessons after lunch so thought I'd come

home and see my big sis. Who knows when you might flit in again. And Soph had to walk into town to pick up some results.'

Tassie was instantly concerned.

'She's fine, don't worry. They're just monitoring her closely. She said she hoped you'd still be here when she got back. When are you planning to go?'

'Soon, actually. I need to get back to London. I left the flat on Friday evening, expecting to be back on Saturday, and it's now Monday. I shouldn't really have come, especially as I haven't done any prep for my next job.'

'So, your visit? Your conversation with Mum? Was it worth it?'

'No. She wouldn't tell me anything. So you and I are still none the wiser.'

Her brother took a bite of his sandwich, munching thoughtfully. 'Tass, does it really matter? All this stuff? It's in the past, and she obviously doesn't want to talk about it.' He swallowed. 'Can't you just be in the present? Live your life now? I'm not sure I understand you sometimes.'

Tassie hated it when her brother spoke to her like this. He could be prone to smugness, with his perfect job, perfect wife, perfect life.

'It's easy for you to say. You've always got on better with Mum. You've got Soph. And *now* you've got a baby.' She was embarrassed that emotion was coming out in a way she'd been able to avoid earlier that morning.

'But Tass, it's a two-way thing. You're always so hard on her. She really is nicer than you seem to think. It's been difficult for her – and not easy for us either.'

'Well, I'm sorry that I've not been here more, but it's hard for me too. I've got work that I have to do. And a mortgage—'

'I'm not saying you haven't, calm down. It's fine. Look why don't you t—'

'Try to forget it? What if I can't?' Her mouth suddenly dry, Tassie went over to the sink and filled a glass with water. Her heartbeats continued to increase as she stared out at a barren patch of garden, where Tom's bike was leant against the fence.

'Tell me about Dan. That's what I was going to ask.'

Just hearing the name made her flinch. She didn't turn around.

'How is he? It would be good to see him again.'

'Well, maybe you could look him up sometime. Because he sure isn't talking to me.' Tassie braced. She wasn't going to cry. Certainly not in front of her brother.

'You're not seeing him?'

She could hear his disappointment and whirled around, her face reddening. 'No, Tom. I'm not seeing him. In fact I haven't seen him since he left here. And yes, just before you ask, it was my fault. Just as it always is. Good old Tassie. Fucking up for ever.'

'Tass, I—'

'Oh can you just stop. Please?' She looked at her watch. 'Shall I get a taxi to the station? If I hurry I can probably still make the one-forty-five.'

'Don't be silly. I'll take you. And, Tass, I'm only saying this stuff because I love you.'

'Well, love me better and don't say anything.'

ON THE WAY to the station, conversation was stilted as Tassie still fumed. Although she was no longer quite sure why.

In the carpark she gave her brother a brief hug. 'I'm sorry. I know I'm not being nice. It's just... hard, at the

229

moment. Really hard. Even if you think it's because I make it so.'

Tom was about to say something, but she turned and opened the door. 'I've gotta run. Give Sophie a kiss from me.'

She got out and started walking away, then ran back to Tom's window, gesturing to him to wind it down. 'God, I'm so, so sorry, Tom. Congratulations.' She was going to lean in and kiss him, but didn't. 'I'm so pleased for you. It's brilliant. Sorry, I can't believe I didn't say anything. Well done, little bro; your dinger finally worked.'

Tom looked at her and shook his head, his eyes amused but wary.

'I did wonder if you'd remember. Now run, I can see the train.'

20

Kent, February 2015
'Spare batteries, flashguns, memory cards, notebook...' Tassie checked her camera bag yet again. Today was going to be difficult and she wanted to be sure she'd not forgotten anything.

Her phone vibrated and a flashing heart with a diamond appeared. She scrolled down. *Happy Valentine's beautiful lady, Oliver and Tilak xxooxx.* With a rueful smile she closed the screen. That would be her only Valentine.

Looking at her watch, she saw it was just before nine. Time to go if she wanted to grab some food on the way – the food in the motel had been horrible.

DRIVING up to the heavily remodelled manor, Tassie considered how, if there was celebrity status A to D, then the bride of the day hovered somewhere around F – a letter that probably matched her breasts.

When she pulled into the courtyard, the woman in question had also just arrived. Tiny, with white-blonde hair down to her waist, she was wearing a black baseball cap with *BOY* written across the front, black and white checked leggings and stilettos.

Seeing Tassie, she shrieked. 'You the photographer?'

'Yes.' Tassie walked towards her, trying to keep her expression neutral.

'Thank fuck for that. I tried ringing the number loads of times last night and there weren't any answer.'

'I think you might have rung the magazine? I don't think you've got my number?' *Thank God – and Syd.*

In the run-up to the wedding, Sadie Manchester had been a nightmare in terms of her fussing, so Syd had decided she would deal with her personally, guarding against the fact that, with her ever-darkening mood, Tassie was not in a good place to deal with highly demanding divas.

Once a year the magazine chose a celebrity to feature and, thanks to a recent scandal with a reality show and some *serious* on-screen canoodling, Sadie was currently hot property. It had been tight, fitting the wedding into the magazine's schedule, but Catrina had insisted they do it. Early in a new year was always a good time for some extra publicity and the fact that *Kiss the Bride* would be photographing the day had already made the news.

Tassie looked around. So far the press hadn't managed to work out the wedding venue. But – she looked at a couple of staff members staring at them from the entrance – it probably wouldn't be long.

'Are the doves 'ere d'you know?'

'Sorry?'

'The doves. For the church. D'you know if they're 'ere?'

'Um, no, I haven't been to the church yet.'

'Well, why don't you go and take some photos there first – of all the flowers and shit – then come back and take some of me.'

'If that's what you'd like.' Slowly, Tassie walked back to the car, bracing herself for the day ahead.

THE CHURCH WAS BEAUTIFUL: light grey, beneath a moss-stained slate roof and three spires rising above a jumble of gravestones. There was a van parked by the entrance with *WHITE DOVE WEDDINGS* written across the side and a man sitting in the front reading the *Sun.*

Tassie knocked on the window. As the man wound it down she could hear gentle cooing coming from behind him.

'Hi, I'm the photographer. I presume you're the dove man?'

'Nah, I'm here to deliver the polar bears.'

Tassie smiled politely. 'The bride asked if I could take some photos of them before the ceremony starts. Would that be possible?'

The man peered up at the sky. 'I'm not planning to unload 'em yet. I need to leave 'em to settle after driving here, and, looking at the weather, I'm not even sure I will be setting 'em off.'

Tassie shuddered. She knew how important the doves were to Sadie: a key accent point, Christopher, the wedding planner had called them. Somehow, whatever the weather, if Ms Manchester had her way the doves would be leaving their baskets.

'What time are you planning on taking them out?'

'About 11.30, weather dependin'.'

'OK. I'll come back then.'

She walked down the short path to the church, taking a sharp intake of breath when she got to the entrance. Two heavy doors led straight onto the main part of it, and just inside the entrance a large archway had been constructed out of white roses and hanging jasmine. Similar arrangements sat at the end of each pew and the aisle was laid with a lilac carpet, its edges decorated with more flowers. It must have cost an absolute fortune.

Slowly, she made her way down the aisle, taking photos in-between sneezes.

WHEN SHE RETURNED to the manor house, Tassie asked at reception for the honeymoon suite and was directed to a room on the middle floor. Before she'd even reached the ornate door she could hear the bridal party – loud shouts still audible above a heavy bass beat. She knocked, then, realising no one would hear her, opened the door.

Inside it was mayhem. Five women lounged or stood around, all in varying states of undress: two wearing matching shocking-pink satin robes, the others in an array of pink and apricot underwear. There were some fantastic breasts on show; not least Sadie's, who was sitting in the centre of the group, dressed in a cream corset, suspenders and lace-topped stockings, her tiny feet up on a low table. She had a large glass of something turquoise in her hand and was smoking a long cigarette, while one of the pink-robed women stood behind her, styling her hair into a small mountain.

Tassie was pretty sure smoking wasn't allowed inside the venue. But then again it was unlikely anyone was going to tell the bride of the moment that she couldn't.

She placed her camera bags in the corner, then looked around more carefully. With sun streaming through the large windows it made a brilliant scene, like a tableau from some decadent royal boudoir, or a Victoria Secret's shoot. Knowing it was a shot she shouldn't take, she quickly changed the lens on her camera and took a couple of wide angles. Nobody noticed.

After she'd changed the lens again, she walked over to Sadie. 'Is there anything particular you'd like me to take or shall I just do my own thing?'

'Did you get the doves?'

'No, but I saw them, they're definitely here. The man didn't want them disturbed after their drive.'

Sadie frowned. 'But you will get them, won't you? Lots of photos. I fuckin' love me doves.' She took a drag on her cigarette.

'Yes, I will. But now shall I concentrate on you? I'll start with the dress, shall I?'

Sadie nodded, and Tassie walked over to the wardrobe where the wedding dress was hanging. It had a tiny shell-pink bodice and a tutu-style skirt fanning out beneath. On the floor were diamond encrusted wedge shoes – at least six inches high.

The room was filled with swirls of cigarette smoke, but the bathroom had wonderful light coming through its windows. She turned to one of the bridesmaids who was busy putting fake tan on her arms. 'Would it be all right if I photograph the dress in there d'you think?'

The woman looked at her blankly – her eyelids coated with heavy black liner and sparkly blue shadow – before turning to Sadie.

'Oi, Sade, the photographer wants to take your dress into the dunny to photograph it. That's all right ain' it?'

Sadie looked across. 'Yeah, that's fine. Just be careful of it. You 'elp 'er will you?'

∾

THE WEDDING WAS due to start at one pm, and when, at twelve-thirty, the skies opened and rain came tumbling down, Tassie feared for the confrontation that would probably be happening between Christopher and the dove man. She'd seen the wedding planner a few times that morning, looking more and more frazzled each time she'd passed him, the damp pages on his clipboard curling.

Standing in the entrance lobby, Tassie took some last photos of Sadie as she walked along the balcony before descending the stairs. Her curled hair was now littered with diamanté butterflies, the skirts of her dress were at least two metres wide and her deeply tanned body was covered in a dust of glitter. She looked, Tassie searched for the words, like a drag queen fairy. Rather wonderful, really.

After dashing to her car, Tassie drove to the church, now buzzing with guests scurrying or tottering through the rain, their Subaro Imprezas and Range Rovers in danger of blocking the narrow country road; fat tyres cutting into the sodden grass verges.

Walking down the path, clasping her cameras under a large umbrella, around the corner from the church entrance she saw Christopher and the dove man having a heated debate, protected from the downpour by a makeshift tarpaulin shelter. Dove Man was waving his hands around, a half-burnt cigarette in one of them. Christopher saw her and said something to the man, who nodded, frowning.

When the planner reached her, his face was bright red, his tie askew. 'I am having the worst goddam awful day. The woman's a nightmare.'

'Why?' Although Tassie already knew some of the answers.

'She's bloody insisting the doves still get let out. Even though the weather's shit and the man said it can't be done.'

Tassie looked around. 'So where are they?'

'They're inside the church, well, fifty of them – it was meant to be a hundred but we both said, no way.'

'Still, fifty doves? That's so many?' Tassie glanced inside.

'I know. They were meant to be released outside but the rain stopped that. So now they're up by the altar – let's just hope the bloody bride can't count. Apparently, they're the type that can be released inside, although he was reluctant with so many of them. Still, he says as long as the doors are open they'll pretty much fly straight out. Let's bloody hope so.'

'And will they be OK outside, in this?'

Christopher grimaced. 'I guess. The man eventually agreed to do it, but only after I offered to pay him another five hundred quid. Cash. I don't think they're actually his birds. He changed his tune about doing it soon enough after I offered him the money.'

Tassie grinned as she walked into the church. The bride might be hard work, but the wedding was very photogenic. She looked towards the altar, where the baskets were lined up under the church's surprisingly big dome, hoping the birds would be safe.

Five minutes later she was back outside, watching a white Mercedes pull up. A young man in a white suit emerged, his dark hair slicked back, skin as tanned as Sadie's.

Dev Stavos.

The driver ran round to him, holding an umbrella over his head as Dev straightened his tie, buttoned his jacket, braced his shoulders then strode towards the church. Tassie took some photos of him coming down the path. His best man, also in a white suit but much chubbier, was running to catch up.

'All right?' Dev grinned at her. 'Shit, hang on.' He turned and spat a piece of chewing gum onto the grass.

Tassie grimaced.

'You taking the photos then?'

'Yes, that's right.'

'Well, you make sure you get as many of me as you do of the missus. Can't 'ave 'er upstaging me.'

He winked, and Tassie instantly liked him even less than she did his bride. Despite the gum he'd been chewing, his breath smelt of alcohol and cigarettes – and not in a sexy kind of way.

'I'll be sure to do that. I love what you've done with the flowers in the church,' she said, politely.

'Woman's work that, ain't got a fuckin' clue what to expect. Not even seen the church yet. Been too busy, ya know.'

By the time Sadie was due to arrive, all the guests were noisily congregating, rearranging hats and hair, their voices loud and shrill as they greeted each other. There were a few minor celebrities, as well as the family contingent; although it was the latter who'd really gone to town on their attire: each suit louder, each tan deeper, each hairstyle more elaborately coiffured than the last.

Watching him standing at the altar, Tassie saw that Dev was chewing on a fresh piece of gum. She frowned, wondering how he'd get rid of that one.

There was a general murmur and Tassie turned to see Sadie's Rolls-Royce pulling up. She glanced at Dev, who looked distinctly underwhelmed by the imminent arrival of his beloved. As she turned to speed down the aisle to get some shots he was still lazily chewing.

The service was as short and secular as a church will allow. Throughout it Tassie could see Christopher and the dove man talking, the latter frequently peering up at the stained-glass windows. The weather had worsened and now the occasional grumble of thunder could be heard.

When the couple returned from signing the register, the vicar addressed the congregation. 'May I be the first to give my congratulations to the happy couple, Mr and Mrs Stavos.' The audience whooped and clapped, phone cameras flashing. He put his hands up to quieten things. 'Please wait, while they make their way out of the church, but first...'

He glanced up as another rumble of thunder trundled across the roof, then anxiously to the side, where Dove Man was busy opening the baskets. At the same moment Tassie noticed Sadie looking at a young girl sitting in the front pew, a huge ghetto blaster now propped up in front of her. She watched as Sadie nodded to the girl, who pressed a button.

Then everything happened so fast.

The first notes of Beyoncé's 'Crazy in Love' blasted through the air, just as a clap of thunder detonated above. Then, five bridesmaids stood up, waving their hands in choreographed unison as fifty doves shot out of their baskets, before – instead of leaving in an orderly queue through the open doors – flying around the church in crazy zigzags.

And *then* it was chaos. Pure, glorious chaos. Birds everywhere, poo everywhere – including on the guests – until, the *pièce de résistance*, a dove took a low flight over Sadie's head and got entangled in her hair.

Sadie screamed, swiping at the bird as it flapped wildly. Meanwhile, the ghetto blaster crashed to the ground but still carried on playing – Beyoncé now belting out 'Love on Top'. Three of the bridesmaids rushed to try and help the bride, all screeching while battling against Dove Man, who was apoplectic with rage as he tried to stop everyone hitting his birds.

And Tassie?

Tassie was busy taking photos.

Eventually someone turned the music off and a sort of calm settled. Some of the doves had flown out of the doors, and those that were left had found various perches. By the time the dove man had managed to release his bird from Sadie's hair it was a toss-up as to who was more damaged. Although, when Tassie saw the bird flapping its wings then settling into the man's hands, she suspected it was the bride who would take more recovery work.

Sadie was panting heavily, her eye makeup smudged down her cheeks as her new husband tried his best to calm her, no doubt reminding her of their public image. Her hair was hanging in stiff shards around her shoulders and Tassie could see spots of white on her dress. This wasn't going to be good.

The vicar returned to the front, nervously looking above him before he spoke. When he did, his voice shook.

'Well, I think we can say that the service has now ended. So if you'd like to *calmly* make your way through the doors, perhaps that's the best way of ensuring the safety of any remaining birds. The groom has asked that you then make your way to the manor, where he and,' – he glanced at the couple – 'his beautiful bride will see you soon.'

It took about an hour to get Sadie re-assembled, during which time Tassie thought it best she make herself scarce.

Slowly, she moved around the guests gathered in the large ballroom. The room was alive with laughter, disbelief and loud exclamations, the air thick with expletives. Dev was receiving lots of sympathy, along with an equal amount of alcohol, and Tassie could see he was loving the attention, particularly evident each time he posed for her camera – always quickly turning to show his 'best side, mate'.

Eventually Sadie appeared in the doorway. When she saw Tassie, she beckoned her over, smiling broadly. 'What a fuckin' nightmare, but this is me big day innit, so let's get it back on.'

Tassie looked at her with newfound admiration. Apart from one small scratch on her forehead, you'd never know that Sadie had been grappling with a terrified bird. Her hair was back in perfect formation and even the spots on her dress had disappeared.

She had to give her credit for being a tough one.

'Right. So shall we start with just Dev and me? Then the families – let's hope they're not all plastered by now. And let's make it as quick as possible. I'm fuckin' starving.'

All through the meal and even the speeches, Sadie continued to fire instructions at Tassie. By seven-thirty, sitting on a chair at the edge of the room scrolling through her shots, she was exhausted, having not sat down once all day.

'I think that you will want this?' A hand holding a plate of food appeared in front of her. Tassie looked up. The hand belonged to a man whose accent was heavy and, looking at his face, possibly Italian.

'Thank you. How did you know?'

'I have been watching you working, I thought that you could not have eaten.'

'Actually I haven't. Thank you.' She took the fork he was holding out. The food was lukewarm, but that was OK. She was hungry. 'This isn't what they had at lunch?'

The man smiled, blue eyes bright above an immaculate beard, cut close to his angular jaw and speckled with white and grey.

'No, I got it from the kitchens for you.'

Tassie was surprised. 'Thank you. That's so kind.'

'Would you like a drink to go with it?'

'Not now, I've not finished my shift yet. But...' She looked towards the bar. 'Maybe later? I'm due to stop working at nine.'

''Is a date, I'll come and find you. *Arrivederci, signorina.*' The man nodded, his eyes warm and encouraging.

Tassie pierced a sausage, watching him walk away. Maybe the day was looking up. She chewed on the meat, which was as bland as the pale pink skin it was wrapped in. The man was now chatting to a younger man, both laughing as they talked. He glanced over at her and smiled.

It was a long time since she'd had any kind of flirtation like this promised to be. For a while she tracked him, moving around the room, chatting to various guests.

It was five months since she'd last seen Dan.

She sighed, twisting some shredded carrot onto her fork. She still missed him. Even searched his name sometimes to see if anything came up. Although nothing ever did: just the details of his cider farm and the same photo of him and Horse Woman, standing in front of the café, each holding a box of apples.

She brought up a photo on her phone, the one she'd taken of him sitting in the pink Nissan. As she ate, she thought back over their time together: sitting by the side of the bank, failing to catch a fish; riding Teela up the mountain; dancing at the ceilidh; the inn, the fire, the ca—

She speared another sausage. *Stop it, girl. It's over. You fucked it. He's not coming back and you need to forget him.* The sausage rolled away from her fork and she speared again, trying to make herself think about Dan and Horse Woman. *Dancing at their wedding. Making bloody cider.*

Shaking her head, she dropped her fork onto the plate. He'd told her he loved her. And she'd... what, fallen in love with him? And yet... What if it was her? What if she couldn't love? Really love. Or she could only love a fantasy – bloody

Alex. But not the real thing, when it was there in front of her.

And I love you too.

Why hadn't she been able to say it? Was she even able to love in that way? Unreservedly, with every part of her being? If she'd said it, at that crucial moment, and really meant it, would he not have walked away?

She breathed in, concerned by how she shook as her brow contracted. Now was not the time for emotion.

When she looked up, the Italian was smiling across at her. He raised his hand, then pretended to look pained, rubbing his stomach to indicate she should eat.

So she ate. The food sticking in her throat.

Maybe she *had* loved Dan. But did she still? Could she, after knowing him for such a short time? Come on Tassie, move on. Now he too was a fantasy, and she knew what became of them. *Eat up. Even if the food's disgusting. Move on with reality.*

Breathing in even more deeply, she bought the phone to her lips, touched the image briefly, then deleted it.

AT PRECISELY NINE O'CLOCK, Smiley Eyes was back at her side, a glass of Prosecco in each hand.

She took one of them. 'How did you know I'd like Prosecco?'

'Everyone likes Prosecco. 'Is Italian.' His eyes creased as he clinked glasses with her. 'Marco Mancini. My pleasure to meet you.'

'Tassie. Nice to meet you too.'

The dance floor was packed and the music loud, so they went and stood by the windows in the ante chamber where it was marginally quieter. It was still raining, but not as hard as before, beads dripping down the ceiling-height windows.

'So, how do you know the couple?'

Marco paused. 'Dev, he's my cousin.'

'Really?' Tassie was confused. 'I thought his family were Greek.'

The man skipped a beat, then smiled. 'They are. But we can still be cousins – distant cousins, granted. The European Union is thriving, you know.'

Tassie laughed. 'Sorry. Yes. Of course you can. And what do you do?'

'I am a stockbroker.'

'Oh,' Tassie sipped her drink. 'You don't look like one.'

'And what does a stockbroker look like, Tassie Morris?'

Briefly, she wondered how he knew her surname, then she laughed. 'I have absolutely no idea. Where do you work? In the City?'

'Yes, but let's not talk about it – my work is as dull as it sounds. Tell me about you. How has your day been? You must have some fabulous shots. I am a bit of an amateur photographer myself.'

Tassie glanced at her camera. There were some incredible shots from the church – she'd eagerly checked them as soon as she'd got back to the manor. Not that they would ever see the light of day. 'I did get some good ones. It was quite a scene wasn't it?'

'Sadly I arrived after the service. I had a few problems with my car. But tell me all about it; I have heard it was dramatic.'

They chatted for a while – Tassie revelling in telling him every gory detail about the church service – then shared a couple of dances before Christopher took over the DJ's mike to announce that the bride and groom were about to make their departure.

Outside, the courtyard was flooded with light and there were some paparazzi waiting in front of the entrance. Tassie was still surprised there hadn't been any outside the church after the service – they'd missed a great opportunity.

Looking at Sadie and Dev beaming professionally for the cameras, she wondered whether they'd informed the press themselves, for they certainly didn't look averse to having their photos taken. Sadie had changed into a skin-tight dress and chandelier crystal earrings, stilettoes and a fake-fur coat. Dev was in a dark jacket, white shirt and jeans. When asked to kiss for the cameras they happily obliged.

She hoped he'd removed his gum.

'The happy couple.' Once again Marco was at her side, now carrying a bottle of Prosecco and two glasses. 'Things seem to be closing. I have a room booked in the hotel. Perhaps you'd care to join me for a nightcap?'

Tassie turned and looked at him. His hair curled pleasingly around his ears, his shoulders didn't slope, and she guessed there would be a great chest under his fine cotton shirt. Desire stirring within her, she automatically moved to trace a finger down the lapel of his jacket.

Then stopped.

'I'm not sure that's a good idea.'

He took a step closer, and she could smell cigarette smoke on his breath as his eyes bore into hers.

'Of course. I am sorry to have asked. How about a drink in the lounge?'

She looked at her watch, and shrugged. It was either that, or back to her soulless motel room and another lonely night.

∽

'Would you like anything else, sir? The bar is about to close.' The woman looked tired as she held out the menu. It had been a busy evening for the bar staff.

Marco looked at Tassie, who was curled in the corner of the sofa, her shoes kicked off, legs tucked under her knife-pleated skirt, an empty glass in her hand.

'Why not.' She smiled at him, feeling as relaxed as she knew she looked.

For the last hour they'd been chatting, and she'd been surprised by how much she was enjoying it. For a stock-broker he knew a lot about photography – including her previous work, which he'd been most complimentary about. They'd avoided much personal conversation, but he'd been to many of the countries she loved and was funny and charming, telling her stories of his childhood, growing up in the rough streets of Naples.

'What would you like, *signorina*?' His rolled 'r' was delicious. 'Something warming for the end of the night?'

Tassie stared at him. She'd already had far too much alcohol to drive, and, let's face it, for a while had known that with every sip, the devil took one step closer. The waitress was looking at her, her eyebrows slightly raised.

'I'll have a Cointreau please, with ice.' And she shifted further back into the cushions, fanning her hair out over the edge of the sofa.

'The perfect choice.' Marco looked up at the woman and the corners of his mouth curved. 'Perhaps you might leave us the bottle and I will settle up in the morning?' He gave a tiny wink. 'I'll pay for a whole one.'

The waitress attempted a smile. 'I'll make a note of it, thank you, sir, madam.'

The way she looked at them made Tassie think of Syd for a brief second.

But Syd wasn't there.

It was just her, and a very attractive man. Slowly, she stretched a foot towards Marco's hand, resting on the edge of the sofa.

WOKEN BY A SHAFT OF SUNLIGHT, when Tassie cautiously opened her eyes the first thing she saw was the empty Cointreau bottle. She groaned and, turning over, put her arm out, expecting to find Marco lying beside her. But the bed was empty and the bathroom door was shut.

She stretched out her legs, pointing then flexing her feet. It had been a good night. A very good night. Although, there'd been a moment at the start when she'd stalled and almost left the room, called a cab. Suddenly semi-naked with a man she didn't know, things hadn't felt at all right. His curves, his smell, the way he kissed her – hard, pushing her against the door as soon as they entered the room.

At that moment she'd pulled away, gone into the bathroom, looked at herself in the mirror, her hair dishevelled, distress in her eyes. But when she'd come out, still half-dressed, the bathroom robe now wrapped around her, he'd understood her change in mood, and had sat on the edge of the bed, motioning to her to join him. And he'd talked, soothed, shared the story of a lost love, as she'd shared brief details of hers; then he'd stroked her back, her hair, her mouth, until, finally, her loneliness had outstripped the doubt.

And after that things had been fine, more than fine. His chest hadn't disappointed, and neither had the rest of him; his skin was smooth and tanned, his hands adept at giving pleasure. And even if it was different, even if he wasn't Dan, he was... nice.

She sat up, smiling, then put her hand up to her head,

inhaling deeply – it was a while since she'd felt this fragile. Breakfast was what was needed. Perhaps they could order room service, maybe go for a walk later, depending on the weather.

She reached down to her bag and started taking out her phone. Then she froze. Beside her bag she saw her camera, which was where she'd left it the previous night. Except, now, the small cover on the side was open and – she jumped out of bed and crouched down beside it – the memory card had been removed.

Her mouth dry, she ran to the bathroom, yanking the door open. The room was empty: nothing but shiny white tiles and neatly folded bath linen. Racing around she could find no sign of Marco ever having existed; until, on the table by the window, she saw a silver tray. On it was a single rose in a crystal glass and, she gasped, her memory card on top of a folded note.

Her hands shaking, she opened it. It was a piece of hotel stationery and contained just one word: *Scusa.* A business card had fallen out and was lying on the table. She picked it up and sank into a chair. *Marco Mancini, Freelance Journalist and Photographer.* Grabbing her phone, she rang the mobile number. Marco's smooth, deep voice soon filled her ear: a voice that last night she'd found so attractive and now just made her feel sick.

'You have reached Marco. Just leave me a message or send me a text. *Ciao.*'

She cut the call then phoned Syd. A muffled voice answered on the third ring. 'Tass? Why you calling so early? Is everything OK? It's only... seven thirty.'

'Syd, no it's not. It's really fucking not OK. I think there's a nightmare about to happen and I can't do anything to stop it. Oh God, hang on—' She lurched into the bathroom and vomited into the sink.

IN THE END it was even worse than she'd imagined – and Syd had been furious enough with her before the story broke. By the next morning her photos (credited with her name) were on the front pages of virtually every tabloid. Most had gone with the shots of Sadie screaming, the dove's wings flapping around her head, but one paper devoted the entire front cover to one of the shots Tassie had taken right at the beginning: Sadie and her bridesmaids, semi-naked in the honeymoon suite. Tassie had to admit that from a professional perspective it was a stunning photo. And probably the one that got her fired.

Catrina was white with anger when she called Tassie into the office. Apparently, Sadie's management was threatening to sue for breach of contract, taking photos without permission and generally inflicting such damage on their client that she was already considering divorce.

'There is a chance this will be the end of the magazine.' Catrina's voice was tight and low. 'I cannot think what you were doing, taking the photos you did. They were always going to be dynamite.'

The discussion had been short and very sour. Tassie was to relinquish all rights to the photos – and any she'd taken for the magazine previously – and never set foot in the building again. As she walked out of Catrina's office, Syd didn't look at her.

Once outside her phone pinged and Tassie opened it, hoping it was Syd. Her best friend. Who hadn't spoken to her for more than twenty-four hours. But it wasn't. It was from one of her private clients, saying that in view of all the publicity surrounding Sadie Manchester, she was sure Tassie would understand why she was cancelling her doing the photography at her wedding.

21

---

ondon, March 2015

It took six days and five hours for Syd to forgive Tassie, after which they were fine again, Syd back to her usual barrage of texts and voicemails, checking Tassie was OK.

When they'd finally spoken, Tassie had been horrified to learn that Catrina had been so angry that Syd's job had been on the line for a while – even though she'd had nothing to do with the fiasco. Which only added to Tassie's already pretty immobilising feelings of guilt and misery.

Fairly quickly she'd lost most of her wedding clients – many making it clear why they were cancelling, a few fluffing other excuses – and all she had lined up now was a few product shoots, which wouldn't be enough to pay the mortgage. But she simply didn't have the heart to start traipsing the streets looking for work – particularly as her name was now notorious.

Marco *Slimeball Dirtheart Twisted Soul* Mancini (just some of Syd's names for him) had tried to contact her a few days after the event, although obviously she'd never returned his calls and had considered suing him for theft.

But, she reasoned, then everyone would find out exactly how he'd acquired the photos, and even now there was a part of her that really didn't want to risk Dan reading about it.

A few days later, when a cheque for £5,000 dropped onto her doormat she'd been incredulous. There was a note. *Best day of my career you turned out to be (and night too). Thought you were probably owed this.* Reading it she'd felt sick, violated, and had instantly taken the cheque into the garden, got a match and watched it burn in a flowerpot.

Now, however, watching her bank balance dwindle there was a part of her that wished she hadn't been so hasty.

She looked at the clock on her kitchen wall. Syd would be here soon, but she still had time to phone her mother. She'd been trying to call her once a week – doing her tiny bit to lighten the load for her brother – but this call was going to be even harder than usual.

'Hello, Sybil Morris.'

'Hi Mum, it's Tassie.'

'Victoria. I'd been wondering when you'd call. How are you?' There was a slight pause. 'I've been worried about you. Although I haven't got long to speak, I need to go and see a new poodle. But, Tom's told me your news. As did Mrs Rushgrove *and* the woman in the local Co-op.'

Her mother's sigh was audible.

'What on earth have you been up to? I saw the photos. What an odd crowd you seem to be mixed up with.'

Tassie almost laughed. 'It's not my crowd, Mum, I just photograph them.' She wanted to say how *her* crowd were friends her mum had never met, or clients like Carlos and Clarissa, but instead she bit her lip. The image of them still caught her. 'How's the farm? How's the land sale coming on?'

'Well, we finally seem to have things sorted on that front,

I think it might be only a couple of months now, which I must say will be a big relief. It still leaves me with all the barns and a few acres, but between me and your brother we'll probably just about manage.'

'Mum... I could come home you know. Come and help out. I've not got much work on at the moment.'

There was another pause – even longer this time. 'Well, we're probably OK, but... If you need to come home, because of... well, how things are with you, you'd be very welcome. What I mean is, if you need any help, you must let me know.'

Tassie looked at the photograph of her father, feeling the ache of his absence. 'No, I'm fine thanks. It's just a slow patch with work. I'm sure it will soon pick up.'

'Well, if you're sure.'

Tassie was certain she could hear relief in her mother's voice.

'And... Do try to be more careful, Victoria. I'd hoped that by now you'd be more settled, and I'm worried that you're not. Anyway, as I said, if you'd like to visit for a while, the offer is there.'

'Thanks, Mum. Listen, one of my friends will be here any moment so I need to go.'

'Yes. And I must get ready to go out. Bye, dear.'

'Bye.'

Tassie barely had time to consider her mother's surprising offer before her doorbell rang.

Syd was standing on the step, her arms full of balloons, roses and a bottle of champagne. She grinned. 'I thought I'd set the scene as best as I can.'

'For me?' Tassie was confused.

'No, you wazza. The boys. Remember? That's why I'm here?'

'Oh God, I actually forgot. I've just had the weirdest

conversation with my mother. Although a nice one. Come in, what time is it? How long have we got?'

~

AT PRECISELY SIX-THIRTY, Tassie's computer began singing the Skype melody and, champagne in their hands and balloons and roses all around them, Tassie clicked *Accept*.

Oliver and Tilak's beaming faces filled the screen, then it was just Oliver's.

'OK, so we've had to do a lot of persuading, but they've agreed that we can prop the phone up on the table, so hopefully you can see all of it. Strangely enough they wouldn't let you be witnesses though, so...'

The view segued into a white and gold-leaf ceiling, then something that looked like a small arrivals board. Next, two unfamiliar faces appeared: an old man, his face eclipsed by a thick white beard, and a woman looking remarkably like an overripe peach – soft, rosy cheeks and a tiny nose.

Then it was back to Oliver.

'That's Dorothy and Dexter, who have kindly agreed to be our witnesses.'

'Who?' Tassie and Syd spoke in unison.

'People who love pancakes.'

Agreement could be heard stage-left. 'Oh yes, we sure do.'

'Specially with bacon grease and sugar.'

Oliver grinned. 'We met them in a diner just along from City Hall, eating said pancakes. Asked them if they'd do it, the witness thing.'

'And we sure said yes. Love a romance, we do. Or is a bromance, Dex?' This time it was the woman's voice.

Oliver laughed, his face filling the screen. 'Dex is shrugging his shoulders. Anyway, we're about to go in – are you ready, ladies?'

Tassie and Syd put their thumbs up. 'We are.'

'Dorothy, Dexter?'

'Just lead the way.'

'Then, Tilakaratne, husband to be, love of my life, shall we go?'

IT WASN'T the greatest way of appreciating a wedding – even one beamed from New York's City Hall.

Oliver had little time to position his phone, so Tassie and Syd couldn't see much. But they heard everything, and that was enough.

By the end of the short ceremony they were both snivelling. And when the broad New York accent announced that the men were now husband and husband, Tassie and Syd's cheers were loud enough that the people there all began to laugh.

Shortly afterwards, Oliver was allowed to pick up his phone and he introduced them to the registrar, a smiley man with a thick black moustache, then again to Dorothy and Dexter, and finally to Tilak, caught wiping a couple of tears away. Everyone was smiling. But no-one more broadly than Oliver.

≈

'So, THAT WAS… DIFFERENT.' Syd wiped her mouth with a dainty hanky.

'It was. But fun. Wow, I can't believe they're actually married. It's a shame we couldn't afford to go, but still, we were there, sort of.'

Tassie had cooked lamb shanks, which they were eating

by candlelight in the kitchen. 'I thought I'd carry on with the romance theme, even if the boys aren't here,' she'd said as she served it up.

As they ate, they touched on the subject of the 'Dove Disaster', although it was a topic they both preferred to forget. Syd was amazed when Tassie told her about the cheque, and horrified when she said she'd burnt it.

'But you need the money? And even if you didn't keep it you could have given it to charity or something?'

Tassie nodded. 'I know, I had all those thoughts... afterwards. But honestly, Syd, I felt sick when I saw it. It was such a dreadful experience, in so many ways. I felt so stupid as well, and...' She paused, her fork mid-air. 'Do you know, for the first time in my life I felt really, really cheap – as my mother would say. Before, you know, the men, the one-night stands... I thought I was fine with it, because it was all on my terms. And I didn't think I wanted anything else. But something's changed. I've changed. And now that life's not for me.'

Syd lifted her glass, grinning. 'Well, here's to no more one-night stands.' She took a sip. 'And thank God for that.'

They ate silently, until Syd looked up. 'And? Any news?'

Tassie shook her head. 'Definitely dead and buried.' She frowned. 'He's probably married by now, it's been what, six months? I reckon Charlotte wouldn't have wanted to wait long before she got her claws fully embedded.'

She looked over at a tea towel hanging by the sink, the corncrake just visible. 'It's fine though. If he was willing to get engaged to someone else so quickly, maybe I was wrong about it anyway.'

Syd shook her head. 'Somehow I don't think so. I read your email. And I thought Sophie and Tom loved him when they met?'

Tassie nodded. 'They did.' She looked away, pulling

down on her top lip. Then she looked back and shrugged. 'I just have to find a new way of living in the moment, don't I?'

'And Awful Alex?'

Now she blushed. After some typically ruthless quizzing she'd told Syd the whole story, which hadn't been comfortable telling. 'Not heard from him either. Not that I expected to.' She took a sip of the surprisingly good champagne Syd had brought – she normally turned up with cheap sweet wine. 'That's the thing that hurts most.'

'What, the fact you kept him secret from me?'

'No. All those years I wasted. I was convinced, *convinced*, that he was the only one. I had him up on a pedestal for so long, and yet I'm not even sure I ever saw the real him. Well, maybe when we were teenagers, but not the years after that. God, Syd, you'd hate him.'

Syd nodded. 'From what you've said, I'm sure I would. I still can't believe you never told me about him. And if I'm honest, I still don't really understand it.' She shrugged. 'But who knows why we do the things we do.'

Tassie pushed a piece of meat around her plate, wondering if she should tell Syd about what the reverend had said about her mother. But she'd not resolved that either, so really, what was the point of bringing it up?

'OK, moving on.' Syd took a sip of champagne – she'd made an exception for Oliver's wedding. 'Work. Life as you're going to live it. What are you going to do?'

Tassie's shoulders slumped. 'Dunno. It's all a complete mess. I've got barely any jobs lined up, my name's mud and I'm wondering how long I'll be able to pay the mortgage. I've been considering renting out the flat; but who'd take the garden on? I'm terrified they'd just let it go to seed.' Her short laugh held no mirth. 'D'you know, my mother actually offered to help me today – a first. And I'm scared I might have to take her up on it. How humiliating, having to slink home at nearly thirty-three. Maybe I should get work in a bar or something.'

Syd undid her knotted mass of curls, shook them out, then twisted her hair back up again. 'Tass, I've got a proposal.'

'Really? I'd have thought you'd learnt your lesson about finding me jobs.'

'It's not about a job, it's about the flat.'

'The flat? My flat? Here?'

'Aye.' Syd coughed. 'I'd, *we'd* like to rent it.'

'What, you and Stan?'

'Yes.'

'But—'

'I know what you're going to say. Politely – or not, looking at your face. That we couldn't afford it. But... the thing is Tass, we can. As of last week.'

'How?'

'Well, Stan loved staying last year, loved your garden and has now decided he wants something like it himself. But I've said he needs to prove it's not just a one-off, that he'll stick to it.'

'I'm still wondering?'

'Right. OK. Well, the thing is...' Syd couldn't keep the pride out of her face. 'He has a job.'

'A new job?'

'Aye. But a proper one. A really proper one. Like, with a proper salary.'

'Oh my God. He actually does? I thought he'd always refused to even look?'

'Well, that's the thing. He didn't actually try. It was someone he was at Oxford with.'

'I always forget he went to Oxford.' Tassie chuckled. 'No offence.'

'None taken, I know exactly what you mean. This guy,

Mark, has his own company which has been given some massive investment. And he and Stan got talking one day and Stan told him all about his spoon. And... well, amazingly Mark thinks it's genius. Has offered to buy the patent off him but also give him a full-time job, with a champion salary. More than double what I earn.'

'So you mean, Stan's now going to get *paid* to invent things?'

'Exactly. And I tell you what, he's in heaven. He's already started – working in some trendy warehouse on the river – and the first day he came home, cock-a-hoop, saying he'd found his tribe.'

'Oh wow, Syd, that's fantastic. And all because of a spoon?'

'Well, not any spoon. It's a self-correcting electric smart spoon that doesn't wobble or tip.'

'So you can feed yourself?' Tassie instantly understood.

Syd paused, her face serious. 'Aye. Because of his mum. He's always said that the thing she hated most when her Parkinson's got really bad was having to be fed.'

'Oh Syd, that's wonderful. She'd be so proud of him.'

Syd smiled. 'I know. She would.'

AFTER SYD HAD LEFT, as Tassie was doing the washing up she thought about Syd's offer, as well as all the life changes her friends were going through. She and Stan were married, and he had a proper job. Oliver and Tilak were now married too. She was the only one who had nothing going right in her life.

She poured herself a glass of Stan's cider – which was pretty good for a first effort – then went through to the living room. But, scrolling through the TV stations, she could find nothing to amuse herself, late on a Saturday night.

22

————

It was just before ten on the Monday morning when Tassie woke up. She lay on her side, curling up her legs, thinking about the day ahead. A day filled with nothing. Just like the previous day had had little in it either. What about Syd's idea? Perhaps she should rent to them? It would be less dramatic than selling; and less painful – for selling would feel like total defeat. She heard the post hit the mat in the living room and got out of bed.

Just as she was bending down there was a knock that made her jump. For a few seconds she felt ridiculously hopeful, but when she opened the door it was just the postman holding a parcel.

'Can you sign please?'

Tassie took the package, signing an unintelligible scribble on the device he held out. 'Thanks.'

Walking back into her bedroom, she shivered. The heating went off at eight-thirty so she decided it would be warmest if she went back to bed. The package had her mother's writing on the front and, she turned it over, the farm's return address written in sloping letters on the back.

Climbing into bed she pulled the duvet around her then unwrapped the brown string and paper. There was a letter and three thin books. She opened the letter first.

Dear Victoria

I have spent a long time thinking about things since your last visit. As you know, I am very worried about the direction your life is taking at the moment, and in all honesty I have been worried for a while now.

Irritation burned her neck.

As you also know, I am not a great believer in harking back to the past. However, it does seem to be something about which you feel strongly. And the fact that your dear father wanted me to tell you is something that, after much thought, I have decided I cannot ignore.

However, and I am sorry for this, the past, my past, is something that I'm afraid I simply cannot, will not talk about. A long time ago I decided I never would again, and it is a promise that I must keep. So instead I am sending you my journals. Perhaps once you've read them you'll understand why some things are better left unsaid.

I love you, Victoria—

Tassie gulped, then read the words again, tracing the ink with her finger.

I love you, Victoria. I might not always be able to show it, but I do. Again, once you've read the enclosed, I think you will understand how very hard I fought to have you. Perhaps it was a battle that in the end proved too difficult not to have left its scars. And, having given careful thought to what you said, perhaps yours and my relationship has suffered, what do they call it, the fall-out from it?

This won't be making any sense, so I would urge that you read the diaries. I am sending them to you in the strictest of confidence (but also with a touch of humility, for sending them brings to mind another occasion. And for that, I am sorry, and will admit it's worried me ever since. Sometimes as parents we do things that we regret, and that was one of them).

Tassie looked up. She knew exactly what her mother was referring to, but wouldn't have expected her to have remembered, let alone apologise for it so many years later.

I would only ask that, once you've read them, you return them and not mention the contents to anyone. Not even Tom. I would also ask that when I die they are burned. There are people around here who still remember the time only too well, and it is something I have tried so very hard to forget.

Mum

Tassie sat on the bed, staring at the letter in disbelief. It was the longest, most open communication she'd ever received from her mother. And the first time she'd been told the words, *I love you.* She got out of bed and walked over to the window.

Looking out at the garden, she tutted. It was looking very sorry for itself. That's what she should be doing at the moment: preparing it for the summer. There was a lot that should be going in now – beetroot, carrots, Swiss chard, to name just three. She'd have to teach Stan all about the different stages of the year.

Eventually she looked back at the bed, and the three thin books lying on it. She had no idea what would be in them and, now that she could finally find out what had happened, she wasn't sure she wanted to know.

She went into the kitchen and made herself a cup of tea – putting sugar in it even though she never usually did. Then she sat cross-legged on the bed and wrapped a grey woollen throw around her shoulders.

The books were A5 in size, all the same light grey, the edges tatty and frayed. She picked up the first and opened it. The paper was thin, yellowing at the edges, and the words *Felton Hall Hospital* were stamped on the inside front cover.

She flicked through the pages, covered in her mother's sloping writing. The other books were just as filled in, all with the same name printed on the inside.

Retrieving her laptop from the floor she opened up her search box. The first page that came up was headed *BBC Domesday Reloaded* and she scrolled down. *This residential psychiatric hospital, centred on a Georgian mansion and park, is involved in a...'*

She leafed again through the pages. Did her mother work there? If so in what capacity?

Come on. That wasn't it.

Picking up each journal, she scanned the pages for dates. Within seconds she'd found the book with the earliest entry and took a sharp intake of breath. July 1982. Three months after she'd been born.

Then, her heart pounding, she started to read.

... BANG! Is that what they want me to write? The doctors who've given me this diary, telling me it will help. What, like taking me away from my baby has also helped? My baby. My beautiful newborn who I've been trying so very hard to bring into being. For YEARS. But I didn't even manage that properly,

did I? For even as one life emerged, death still crept in and stole its twin.

Her heartbeat quickened.

Will they read this? Those oh so concerned doctors. If so then I'll write what they want to hear. That yes, I took Alfred's gun. Took it from the cupboard. And yes, I sat with it across my lap. But I would NEVER, NEVER, NEVER have used it. I WOULD NOT. Because of my baby. My beautiful little girl. Victoria.

Do you know why I chose that name? Because of Queen Victoria. I knew, you see, knew that this baby, this tiny miracle, who survived when none of the others did, was going to be strong, tough, beautiful – like a queen. And so I called her Victoria. Alfred didn't want to, I think. But he wasn't going to say no. He was as delighted as me. Back then, when she first appeared in our lives. When everything was perfect. For a while. Until *&*Sd*–

Something had been scratched out.

But she remains. My beautiful, perfect, healthy Victoria Queen.

Tassie could barely breathe as she read on through pages of tightly crammed words.

... Today's question was a classic. 'How did it feel, Mrs Morris, to lose your babies?' How did it feel? HOW DID IT FEEL? HOW DOES IT FEEL? STILL? EVERY SINGLE DAY???? Let me tell you, dear diary, how it felt. Each time I opened my legs and a dead baby fell out, it felt like my heart was being ripped out with it. And what's a body, I ask you, without a heart or a soul? It's the living dead. That's what it is. And that's what I've become.

The first, second, even third time I still felt the elation of being pregnant. But the fourth, fifth – I dreaded each day that came. Knowing that each could be the day when the thing that pulled the life out of my babies would also pull the life out of me.

At least the question was asked with more care than that nurse. That bloody nurse. Three times she was there when I went in. Three times she said, 'It's nature's way, dear.' I swear, the third time I thought I'd kill her. 'Sorry, it's nature's way, dear.' That's what I would have told her as she went puce, my hands around her throat.

Tassie read faster and faster. Pain and despair imprinted every page.

... It was better when they were taken earlier. The ones that just slipped out at home, the smallest, flushed away with the bloodied paper I wiped myself with. Although not always. Shall I tell you what a baby looks like at twelve weeks? It looks like... a baby. He was a marvel. With perfectly formed fingers and toes. Completely identifiable ears, nose and mouth. Baby three. They just took him away after that. I've often wondered what they did with him.

... I hate the bloody music they play in here. I think it's meant to soothe us. I hate it.

A few months later:

... They've said I should remember, that it's bad to suppress. So, let's write it all down then shall we?

No. 1: lost at six weeks

No.2: lost at four weeks.

No 3: ~~born~~ lost at twelve weeks

No 4: born dead

No 5: I don't even know what to say. We buried her on top of the hill. Sometimes I think I see her.

Tassie gasped.

... I need no more than this for my memories to flourish, or is it fester? I remember everything: the pools of blood, the jellied, scarlet bits of liver, the excruciating pain. The emptiness. I remember it all, and I don't want to remember anything.

... Last night I dreamt they couldn't hear the baby's heart. I woke up screaming.

... The rage I feel at women smugly pushing their prams around the village. Like some kind of pack.

... Holding your foetus is more than holding death. It's the deletion of life itself.

... Alfred came today. Alone. He brought oxeye daisies — a huge bunch of them. I hate being reminded of the seasons blossoming, life moving on for everyone else. My baby growing every day. Victoria. Beautiful strong, miracle Victoria. Who I've not seen for five weeks. My choice, for I've seen how it stresses her to come here. How I stress her. Grieving still for her sister.

So, finally, she knew. Everything. Tassie clasped the diary to her chest. Three times, she'd seen her. Eyes welling, but her mind full of light, she carried on.

Not knowing how to be. So I told him to come alone. And he did.

By the third journal, the tone had begun to change, and by the end Tassie was reading a person who sounded more like her mother. Controlled. Restrained. As she read, it was like she could see the emotional barriers going up. Until the last entry, dated January 1983.

... Alfred and Victoria visited today. She has grown so much, she's beautiful. She didn't know me at all, cried when Alfred handed her over. Watching the two of them, I know that they've been fine, that Alfred has been a good father. His lambing approach seems to have worked. Along, no doubt, with the ever-willing attentions of Geraldine Rushgrove. I know I should be grateful for her help, but how I hate the woman. Hate the fact that she knows where I've been all these months. She's promised not to tell anyone. I doubt that. The woman's a born gossip.

And what of me? What have I left to offer as a mother? How will it be when I go home next week? I'm terrified. The crazy woman who lost five babies. The woman who considered shooting herself when she lost her fifth. Couldn't even cope with the sixth who survived. My beautiful, perfect daughter. How ungrateful that woman must seem. How can I possibly be a good mother? How will I even know how to mother, starting from where I am now?

Sybil Morris. ~~Inmate.~~

Tassie stared at the words, her face wet with tears. Her mother had lost five children? How utterly dreadful for her.

But her tears were for more than that. For now, it was all making sense. The loneliness she'd felt all her life, the continual sense of something missing. She had a sister. And she'd seen her, she was certain. *Three times.* For that at least she could be grateful.

For a moment the magnitude of it all threatened to overwhelm her. Then anger erupted. Her mother should have told her. Surely she should have? Although, what good would it have done?

But... She threw the diary on the bed, then picked it up again. Reading through the pages, she saw the anguish her mum had suffered. She could see why it was something she just couldn't talk about.

And she'd seen her! *Three times!* The wonder of it exploded in her brain. She'd seen her sister! And, she smiled, she was sure Dan had seen her too. She hugged her arms around herself, comforted by the knowledge. Although... How she'd have loved to phone him and tell him. She took out her phone, glad his number was still on it. Staring at it, she thought back to their time together, her time with... the one.

Sighing, she switched to her 'favourites' and scrolled down to her mother's number. Perhaps she could talk to her, give her some kind of comfort. But she knew that wasn't the right thing to do. That it wouldn't work. *Love.* So bloody complicated. Slowly she read through the pages, again and again. Then she pulled her laptop towards her.

From: Tassie.Morris@morrisphotography.co.uk @ 11.45am
   To: S.Morris@gmail.com
   Monday 9th March 2015
   Re: Coming Home?

Dear Mum

   Thank you so much for your letter. I understand. I truly do. I am so very, very sorry. And I have no need to talk about it either.

   I think, if it's still OK, I might take you up on your offer of coming home for a while.

   One of my friends, Sydonie, has offered to rent the flat from me and I think that for six months (can you cope with six months?) that would probably work well.

   I actually have a plan that I've been thinking about for ages. I would love to talk about it when I see you.

   If it suits, then it will take me a few weeks to clear everything here, so I'll be home at the beginning of May. I do hope that's all right.

Mum, I love you too, and, again, I'm so sorry – for everything.

Love,

Victoria

xxxx

23

————

London, April 2015

'Are you sure that's it?'

Tassie looked around her living room and nodded. 'I've left the gramophone and records for Stan; it was kind of part of the rental agreement.'

'And the shoes? Over there. Plastic pink ones?' Tom stepped aside so she could see.

She grinned. 'They were too.'

He shifted a big cardboard box in his hands. 'Come on then, Sis, let's go.'

All the way back to Shropshire they talked about what she might do now she was coming home. Tassie shrugged off Tom's suggestion of taking local wedding photos, so then they discussed how she might do them for local artisan food producers. Apparently, the market was thriving, especially in Ludlow.

Eventually she admitted she'd been thinking about setting up as a cheese-maker. At which point, he turned to her, excitement in his voice.

'Do you remember Annette Barney? The goat lady Mum and Dad know?'

Tassie nodded, thinking how strange it was that they couldn't stop saying 'Mum and Dad', like the words were stuck together. 'I've often thought about her.'

'Mum was telling me the other day that she's thinking of retiring soon. So it might be that she could help you. Perhaps you could buy some of her stuff?'

'D'you think?' Tassie felt excitement trickling through her veins. Maybe her dream wasn't so far-fetched.

An hour later they were driving through Shropshire's narrow roads when Tom glanced over. 'Are you sad to be leaving London?' He slowed to avoid a man on a bicycle who'd swerved out around a pothole.

'No, not really. It's rather lost its appeal over the last few months. Especially as things have moved on so much with all my friends. And I think it's about time I came home. Do more to help. You've had to deal with a lot, you and Soph, and you've got the baby coming soon. Only a few more weeks. You must be getting excited?'

Tom's face lit up. 'Like you wouldn't believe.'

'How's Mum been with it all?'

'She's been great, really pleased. And...' His fingers tapped on the steering wheel. 'I'm not sure what it is...'

'Nervous?'

'Nervous? Why do you say that? No, she's actually been pretty chilled.' He chuckled, 'Maternal, was the word I was looking for. It's seemed a bit like, in her head, Soph's one of her dogs, so she knows exactly what her role is.'

They both laughed.

'Actually she's been brilliant. Never too invasive, but always there when Soph's needed her. Attending any appointments I've not been able to go to, helping choose stuff for the nursery. She's changed, I think you'll find. She misses Dad a lot, so much more than I thought she would, and is happy to have us around. It suddenly feels like she needs us.'

'Then it's good I'm coming home.'

For a while they drove on in silence, Tassie contemplative as the villages became increasingly familiar. She looked over at Tom, smiling – although he was too busy concentrating on the road to notice.

For the first time in her adult life there was no knot of tension growing in her stomach, no nervous anticipation of squalls that might lie ahead. She sunk her nose into the bouquet of sweet-peas and peonies she'd bought en route. For the first time ever, she was looking forward to going home.

She sniffed the flowers again, tears pricking the corners of her eyes. Except they might still say "Mum and Dad", but it would never be that again.

WHEN THEY REACHED THE FARM, they found their mother sitting in front of the fire, Honey at her feet. They unloaded some of Tassie's boxes, and Tom said he'd come back and help unload the rest in the morning.

'Are you sure you don't want some supper before you go? I've made enough.' Sybil gestured towards the kitchen table, laid for three.

'Thanks Mum, but I think I should get home.' Tom kissed her cheek.

'OK. Love to Sophie.'

'And from me.' Tassie gave her brother a long hug. 'And thanks for today.'

As he left, she turned to her mother, who was placing a dish on the table. 'Can I do anything to help?'

'Just sit down and eat, it's all done. I've made toad in the hole. I hope you still like it.'

After supper her mother returned to her chair by the fire, and Tassie pulled up the big armchair her dad had used to sit in.

They'd been chatting for a while when her mother looked at her, a new softness in the crevices of her face. 'It's funny. Seeing you in Alfred's chair. You remind me so much of him.'

Tassie smiled. 'I have his eyes.'

Her mother nodded, then bent to stroke Honey.

Tassie got up and walked over to her bags. Unsure whether she was doing the right thing, she pulled out her mother's diaries then returned to the fireplace. When she held them out, her mother flinched.

'I wasn't sure what you wanted me to do with them?'

Sybil took them from her then placed them on her lap, sighing. 'I'm not sure either.'

'Mum?' When her mother looked at her, Tassie saw the wariness in her eyes. 'It's OK. I'm not going to talk about it. I respect what you said.'

Her mother nodded slowly. 'Thank you. I appreciate it.'

Tassie took a deep breath. 'It's just, I just wanted to say... in person. That I'm sorry. Because I understand more now. And I'm sorry... for how I might have been with you. Because I didn't know.'

Her mother shook her head. 'You couldn't have; it was my choice not to tell you.'

'I wish you had, Mum. It might have...' Tassie looked for the right words. 'Made things easier. Between us.'

There was a long silence, and when her mother spoke her voice was cracked and low. 'I couldn't stop the grieving.'

Tassie wasn't sure what to say, so she said nothing.

'It seemed so ridiculous. There you were, the baby I'd always wanted – longed for – *we'd* longed for. And all I could do was grieve for the ones I'd lost.'

Now her mother looked straight at her.

'I'm sorry. You should have been enough.' She smiled. 'And you were. You are. You and Tom. I'm so lucky.' Her smile broadened, stretching further than it usually did. 'I'm so proud of you both. I hope you know that. I know I don't always show it.'

She withdrew into her thoughts, and when she spoke again her voice was calm, reflective.

'It was like... with the loss, not just of your sister but all the babies before, a part of me died, that I could never regain. And this struggle, between moving on with my life, our life, and being pulled back into the past. For a while... for a long while, well, I think the past won. I just couldn't see how I was going to get better. But I know that wasn't help-ful... for anyone.'

Still Tassie didn't speak and it was a few moments before her mother spoke again. 'That vicar. The one you spoke to?'

Tassie nodded.

'What did he say? What were you going to tell me that day?'

'She. It was a female vicar.' Tassie shrugged. 'I'm not sure it matters. Whatever it was, it's sorted.'

'I don't understand. What is?'

Tassie took a deep breath and when she spoke her voice was shaky. 'It's just that, well, I've found it quite hard, to have... Well, to find anyone I could really love. Which sounds so stupid.'

'Apart from that awful Alex.'

Tassie started. 'Awful? I thought you adored him?'

Her mother shook her head. 'Why would you say that? I always thought he was far too arrogant, and your father couldn't bear him.'

'But you always... You were always telling me about him. His news.'

'Because he was the only person I knew that you knew.' Her mother shrugged. 'You were never keen on bringing anyone else home. And,' – she nodded slowly – 'his mother, over the years, has been very kind to me. Especially after your father died.' She huffed. 'But that doesn't mean I have to like her son. Especially after how he treated you. I saw all that, how he was with you, although you never wanted to listen to me.'

Tears filled Tassie's eyes. All this time, she'd got it so wrong.

Her mother leant forward, putting her hand on Tassie's knee. 'What about that man you came home with when... Who helped on the farm that weekend?'

'Dan?'

'He seemed like a good man. Reminded me of your father in some ways.'

Tassie's shoulders slumped. 'He was, Mum, he was. But,' – she straightened – 'let's just say he's the perfect example of the problems I've had.'

'I'm sorry. I liked him.' Her mother sat thinking for a while, then looked at the diaries sitting on her lap. 'You asked me what I'd like to do with these?'

Tassie nodded.

'I'd like to burn them.' She gestured towards the fire. 'Strikes me they contain secrets that haven't done anyone any good.' She held one of them out. 'Can you help me?'

It took a while to burn the three books, her mother slowly tearing out the pages while Tassie dropped them into the flames. Finally, all that was left was a stream of ashes cascading into the fire's grate.

Her mother crouched down in front of the hearth, moving stray bits of paper into a central pile. Then she looked at her hands, the tips of her fingers blackened with soot. 'We should clean up, then it must be time for bed.'

Tassie knelt down beside her, briefly resting her head on her mother's shoulder as she handed her a dustpan and brush. 'Thanks for supper, Mum.' After a brief hesitation, she kissed her mother's cheek, warmed by the fire. 'Love you.'

Her mother looked at her hands, then Tassie, then again at the fire. 'I think we can do this in the morning. It'll keep till then.' Slowly she stood, smiling. 'I won't hug you, dear, or I'll cover you with soot.' When Tassie stood, she kissed her forehead. 'I've made you up the bed in the room next to mine. We can sort where you want to go more permanently in the morning.'

As Tassie turned to follow her, she knew that her response hadn't been exactly what she wanted. But that was her mother. And even without the 'I love you too', she absolutely knew that she did.

∿

Lying in bed, the narrow mattress covered with a patched and faded quilt, Tassie found that sleep eluded her – despite her tiredness.

She decided not to read, and instead lay thinking about her garden: what Stan would do with it, whether she'd left him sufficient instructions. When she heard faint sounds coming from downstairs, she realised her mother had forgotten to lock Honey in the pantry when they'd come up. Remembering the box of chocolates they'd left on the kitchen table, she pushed the quilt off and went to investigate.

When she reached the bottom of the stairs, she stopped. Honey was sitting in the kitchen doorway, transfixed by something beyond. She called to her, whispering her name, but the dog didn't move.

Quietly, she walked over and crouched down next to her, ruffling the top of Honey's head as the dog growled softly. Outside, the moon was low and bright, throwing the palest blue light onto the walls and floor of the kitchen.

And then she saw it.

Almost as if suspended in water, the air was filled with tiny particles, which she first assumed to be dust. Yet as she watched, she realised it was the ash from the fireplace, rising so slowly as to be almost imperceptible.

Thinking there must be some sort of draft, she glanced over to the window and... there she was, sitting on the window seat.

Not the little girl. Although it *was* the little girl. But this time Tassie knew to call her, her sister.

Dressed in a pale pink dress as delicate as a cobweb, the child's hair hung almost to her waist. Tassie took a deep breath, then found herself too scared to breathe out again for fear of frightening her away. The child waved, and particles danced in the invisible wind.

Her hand on Honey's neck, Tassie was grateful that the dog remained stationary, although she was still growling softly, her tail swishing on the stone floor. Cautiously, Tassie stood to take a step forward. Then she stopped. For the girl also stood, shaking her head with a quick, sharp movement.

'You want me to stay here?'

A single nod.

'You're. We're—'

Again the girl nodded, then giggled – and a faint sound, like the gurgling of a sun-filled stream, filled the room.

Tassie took another step forward, and this time the child put up her hand to stop her.

So Tassie stopped, although there were tears in her eyes and she desperately wanted to go closer – to know her – even though she knew she couldn't.

'What's your name?'

The little girl looked towards the fireplace, into the light thrown by the moon.

Honey growled louder and Tassie knelt down beside her. 'It's OK, Honey, there's no need to be afraid.' She looked over to the child, who was still looking towards the fireplace. 'She's... well, she's part of me really, we're sisters.'

There was wonder in Tassie's voice as she bent and kissed the dog's head, aware of the animal's solidity. When she looked up again the little girl was pointing.

In the pool of moonlight, the ash was gently shifting and Tassie realised that faint letters were being spelt out, although it was hard to see what they said.

'R?' The child shook her head and frowned. 'E?' Another shake. 'C?' A vigorous nod, and a giggle. Tassie carried on spelling letters out, her guesses earning either a nod, a grin or, once, a frustrated stamp of the little girl's foot. Finally, she worked it out. 'Claire?' She looked at the child. 'You're called Claire?'

The ghost child beamed, gave a little jump – or more of a float – then curtsied.

'Oh, how beautiful.' Tassie smiled at her. 'Claire. Hello.'

The child waved again, her fingers spread wide, and Tassie did the same. For a few seconds they just stood, Tassie trying to drink in her every detail. Eventually the girl pointed to the fireplace and Tassie saw that a scrap from a page of her mother's diaries was sticking out of the grate. 'Do you want me... ?' She looked at the child, who nodded.

When she reached the fireplace, Tassie bent and pulled out the charred scrap. Instead of the thin, lined paper she'd expected, it was cream parchment, from the letter her mother had written when she'd sent the diaries. Now she remembered that she'd put it in one of the books, and they'd obviously ripped it up by mistake.

But there was nothing on it. She stared at it for a few seconds, scared to turn it over for fear of there being nothing on the back.

Honey gave a short bark, and even as Tassie looked across to the window, she knew that Claire would be gone.

And in that moment, she felt a sense of loss so intense it seemed to twist her heart.

Walking over, she touched the space where the little girl had been, then stroked her hand down the window. Outside, an old apple tree was silhouetted against the moon, and Tassie felt her heartbeat quicken when, peering out, she saw the little girl's outline, high up on one of the branches, where she sat, kicking her legs.

Pressing her nose against the glass, Tassie stared harder. For alongside the girl – she strained to see, desperate to work it out – she was sure she could see the faint outlines of other tiny figures. She gasped, banging her head on sharp wood, the pain instinctively making her close her eyes.

Honey barked again, and when she'd relocated the spot in the branches, there was nothing there.

She searched every part of the tree before looking up at the moon. Then she raised the piece of paper to her lips and kissed it. 'Goodbye, Claire. My twin. I'm so glad I know your name.'

There was a sound, and she looked back to see Honey padding towards her.

'Come here, Hon, let's see what this says.' She patted the window seat and when Honey jumped up, she sank her head into the dog's fur as she turned the paper over.

She breathed out a sigh. Just as she'd hoped, she saw her mother's sloping letters, still just visible, despite the charring.

In the middle of the paper there were four words, and she read them, then held the scrap of paper to her chest.

I love you, Victoria

She looked towards the window, her reflection bouncing back. 'Is that from you, or Mum? Or both of you?' She smiled. 'I think I'll just go with that. Thank you, Sis. I love you too.'

The kitchen was still filled with light from the moon and the air was now clear, ash having settled like a dusting of fine snow. Quietly, she removed the dustpan and brush from the fireplace and began to sweep, wondering whether she'd ever see the little girl again.

She hoped that she would – but guessed she probably wouldn't. But she had the paper. And, she smiled, she had her mother too.

~

FOR THE NEXT FEW WEEKS, Tassie worked hard creating a new life for herself. With everyone's encouragement she went to see Annette, who was thrilled to hear she might want to set up a cheese business and immediately offered to sell her everything from hers.

At their first proper meeting she took Tassie's hands in her considerably rougher ones, saying that she'd prayed something like this would happen, that Tassie was the heir she'd always wanted. 'I'm just so delighted,' she beamed.

Tassie squeezed her hands. 'So am I.'

Her mother proved remarkably tolerant as every surface in the kitchen gradually became covered with cheese-making paraphernalia: muslins, thermometers, cheese moulds, draining mats, waxes and wraps.

And Tassie was over the moon.

~

It was on the day before Tassie's birthday that her mother suggested they pack a picnic basket and have a celebratory tea on the hill.

She'd asked Sophie and Tom whether they wanted to join them, but Sophie had been concerned about getting too hot on the climb. Which was probably sensible. They'd had a succession of glorious summer days, with heat gathering strength early in the mornings and little wind to disrupt it.

Despite not leaving the farm until late afternoon, the sun was still hot as Tassie and her mother climbed up Alfred's Hill – as Tassie and her brother now called it – their father's ashes having been dug into the oak tree's roots.

When they reached the top, Tassie stared up through the profusion of green leaves and twisting dark branches to flashes of blue sky beyond. Then her eyes travelled down the trunk to where, at its base, there was a jar of wild flowers she often replenished.

Her mother had nodded when she first saw it, saying nothing. Tom had assumed she put them there for her father, and Tassie couldn't tell him they were for their sister too. *Claire.* Their sister. Her twin.

'Happy birthday.' Her mother held out an envelope.

'Thanks, Mum. But it's not until tomorrow.'

'I know, but I have to leave early in the morning, so I thought it would be better to give it to you now.'

Tassie opened the envelope and took out a card. It was a crudely drawn picture of a black and white goat eating a yellow birthday cake; green scribbles representing grass. She laughed.

'Yes, sorry about that. It was the most appropriate one I could find.'

Tassie read the words *Happy Birthday Kid,* scrawled in red writing, beneath which her mother had added,

'Dear Victoria,

Please forgive the card, but all will become clear,
much love, Mum.

There was a second, smaller envelope inside. Intrigued, Tassie ripped it open then took an intake of breath. It was a cheque for £15,000. She looked at her mother, her eyebrows rising as her mouth fell open.

'For your business. Money to convert one of the barns and buy in the equipment you'll need. I think it's about time you moved the operation out of the kitchen. Especially as the results have been so good.'

'But...' Tassie found herself speechless. All she could do was stare, first at the cheque, then her mother. Eventually she found her voice. 'Tom?'

'Don't worry about him; I've given him the same. With the baby coming they could do with two cars, so I'm sure he'll put some of it towards that. Although obviously it's up to him and Sophie.'

Tassie leant over and, putting her arms around her mother's shoulders, pulled her into an embrace. The moment was brief but relaxed.

'Thank you. Thank you so much.' Now there were tears in her eyes. 'This means so much to me. And will make such a difference.'

Sybil's smile was equally full of emotion. 'Well, we did well with the sale, and I know you'll spend it wisely.' She reached into the pocket of her overalls and pulled out a small package. 'And, as you've both had the same, but it's your birthday, I've also got this for you.'

Tassie noticed that her mother's hand shook slightly as she handed the package over.

Slowly she peeled back the tape, then opened out the neatly folded wrapping paper. Inside was a red leather box, clearly old but still pristine. It opened stiffly, and this time she gasped out loud. For nestled in black velvet was an emerald and diamond ring, intricate carvings etched into its sides of gold.

She held it up, the precious stones catching the light. 'It's exquisite.'

'Can I see?' Sybil held out her hand and Tassie handed it over. For a while her mother sat staring at it, then she slipped it onto the top of her middle finger, holding it up to the sun. 'It originally belonged to your great-great-grandmother.'

'The one who lived in Wales?'

'No, on your father's side. She lived in India, well, Pakistan now. He gave it to me when he asked me to marry him.'

Tassie looked at her mother's hand. On her wedding finger was another ring – the one she'd always known.

Sybil was still staring at the ring. 'I stopped wearing it after I came out of... after... when things happened.'

'So what's the ring you wear now?' Tassie studied her mother's hand, noticing for the first time that the skin was speckled with faint liver spots. The ring was platinum, with round and oblong diamonds set in half the band.

'An eternity ring. Your father bought it for me in Shrewsbury, twenty years ago.'

They sat in silence, Tassie wanting to know more, but afraid to ask.

When her mother spoke again, her voice was fragile. 'He had an affair, you see. And although I understood why, how it could have happened, I was very angry—' She shook her head, the line of her mouth set. 'Actually, I was distraught. For a long time.'

Tassie remembered the journals. Her mother's long-standing hatred of Mrs Rushgrove, who still lived in the next village. 'It wasn't—'

'Geraldine Rushgrove.' Bitterness curdled her mother's voice. 'Eventually I forgave him. As I said, I could understand. But not her.'

Tassie shifted closer to her mother until their shoulders touched. She instantly understood the humiliation her mother had felt every time they'd bumped into the obsequious woman, as they often did, at church events, local concerts, fundraisers.

'She was widowed, soon after she got married. But that doesn't mean she should have gone for Alfred.'

Her teenage diary... She'd written about seeing her father in a café. Tassie breathed in, stretching her mind back as she then breathed out. Seconds before she'd seen her father, she now had a faint memory of seeing Mrs Rushgrove. A much younger version, long glossy hair, wide hips and a tight waist in a red pencil skirt. It was the skirt she could remember most clearly. She'd thought nothing of it at the time. But now...

Her mother handed her the ring. 'It was a long time ago, and, as I said, your father and I got over it, eventually. Geraldine moved away for a while, which made things easier.'

'But she came back.'

'Yes.'

Sybil's sigh wrenched Tassie's heart.

'She did.'

'Mum. I'm so sorry.' Tassie gently put her hand on her mother's, who stroked the antique ring that she now wore.

'It's OK. Time has healed most of the hurt.' She looked at Tassie then squeezed her hand. 'And sitting here, with you, now... is very special. Nothing will replace your father, but...'

Tassie squeezed back. 'It's funny you know. Now, whenever I think of Dad, I'm not thinking that I miss him.' She paused. 'I guess I didn't see him that often – so those feelings will probably come later. But every morning when I wake up and it's a beautiful day, or here, sitting with you now, I feel so sorry for him. That he's missing this moment. Which is one he'd have loved so much.'

Her mother nodded. 'Sometimes I think your father is still with us. Out there, in the fields, checking the fences, watching over the cows. He was so attached to this land: it doesn't feel like his spirit has moved very far away. Your sister's here too. I know it.'

Tassie stared at her mother, whose face was peaceful as she looked ahead. Hand on hand, they sat looking out across the landscape, down the hill to where swathes of rapeseed daubed gold stripes across the fields, stretching out to the dark horizon of the hills beyond.

Neither said another word, but Tassie felt a soft calm in the air, a quietness that did indeed remind her of her father, just as light refracting through leaves would always make her think of Claire.

24

Londmon, September 2015

Tassie looked around the table, hoping it would be big enough. She'd forgotten how busy Soho could be on a Friday night.

She felt her heart fill with warmth. It would be so lovely, seeing everyone again. Although Oliver was already there.

She put her arm around his shoulders and squeezed. 'Thank you for having me to stay tonight.'

'Our pleasure, although why you didn't want to stay in your flat I don't know.'

'Because it's Syd and Stan's flat now, and they don't have a comfy spare room like you do.'

'What time are they getting here?'

'Any time now. And Tilak? What time does he finish?'

'I was hoping he'd be here by now. Let me call him.'

She watched him phoning *Hubby* and smiled.

Oliver had a quick chat then put his phone down. 'He's not far away. So, come on, while I can still hear you, spill the news. How's the cheese?'

'Well...' Tassie delved into her bag and pulled out a black wax cylinder. On the top was a cream label with a pen and ink drawing of two goats: one standing in a field, the other climbing a hill behind.

On the side was another label, printed in a selection of delicate black fonts.

THE TEELA CHEESE CO.
GOAT CHEDDAR
Hand-made in Shropshire, England

Oliver squeezed his palms together. 'Oh my God. I can't believe you've already done it. It's only been... what? Less than six months? Tassie,' – he leant and kissed her cheek – 'you're a wonder.'

She grinned. 'Just over four actually. I know, I am rather chuffed with myself. Although I did get a bit of a leg up from another cheese-maker.'

Oliver twisted the cheese over and over. 'I love the picture on the top. Who did that?'

'Sophie, my sister-in-law. Turns out she draws brilliantly. Along with everything else.' She pointed to the drawing. 'And that's actually our hill at home. Tom proposed to Sophie on it and... Isn't it lovely to have it as part of my brand?'

'I genuinely think it's awesome. Well done, babe.'

'So far I'm just doing soft cheese and Cheddar, but I have plans to extend to others as well.'

'And how is it? Living with the ogre.'

'Actually, Oliver, she's all right. Going home has made a big difference. We even laugh sometimes these days. And she's been brilliant at helping me with the business. At the moment I'm still buying milk from other producers, but we're seriously considering getting our own goats. Apparently they come second only to dogs in terms of her favourite animals.'

'Can I keep this?' He held up the cheese.

'Yes, of course. I brought one for Syd too.'

'And Teela? Why the name?'

Tassie felt herself blushing. 'It means strong-willed, and goats are known to be really stubborn.'

'Well, I'd have thought Billy, Nanny or something like that. But everyone to their own – and, Tass, I'm so proud of you. My little entrepreneur. Who'd have thought? Here, give us a hug.'

'Can we join in?' They looked up to see Syd, Stan and Tilak standing there.

'No, I got here first. And look what I've got.' Oliver held up his present. 'Tassie's officially a cheese-maker!'

Once everyone was seated, conversation whirled around the table, for there was a lot to catch up on. Tassie, now sitting next to Stan, was delighted to hear he was still loving his job. She nudged his shoulder.

'As your landlady, that's something I'm pleased to hear.'

'Honestly, it's sick, Tass. Not only am I having more fun than I've ever had, but I feel I'm doing some good as well. The spoon's selling great, and I'm now on to getting people with disabilities playing video games.'

'I'm so pleased for you. And, dare I ask, the garden?'

'Ah, the real reason you wanted to sit next to me. That's good too. Even Syd's impressed. I'd have brought you some spinach, but the missus didn't think it would be very good after a day on the bike. Actually, Tass, there is something we need to talk to you about.'

Tassie was instantly wary.

Stan put his hand on hers. 'Don't look so worried, it's nothing bad. Definitely sound in fact. It's just—'

'Stanley Matthews, don't you dare.'

They looked at Syd, glaring at her husband from the other side of the table.

'Swap with me. Now.'

Stan laughed as he got up, kissing Tassie on the cheek before he moved away. 'It's good to see you. And I'm loving the cheese.'

'So, Sydonie, what's up?' Tassie linked her arm through Syd's as she sat down.

Smiling, Syd patted her stomach. 'This.'

Tassie gasped. 'You're not?!'

'I am. Ten weeks. Isn't it amazing?'

Images of her mum's journals flashed through Tassie's mind, but she quickly dismissed them. Times had moved on and Sophie had been fine – eventually. She put her arm around her friend. 'It is. And *you* will be wonderful as a mum. You were born for it.' She looked at Oliver and Tilak. 'Did you know?'

They both nodded.

Irritation prickled her neck. 'For God's sake. What is it about me always being the last to find out? About *anything*.'

Syd looked concerned. 'You're not cross are you? Oliver's only known a couple of days. He happened to come into the office just after I'd had my scan. And I really wanted to—'

'I know,' – Tassie kissed her cheek – 'tell me yourself.' She kissed it again. 'And I'm delighted you saved it until I could do that.'

Oliver clinked his glass. 'Well, if we're in the "tell zone", Tilak and I also have some news.'

Everyone looked at him expectantly as he puffed out his chest. '*We* are also going to have a baby.'

'Well done, mate, it hardly shows.'

Oliver glared at Stan.

'Obviously, we're adopting. And this,' – he pulled out a photograph – 'is he.'

There was a sudden flurry as everyone stuck out their hands.

'Shall we let Tassie go first? For once.' Oliver winked at her.

She reached over and took the photo from him. Then laughed. It was a baby, definitely. A *very* cute baby. With enormous, slightly quizzical black eyes, white eyebrows, chin and paws. 'He's gorgeous. What kind?'

Stan snorted. 'You can't ask what kind, Tass. That's not very PC.'

She held the photo up.

'Oh. I see. Very funny, guys.'

Laughing, Tilak answered. 'He's a schnauzer. Isn't he beautiful? We pick him up on Sunday.'

'How are you going to look after him, with you guys working all the time?' Tassie raised her eyebrows; it was one of her mother's stock questions.

'That's all sorted. He's allowed to come to hospital with me,' Tilak said. 'Some of the staff complained about it only providing a crèche, so it's now got a doggy day centre too. Actually, there's been some interesting work with patients visiting the dogs. Some encouraging results.'

'Any more potential barriers to ownership?' Oliver waved a breadstick at her.

Tassie shook her head, smiling. 'No, but do make sure you get all the proper paperwork, especially if he's a pure breed. I'll go over it with you.'

'Oh yes. I forgot you are an expert in the trading of puppies.'

'Breeding of puppies, Oliver. Breeding. You make Mum sound like a trafficker.'

Tilak turned to Stan. 'So, tell us a more about your inventing...'

Tassie turned to Syd, 'So, have you thought about names...'

Oliver leant towards them. 'How about Olive, if it's a girl?' He twirled his breadstick.

~

TASSIE and the boys were up early on the Sunday morning. She was working and it was the day they were travelling out to Hampshire to pick up their puppy – still arguing about the name as they ate breakfast. Oliver wanted to call him Hudson; Tilak had suggested Jayasinha – Jaya for short.

'What do you think, farmer girl?' Oliver raised his eyebrows at Tassie as she slathered a croissant with strawberry jam.

She laughed, then stuck out her tongue. She was wearing one of her dad's old checked shirts, with faded jeans and her favourite silver trainers. 'Leave me out of this. It's your baby.'

'Well, I understand it represents the Sri Lankan flag. But look,' – Oliver brandished the photo – 'he's not looking very *Victorious Lion* is he?'

As they kissed her goodbye and ran out the door, she suspected Hudson would win.

When her phone pinged it was Giles.

Prob 45 mins away. Ready for our sunny day in the Smoke?

She texted back. *I thought you were always in the Smoke? See you soon.*

Giles Geldron, someone she'd known from childhood, had his own meat-curing business in Ludlow and he'd offered to bring her cheeses down for her in his van. They often did events together, and today they were doing a big artisan food event in Borough Market. Although it was the most expensive thing she'd done, Tassie had decided it was just the kind of publicity she needed to really get her business going.

Washing up the breakfast things, yet again she totted up how many cheeses she'd need to sell in order to break even. It had cost a lot to set up her production cold stores, and goat's milk wasn't cheap. Even with the money her mother had given her she needed to keep a strict tally of her finances.

She looked at her watch: 7.35am. She should probably get going as it would take her at least an hour to get to Borough from Chalk Farm. Although it was straight down the Northern line, she knew not to trust the Tube on a Sunday.

GILES WAS THERE by the time she arrived – for as she'd predicted, the trains had been slow. The weather was perfect for a market: one of those gorgeous sunny September days that manage to prolong the relaxed vibe of summer.

'Hi Tass, looking lovely as ever. How's your weekend been?' Giles looked at her for a few seconds longer than necessary, then carried on hauling huge plastic trays out of his van, his long hair swinging jauntily in its ponytail.

'Here, let me help.'

'No worries, I got here earlier than expected. I've already taken your stuff out.'

Tassie looked over to where her stall had been allocated, next to his. 'You've put my table up as well. Thank you.'

'Pleasure. I thought if we got everything set up we could maybe grab a bacon sandwich or something, before things get too busy?' He shifted the trays in his hands as he looked at her.

'Oh, I'm sorry, I've only just had a big breakfast. Maybe a drink later?' She smiled at him.

· · ·

By TWELVE O'CLOCK the market was buzzing, smells of freshly baked bread, melted cheese, paella and charcuterie filling the air. The sun had continued to strengthen and Tassie had tied her shirt around her waist and stripped down to her white vest top, her hair piled on her head.

As well as enjoying the sunshine, she was gratified that her stall was getting a lot of interest, mostly for the beautiful drawings on her packaging. Her present customer, a designer, was asking if the artist did commissions.

'Well, at the moment she's a bit busy with a baby, but I can ask her,' Tassie said, taking the card he was holding out.

As she watched him walk away, carefully examining the product packaging on every table, she took her phone out of her satchel, stashed at the back of the stall, and started texting Sophie. *Hey guess what! I think I might have found you a new career! Sunny here, all going well. Hope it's good in Shropshire. How's my niec—*

'Oh look, goat's cheese, I love the packaging. Shall we try some?'

Tassie froze. She knew that voice. Without looking up she bent over her boxes, pretending to be busy sorting something out.

'Excuse me?'

Had her heart actually stopped? What the hell was she going to do? She couldn't just ignore her. *Breathe, girl. That's what. Just breathe. And don't say, Oh.*

Slowly she stood.

Charlotte was standing with one of the cheeses in her hand. Her face was warm and open, but it shut like a crab's claw when she realised who the seller was. 'Oh. It's you.'

Tassie willed herself to look at who she was standing next to. He had his back to the stall but, on hearing Charlotte's exclamation, turned around.

His hair was slightly longer, but otherwise he was just

the same. Still tanned, he was wearing an old brown suede jacket and a white T-shirt. He looked every bit as good as she remembered.

'How can I help you?' She looked at Charlotte, then Dan. 'Hello. Long time no see.' She desperately hoped that the calmness she was willing into her voice belied her heart's thumping.

'Tassie?'

'Yes. Indeed. What can I help you with?' Feeling herself blush, she turned to Charlotte. 'Would you like to try a sample?' She held up an oak board. 'I usually recommend it with this chutney.' She picked up a small white dish.

'Tassie!'

'Yes, Dan.' Despite her nerves, his look of total shock enabled her to smile. He smiled too, and her heart contracted.

'No, thank you,' said Charlotte. 'Er, Dan, do you want to chat, or shall we go?' Already her shoulders were turning.

Tassie glanced at her. No wonder she was looking uncomfortable, considering how vile she'd been the last time they'd met. Her eyes went to Charlotte's fingers, but they were in her pockets. She considered grabbing her arm and inspecting her hand.

Not cool.

'How have you been, Dan?' Lord knows, she didn't have to be polite to his wife.

'Great. Thanks. Although I'm currently in shock. What are you doing here?'

'Oh, you know. Life moves on. I did my dream, finally, you know... Do you remember?' She hoped he wouldn't notice the name.

'Teela Cheese.' He smiled his familiar crinkly-eyed smile. 'That's nice. Are your goats as strong-willed as horses?'

293

Charlotte looked at Tassie, then Dan. 'It's nearly time for our meeting.' She tried to look suitably apologetic. 'I'm sorry, Tassie, but we've got an appointment with a journalist, can't be late.'

Dan looked confused. 'I thought it was at one?'

'No. Twelve-thirty. Didn't I say? He phoned to make it earlier. And I'm not sure where the café is so we really need to get going. Bye, Tassie, good to see you. Your cheese looks great.'

Tassie looked at Dan and thought her heart might actually break. 'Bye then.' She put out her hand and touched his, still hovering over her table. 'It was good to see you. Really good.'

'You too. And...' he hesitated. 'If you don't think this is too inappropriate, I'm proud of you. What you've done. Your stuff looks great.'

He turned to go, Charlotte droving the way. After they'd taken a few steps Tassie called out. 'Dan?'

He turned instantly.

She squeezed past the edge of the table and, picking up two of her cheeses, walked over to them.

'I was so sorry to miss you when I came to your farm. And... well, you had some part in all this, so take these.' She made herself look at Charlotte as well. 'I hope you enjoy them.'

When she returned to her stall, Giles was staring at her.

'Who on earth was that? It was like being at the cinema, watching the three of you.'

Tassie forced a smile. 'Just someone I used to know. And his wife. How are you doing with sales? You seem to be keeping busy.'

. . .

FOR THE REST of the day Tassie was on tenterhooks, convinced that at any moment Dan would reappear. Every hour that he didn't she felt more and more dispirited, and not even the delicious hummus and salad wrap that Giles fetched for her gave her any solace.

'Thank you, Giles. Again.'

'And, again, no worries, Tass.'

She looked at him. There was something of the new-born calf about him, with his lanky legs and doe eyes.

'So, do I get the pleasure of your company going home tonight?'

She started. 'Shit, Giles, I'm sorry, I forgot to say. My friends are getting a new puppy today, and I said I'd go back there this evening.' She laughed. 'They're a bit worried they won't be able to cope – even though one of them's a doctor so I'm sure they'll be OK.'

Giles tried hard to hide his disappointment, but didn't quite manage it. 'No worries. I'll just drop your cheese back at the farm, shall I?'

'Would you mind? That would be great – although I'm hoping not to have much left by the end of today.' She turned to the couple who'd stopped in front of her stall, her smile suddenly radiant.

'Hello, would you like to try a sample.' She held up her board. 'I make it all myself.'

≈

'So, that's all that's left. Good eh?' Tassie slipped two trays of cheese into Giles's van. 'Why don't I just come and pick them up when I get back to Shropshire? Have you got enough room in your fridge until then?'

'Yes, that should be fine. Maybe we could grab that meal when you do?'

'Maybe.' He was persistent, she'd give him that. 'Although – I think it's OK to leave the van here for a bit. Why don't we go and get a drink now? Before you go? Someone was telling me there's a pub near here that Shakespeare used to use?'

Hope flittered across his face. 'OK, sounds great. Let's do it, baby.'

The pub was as old as it was characterful. As they entered the courtyard, Tassie read the blue plaque on the wall. 'I was right, Shakespeare used to drink here, and Charles Dickens. Although it was a coffee house then. Now it's the "last remaining galleried inn".' She looked up at the white balustrades. 'Very Romeo and Juliet.'

'You want to climb up there then?'

'Sorry?'

Giles was grinning at her. 'You go up there and I'll serenade you from below.'

Tassie felt a stab of sadness, which soon switched to irritation. Where was Dan now? Would he have left London? Clearly, he'd felt nothing on seeing her again. She shouldn't have wasted her cheeses on him. She smiled at Giles. 'Or we could go inside and have a beer. Come on, I'll buy them.'

Over two rounds Tassie reconfirmed why she and Giles would never work. He was sweet, but the conversation couldn't be called scintillating – although by the end of her second drink she knew an awful lot about the process of curing meat.

Finally, he looked at the huge clock on the end wall. 'I should be going: it'll take me a while to get back home. You sure you don't want to come?'

'No, that's fine, I'll see you back in Ludlow.'

'OK.' He stood up. 'Shall we?'

'Actually, I'm going to look around here a bit more. I find it fascinating – how old it is.'

'All right. I'll see you soon then?' He bent and kissed her cheek. His breath smelt of beer and, was she imagining it, milk?

After he'd gone she wandered around the pub, reading all the information on its history before placing her empty glass on the bar.

The barman had been watching her. 'You can go upstairs too, if you're interested.'

'Can I? Is there much to see?'

'It's mainly just function rooms, not very atmospheric. But you can get out onto the galleries, or balcony as we'd call it. That's good.'

Tassie climbed a staircase crammed with photos from many decades, then walked across an empty function room to a misshapen door by the window. Stepping out onto the balcony she was struck by how old it felt. The thick wooden planks were delightfully uneven, blackened and split in places, and she could see many neat repairs in the white painted balustrades. The farm could do with some of this expertise.

Her eye was caught by someone entering the courtyard, first at a run then slowing to a walk as he neared the pub's entrance. Brown suede jacket. Dark blond hair. She was still recovering from her surprise when, after glancing at the plaque, he opened the door and disappeared.

What goes in must go out. Ten, nine, eight, seven, six... She counted down with a delightful certainty. It was on three that he reappeared, head down, his pace now despondent.

'Ahem.' She leant over the balcony.

First Dan looked behind him, then towards the road. Finally, he looked up.

'If only I knew my Shakespeare, I'd know what to say.' Her grin was almost as wide as the balcony on which she stood.

Dan looked up at her, his expression matching hers. 'I think Juliet's currently asking "Wherefore art thou Romeo?"'

'And what does Romeo say?'

'Doesn't he climb up the balcony to be with the love of his life? Or was that just DiCaprio? Anyway, as the property is owned by the National Trust,'– he pointed to the sign – 'I'm afraid Romeo will just have to come up the normal way.'

'Hang on.'

He was turning, but stopped.

'Or Juliet could come down?'

'That's true. Juliet could come down. Or, let's be modern about this: we could meet halfway.'

Tassie laughed, held up a finger and then, shaking her hair out of its messy bun, leant over the balustrade. 'And so, she rescues him right back.'

'Who does? What? Have we moved onto Rapunzel?' He shook his head. 'I know your hair's long, but, trust me, that bit of the story would never have worked.'

She laughed again as she leant further forward, every atom in her body wanting to reach out and touch him. 'No. It's *Pretty Woman*. Surely you know that?'

25

There were a few moments in Tassie's life that she knew would remain unforgettable. And, walking slowly back down the narrow stairs, this was definitely one of them.

Questions were racing. Why had he come to find her? *How* had he found her? She guessed through Giles, bless him. What if he was married? Or still just engaged?

Despite the lack of answers, there was still enough of the old her deciding to go with the moment, to make the most of anything she was given. God knows she'd missed him for long enough.

When she pulled open the door, he was standing there.

'Hello again.'

'Hello.'

Silence.

'Tass, I'm so sorry—'

'Dan, I'm so sorry—' They both spoke at once. Then laughed.

'Shall we get a drink? Sit down?'

Tassie looked around the noisy pub. 'Actually, I don't need one. Unless you do?'

Dan shook his head.

'How about we go for a walk then?'

THE SUN WAS STILL SHINING as they ambled along the side of the Thames. A party boat was making its way down the middle of the river, disco beats of 'Hold My Hand' blasting out from its open windows.

All along the pavements people were sitting at tables, drinking and chatting. Two joggers swerved around those walking, their faces red with the effort of both running and dodging, and at a sharp turn in the walkway a man sat wearing a scraggy pink wool hat, Mad Max glasses covering his face and a sign saying *Fuck the World* propped up in front of him.

Tassie pointed. 'Only in London.'

As they walked, neither said much, clearly happy to be in each other's company while taking in the sights; until finally, outside the Tate, Dan turned to her. 'Shall we go on the bridge?'

Tassie glanced up at the strands of steel traversing the water, the vast dome of St Paul's framed by buildings on the other side. 'Good idea.'

It was slightly less busy on the north side, just a sprinkling of tourists taking photos of the cathedral. Dan pointed to the steps at its front. 'Let's sit down.'

So they sat, looking around at the streets where crowds filled the restaurants.

'How have you been?' Dan kicked at a stone on the step below.

'Oh, you know. Busy.'

He cleared his throat, looking straight ahead. 'Tassie, Charlotte told me what happened. I'm so sorry.'

'Talking of which, where is she?'

His expression hardened. 'I have no idea.'

'Meaning?'

'Meaning she told me everything, and her behaviour was unforgivable. Well, she didn't tell me that, she said she was protecting me. But it was.'

'I like your Bedford.'

Dan winced.

'Who's Betty?'

'My mother.'

'And I saw Billy. He looked... silly.' Her laughter broke the tension.

'Tass, I am so sorry. When Charlotte told me, how she swapped her ring—'

'Hang on, she swapped her ring... So you're not engaged?'

'To Charlotte? God no. Never.' He snorted. 'I told you, it would be like marrying my sister.'

Tassie thought back to the meeting, how she'd noticed that Charlotte was standing in an odd way, hands behind her back. The cunning mare.

'Were you in Ireland?'

'Yes, I was. That bit was true at least.' He turned towards her. 'I've been negotiating with a company to buy the farm. And it actually looks like it might happen. I still can't imagine the freedom I might have.' He paused, looking away, then back at her. 'But I'm so sorry I wasn't there when you came. I can't believe you came all the way down to Somerset.'

'With a witch.'

'A witch? Don't tell me, on a broomstick?'

'No, in a red Honda Civic.'

He laughed. 'Most people would have got the train. But that's what I love about you, Tassie Morris. Maker of a goat's cheese called Teela.' He paused, aware of what he'd just said, then he smiled and put his hand up to her face.

His touch was delicious.

She leant towards him and put her hand on his. 'So, let's get this straight. You're not married.'

'No.'

'Engaged?'

'No.'

'Girlfriend?'

'No.'

'Boyfriend?'

'Er, no.'

'Any sheep?'

Dan laughed. 'Stop. Anyway, what about you?'

She shook her head. 'No one.' She blanched, then looked at him. 'I guess you don't know?'

'Know what?'

She still felt repulsed thinking about *Muck-fucker Mancini* – Syd's best.

'Doesn't matter. One day I might tell you.'

'Is it about that guy? The one in your flat?'

Tassie sighed. 'No. It's not. Again, long story, but one which I *will* tell you, at some point, I promise.' She paused. 'I did see him again, actually, a couple of months ago.'

'Tass, I have no idea who he is or anything about him. So maybe we need to get him out of the way, right now. Given the trouble he's caused.'

She sighed. 'It was at a drinks party, given by his parents. My mother knows them and wanted to go and... well, let's just say things are a lot better between her and me these days, so I went too. And he was there, with his beautiful American wife and children.' She looked at him. 'I told you he was married.

'Anyway, I chatted to her for a bit, found out that she's

actually nice – in a sort of worthy Gwyneth way – and I watched one of her children run riot around the house – and thanked God he wasn't mine. And then, sorry, this won't sound good, but when I was in the kitchen getting some water, he cornered me. Alex. And...' She sighed. 'He was drunk, very drunk, and he... Let's just say that he suggested things that were highly inappropriate, given his wife was in the next room.' She sat staring out at the wide curve of pavement. 'And, again, this isn't going to make much sense to you as you don't know the background, but I just felt pity for him. For he is pitiful. And sad. And quite dull. And deeply unhappy. And all the time I was looking at him I...' She turned to Dan, her heart slowing. 'All I could think about was how much I missed you.'

Dan's expression was unreadable. 'I'm guessing we didn't do all the talking we needed to when we first met.'

'No. And I'm sorry. That was my fault. But this "thing" was so big for me. Had affected me all my adult life, and I hadn't worked it out then, so couldn't solve it. But I have now.' She stopped. 'And do you know what?'

He shook his head.

'Turns out it was actually all about my mother.' She smiled. 'One day, I promise, I'll tell you everything.' Her face grew serious. 'Well, I'll tell you the bits of the story that are mine to tell.' She paused. 'OK, so here's a question for you. Why did you react so quickly, not even give me a chance to explain?'

Dan scratched the side of his face. 'I don't know. No, actually I do. I guess after Mum and Dad died I learnt to protect myself. I had to. Otherwise the pain was too much to bear. And that kind of crystallised within me. I became, not a three-strikes, but a one-strike guy.'

'And not even the card was enough to change your mind?'

Dan looked at her, surprised. 'You sent me a dodo. Which is extinct. I thought it was your metaphor for our relationship. An angry jibe.'

'You're as bad as Oliver. I sent you an albatross, with, I might add, the words "miss you". An albatross because... God it sounds so cheesy... they mate for life.'

Dan laughed. 'I can promise you it was a dodo. Embarrassingly, I've kept the card so can prove it.'

'Tenner it was an albatross.'

'Dinner it was a dodo. Albatrosses are white, dodos are – were – brown and black.'

Tassie thought for a moment, then put her hand on her forehead. 'Oh hell. I can remember the colours. Bugger. I can't believe I got the wrong bird. I'm so sorry. What a numbat.' But she was laughing as she said it, as was Dan.

When their laughter stopped, silence stilled the air and when she spoke, Tassie couldn't keep the nerves out of her voice. 'So, Dan Jacobs, where do we go from here?'

'Well, I was planning to drive back to Somerset tonight. But as Charlotte has Daisy,' he winked, 'I guess my plans have changed. What about you?'

'I'm going back to Oliver's: they got a new puppy today.' She looked at him, suddenly shy. 'If you think it's appropriate, I'm sure they'd love to meet you.'

'It seems a little early for plans like that.'

Immediately she felt crushed. Perhaps everything wasn't going to be OK.

Then he turned and put his arms around her, his face flushed. 'You see, if we're with other people, then I won't be able to do this.' Slowly, softly, he put his lips to hers and heat, like melted chocolate, poured through her veins. 'Or this.' He stroked his hand down the length of her hair, then twisted it up so his hand could also cup her head. 'Or this...'

He slid his other hand under her shirt, then around her waist, pulling her to him.

Tassie: *What are you and Stan doing tonight?*
Syd: *Just chiln. Y?*
Tassie: *Fancy supper at Oliver's?*
Syd: *Spur of momt? If he dozn't mind, b lovely 2c you b4 you go.*
Tassie: *There'll be one other.*
Syd: *Who? Sum1 you picked up at the market?*
Tassie: *You'll C Oliver said 8. Laterz babe xx*

EPILOGUE

Shropshire, June 2016

Shropshire, June 2016
The bride looked hot as she walked up the hill. The sun had speared the land with its most powerful rays since morning, and by midday the corn in the fields felt warm to the touch.

Now, even though the sky was still bright, a pearlescent moon hung serene on the horizon – so resplendent it felt like you might stroke it. It was a summer moon: an auspicious day in the Wiccan calendar.

Dressed in a vintage lace frock, the bride wore gold leather sandals and there were pale roses and gypsophila woven into her long blonde hair.

Holding her hand as they walked was her mother. She wore a plain white shirt and knee-length skirt, but her shoes were heeled and polished, and for the first time in thirty years she'd applied lipstick that morning.

The man standing at the top of the hill watched the two of them. His eyes crinkled and, if you were to look closely, you would see his heart expand then tighten.

Meanwhile, the reverend standing next to him hoped the two women would hurry up. For much as she loved watching their approach, her robes were heavy and beneath them she was melting.

Guests congregated just below the top of the hill. Two had babies in their arms: one, a sleeping new-born; the other crying fretfully in the heat. The father rocked his daughter until she too was quiet, lulled into drowsiness by the breeze now filtering through the branches of a solitary tree.

Almost as one, everyone turned towards the ruffling air, sighing with relief.

Eventually the women reached the hill's crescent, where, smiling, the bride directed her mother to a bench that had been there for decades.

Nodding gratefully, the mother sat in order to catch her breath. But really it was so that she could feel the sense of peace she always felt when sitting there, often with her husband.

For a few precious seconds, mother and father – flesh and spirit – watched with pride as their daughter looked deep into the eyes of the man she truly loved.

While high in the sky, like particles of stars dancing in the beams of the moon, fragments of two older spirits sent blessings and love to their son.

And in the ancient oak, a little blonde child nestled into the crook of a bough, shimmering light bouncing off the sparkles of her party dress, her face luminescent with its pixie grin.

On the hill there were quiet murmurings amongst the guests – and a few sniffs – as in the distance a soft bleating of goats could be heard; and, if you listened carefully, the sweet tinkling of the bells hanging around their necks.

Finally, the mother stood, returning to her daughter's side. Once more, they took each other's hands.

The reverend held up a leather-bound book as she

smiled at Tassie and Dan, then smoothed down the sides of her robes.

Tears glistening in the corners of her eyes, she looked out at the gathered congregation.

'It is with my *very* great pleasure that we are gathered here today...'

The End

ACKNOWLEDGMENTS

'She believed she could, so she did.' But not without a lot of help from those who believed in her too.

Firstly, I must thank those closest to me: Pete, Imani and Jai. I've been working on this and other books for a long time - and haven't always been easy to live with.

For the, 'It's *always* about the light' advice, my love and thanks to my friend and photographer extraordinaire, Susie Lawrence - who not only captures weddings beautifully, but can help you find your groom. And to Jax: for being the light. I love you.

Thank you to Matthew Oliver for planning my own wedding so meticulously, and Susie Edwards - who was a wonderful florist and is greatly missed. To Kat Williams: because *Rock n Roll Bride* magazine was the original inspiration for this tale; Annette Lee, who taught me all about goat's cheese; and JJ: my favourite. Obviously.

If you google, 'how to break an addiction to a person,' you'll find a book of the same name. Thanks to Howard M. Halpern, PhD for writing it. It really helped. Thank you to Dr Lily Hudd - you're a "just need to check this bit" star. Thanks also to Beverley Blackman for being my psychotherapy sounding board, and Jane Brewin of Tommy's for the Sybil chapters. Thirty years of thanks go to Sophie Corbett for welcoming me to Shropshire; to Stuart Wakefield, for answering 1,000 questions and being my partner in writing, and Danielle Simpson: for your encouragement when it was needed most.

Thank you, Darren Bennett and Andy Bridge, for my brilliant book covers, and David Bamford for using your weekends to do some speedy final edits. To Annie Chillingworth for my beautiful goat, and Joanna Penn, for brilliant free advice.

I literally couldn't have written this novel without those many, *many* friends who've read numerous drafts of numerous novels and generally been so encouraging.

These include: Annie G, Anne Y, Arminal D, Bryony J, Chris B, Christina H, Chrissie T, Emma G, Emily W, Eira M, Fi L, Harriet W, Helen S, Honor B, Jackie R, Jenny B, Kate K, Karen B, Louise E, Mary D, Mark W, Moger, Nick & Olivia, Nickie D, Rebecca dP, Rosanna L, Sally F, Sara M, Sarah C, Suzy J, Sylvia B, Tracy C, and Tamsin B. And if I've left anyone off this particular list, I'll bake you a cake.

Huge thanks as well to Ella Berthoud, Helen Corner-Bryant, Helen Baggott, Ayisha Malik, Janet Gleeson and Rose Tomaszewska for your expert help and advice.

Thank you to all the brilliant agents who've given me their time: Jenny B, Nelle A, Cath S, Jo U, Jo W, Robert C and Sheila C. I haven't yet found my perfect match; but one day I will.

Darling Dad. Thank you for decades of hand-holding and the excellent tax advice.

And lastly, I love you Mum, and wish you were here to hold your own copy of SHOOT THE MOON. We miss you.

ABOUT THE AUTHOR

Bella Cassidy lives in Dorset with her husband and two children.

She's a bit of an expert on weddings, having had two of her own. For the first she was eight months pregnant - a whale in bright orange - and married in a barn with wood fires burning.

The second saw her in elegant Edwardian silk, crystals and lace, teamed with yellow wellies and a cardigan.

Both were great fun; but it was lovely having her daughter alongside, rather than inside her at the second one.

If you enjoyed Shoot the Moon, it would be brilliant if you could rate the book, and perhaps leave a review on Amazon. With eight million titles to choose from, getting noticed is a bit like searching for a needle's eye in a hay stack.

Love the places Tassie visits? Then follow Bella's TOUR OF THE BOOK *on Facebook and Instagram. She's starting in Scotland, visiting Schiehallion, Aberfeldy, Castle Menzies and the Isle of Skye. Just look for @BellaMoonShoot.*

Printed in Great Britain
by Amazon

75557128R00189